# LOW SIDED

SACRED HEARTS PNW CHAPTER - BOOK IV

## ANDREA DOWNEY

# COPYRIGHT

Editing & book design by Maggie Kern @ Ms.K Edits

Cover art by Dar Albert at Wicked Smart Designs

# DEDICATION

*To Jared, I literally could not have done this one without you. Seriously.*

# PROLOGUE

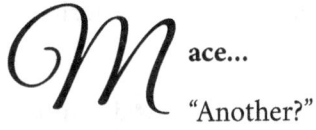ace...

"Another?"

I looked up, squinting at the plucky bartender chick that was serving 'em up.

"Yeah," I murmured and nodded. She gave me a look that was somewhere between empathetic and sympathetic.

"Okay, but this is going to have to be your last one, man. I don't need to get busted for overserving you, no matter how good looking I think you are."

I gave her a watery smile and swayed a bit on my barstool and nodded as she poured me another whiskey.

I was at this shithole bar in White Center, probably a quarter mile or so from the club. I honestly needed a fuckin' break from the fuckin' lovefest going on over there. Guys were gettin' girls and settling down left and right, and shit if I didn't want that.

I was a jealous bastard. Weren't no bones about it.

"What's your name?" she asked me as she tipped the bottle back up and set it just out of reach.

"They call me Mace," I said, and took a sip of the smoky amber liquid in my glass.

"Oh, yeah? Why's that?"

"Not supposed to ask me that, sugar."

"Well, I apologize then."

"'S no worries, you didn't know."

She was quintessentially Pacific Northwest – her clothing organic, a mix between steampunk and hippy tree freak. Her top was a tank top looking thing with lacing like a corset in the front. Her shoulder was tattooed with a Raven, the rest of her arm crawling with lush ivy vines.

Her hair was a brownish blonde, and in thick, ropy dreads down past her waist. Wood and metal beads with runes on them decorated her thick locks in irregular intervals.

Her skin was on the pale side, a scattering of light freckles over her nose and cheeks, barely there and almost unnoticeable in the dim light of the bar. She was thin, but wiry. I didn't think she was weak, but she certainly was willowy – almost looked vegan, but that could have just been the Burning Man style she had going on.

Burning Man was popular up here, even though it was a big musical festival, rave, party thing that happened down in the California – *or was it Nevada?* desert. A lot of people from up this way went down there and partied hard for like a week or two every year – pitching tents, a bunch of crazy art installations – you name it.

"What's your name?" I asked her and she smiled at me with a wry twist of lips.

"Most of my friends call me Raven," she said.

"Nice to meet you, Raven."

"Nice to meet *you*, Mace."

A few guys came into the bar. Frat types. Asshole types, and Raven gave me a wink.

"Duty calls," she said with a breezy sigh. She moved away from me, carrying her herbal scent down the bar with her. I smiled and thought through the haze of my drunk that she probably used essential oils for all the things.

She was pretty, and I liked the sparkle in her light eyes, but she probably wasn't the girl for me. I mean, she was a lover-not-a-fighter type and probably couldn't hang or go my speed. Her speed was probably saving the spotted owl on the weekends or something, spending forty-nine days camped in a tree so the man couldn't cut it down.

I chuckled to myself and shook my head. I could respect sticking it to the man every which way, but I needed somebody that could stick with me. This life wasn't for everyone. *Still,* I thought to myself, looking down the bar where she was at the opposite end talking to some old barfly regular; *I could tap that.*

Her legs were encased in tan leggings that looked like leather, a bunch of bronze zippers along her hips and thighs, but there were definitely no pockets. The way the material clung to those long stems of hers left nothing to the imagination. Her tank boots finished off the look she had going quite nicely.

I heard laughter and muttering behind me and turned a bleary eye on the three frat-lookin' motherfuckers. They were sizing me up, and I turned back forward.

Little shits could fuck off into oblivion for all I cared. It happened a lot, two or even three guys getting it in their heads that they could take on a Sacred Heart. That we weren't nothing. That was, until they lay on the pavement broken and bleeding, or until we fuckin' caught up to their little asses later – whichever came first.

They burst out laughing about something and high-fived each other. I didn't care except they were ruining my peace and damn quiet.

"Hey, hey yo!" one of them called out, and I knew it was to me. I just ignored them. I was on parole for another year, and I had absolutely no desire to go back to the state pen and finish that bid off, fuck them very much.

"I'm talking to you!" he shouted, irritated.

"Hey! Knock it the fuck off, boys, or you can get the fuck out my bar," Raven told 'em.

"Shut up and just keep pouring the fuckin' drinks, sweetheart," one of them called out. I turned, just in time to see him grab his crotch and tell her, "I'll deal with you later."

Nice.

"Some people's fuckin' children, man," I said slowly. "You kiss your mother with that mouth?"

"Man, fuck you!" the dude's buddy, some Asian kid, said laughing.

"I don't swing that way," I said, turning back to the bar. "More power to you if you do, though."

I have no fuckin' idea what happened next. I heard something snap, shouting, and a white light flared through my vision as the back of my head erupted in pain. Next thing I knew, I hit the sticky barroom floor, face-first and next, my ribs exploded in fire.

I managed to get up and heard more shouting, as I groped blindly and spilled out of the exit and onto the front sidewalk.

I couldn't get air, I couldn't breathe, and I had a second to think through my drunken haze, *goddammit! They got the drop on me.*

What came next was probably the most brutal ass kicking of my life, and that's including the one I took in that yard fight when I was locked up.

4

I took a sneaker to the face and grimaced, immediately tasting blood as kicks and blows rained down on me.

*Boom! Boom! Boom!*

Three deafeningly loud rapid reports sounded. I heard some muffled shouts and screams, the thudding of rapid footsteps down the sidewalk, and then the smell of essential oils assaulted my nose.

"Come on, Mace, you gotta get up! Cops are coming for sure, and we need to not be here when they do."

I struggled, but things didn't want to quite work. My eyes were swelling shut and every time I breathed in, it was like breathing so much bitter broken glass. I spat and tasted nothing but copper.

"Come on, Mace! *Help me!*" a woman's voice cried, and I struggled to my feet. My head swam with liquor and the beatdown. I don't remember shit else after that.

## 1

*M*ace...

"Easy." A light hand fell on my chest and pressed me back down onto the uneven surface I was lying on. I rested my head back on the arm of what I assumed was a couch just by feel.

"I can't see," I complained, then I tried to look around. Everything hurt, and it was dark.

"Your eyes are swollen shut, hang on. Let me finish what I'm doing here, and I'll get some ice on that." The voice was kind, soothing, and female.

"Who are you?" I asked the voice.

"Raven," she said gently, and I felt a stinging touch against my eyebrow. I flinched. "Shhh, it's okay. I'm just cleaning your cuts."

"Where am I?" I demanded.

"My place."

"You call the cops?"

"No. The cops aren't my friends. You're going to be okay, I'm a trained medic... take it easy for me, would yah?"

"I've never called a pig friend either..." I grunted, laying back, at this woman's mercy. Her voice was soothing, and instilled a touch of trust. It was sort of familiar, but I couldn't place it in my haze of pain. "Do I know you?" I asked.

I could hear the smirk on the tail of her slight laugh. "I told you, I'm Raven... you might remember me as your friendly neighborhood bartender." I reached out, groping blindly, and captured her upper arm. Her skin was soft as silk and I felt my way to her face, startled when I encountered equally soft, silken hair. I remembered; Raven had had dreads.

"You're lying."

"I'm not," she said softly.

"Raven had dreads," I said.

"A wig," she murmured. "My own hair, I made it myself." A rough dread was pressed into my hand.

"That's actually kind of gross," I muttered, and she laughed.

"Yeah, well, all that aside, I'm going to need you to try to rest."

"My phone..."

"Trashed, I'm afraid." She had gone back to doctoring up whatever cut was on my face, and I tried not to flinch.

"Fuck," I muttered, and she chuckled again.

"Only thing that matters is that you're going to be okay," she said, low and conciliatory.

"You're doing a lot for a man you don't know," I said, and she was quiet. No touching. I waited and heard nothing. I was starting to wonder if I were going crazy, if I were dead or some shit and having some weird Hell experience. There was no way I would have got into Heaven. "Raven?"

"Yeah, I'm here," she muttered. "Some people helped me once… guess I just need to pay it forward."

I was quiet, turning her words over in my head. Her voice had been the softest yet, and incredibly sad.

"Thank you," I said. "For whatever you did to get 'em off of me."

"Just stay right here, don't move," she murmured. "I'll get you some frozen peas for your eyes and then we'll get into the really not fun stuff."

"What's that?" I asked, a slight smile curving my lips.

"Pretty sure you've got some busted ribs; we need to bandage you up and keep shit from moving. You're lucky; you don't seem to have punctured a lung."

"Shit, this gonna require I move?"

"Yup." Her voice was strained and ended on a whoosh of breath as she heaved herself to her feet.

"Fun," I muttered.

I waited, listening to her footfalls retreat, a fridge or freezer door open and shut. She laid something cold across my eyes and face and I put a hand over it. I wanted to see her. I wanted to see myself.

"Think you can sit up, Mace?"

"I don't know," I said honestly. "Can you do something for me?"

"Depends on what it is," she said.

I sighed out, "I need you to let my boys know where I am, that I'm still alive."

"What, like your kids?"

I chuckled. "No, my club."

"Oh, I don't know…"

"They need to know. They might think the police grabbed me, or something worse. They could go looking for me or go looking for a fight. Fuck… I don't know where we are. Are we still in White Center?"

"Yes," she said softly, hesitantly. "It's not much, but we're in my apartment, a one bedroom above Excelsior Ice Cream."

"That's on fifteenth, right?" I asked.

"Sixteenth," she answered.

"Okay, seriously, I need you to go like one block east and seven blocks down to Iron Heart Salvage. You know where it is?"

"Yeah, I know where it is. I also know the Sacred Heart's clubhouse is across the street, but I *really* don't know about all that—"

"You don't have to be scared?" I said.

"Uh, *yeah*." She sounded like I was crazy for even asking.

"Do I scare you?" I asked.

"Not right now," she said softly.

"Did I scare you before? In the bar?"

"No…"

"Then *please*…"

"Let me get you fixed up and let me think about it," she hedged, and I wondered what she was hiding from. What had her hardcore lookin' to get out of drawing any kind of attention to herself?

*Shit, that hurt.*

"Sorry," she murmured quietly.

"It's alright," I said gently. I could feel she was trying to be careful. That didn't make it any less painful.

"Look, you'd be a lot more comfortable in the bed, and you're gonna need a day or two before you can really start moving."

"You tryin' to get me in your bed?" I asked with what I hoped was a reckless grin.

"You're seriously trying to flirt with me right now?" she asked, surprised.

"Gotta find the little joys no matter what you've got going on, sweetheart." She touched along my ribs and I jumped crying out, "Ow!"

Her voice held a hint of a smile when she said, "Sorry."

I tried not to laugh, laughing hurt. "If you don't like me calling you sweetheart, all you have to do is say so. I can't exactly see and I honestly didn't mean anything by it, just habit I guess."

"No, it was fine," she said and sounded almost startled. "I would never hurt somebody over something so petty. I'm really trying to be gentle."

"Appreciate it," I grunted as she prodded another tender spot.

"Okay, come on, we've got to get you sitting up."

Fuck, that was no fun. I didn't know what part was worse—the sitting up, her helping me out of my jacket and then my shirt, or the whole binding up my ribs thing.

Scratch that.

The worst thing was levering me up onto my goddamned feet and helping me shuffle over to her bed, which was low. *Really low*. Like a mattress on the floor low. Maybe I should be glad that I couldn't see much.

"Easy, easy!" she hissed, and I finally made it down onto the edge.

"Fuck, I'm gonna puke," I said – that weird taste invading my mouth, the one that was a precursor, a warning sign of things to come.

"Hang on, no, no, no, gah!" She thrust a trashcan or something into my arms and my stomach rebelled. I swear to Christ in doing so, it pulled on *everything* from the inside.

"Oh, God! Oh, fuck!" I moaned and I heard Raven sigh.

"Easy, it's okay, you're okay."

Bullshit. I most definitely was *not* okay.

"My boys," I grunted, grinding agony twisting throughout my torso. "Please tell me you'll go get my boys," I said as she helped me to lie down.

"I promise," she finally said. "Just rest now."

## 2

_____

*R*aven...

"Woo boy," I muttered under my breath and stared down 15ᵗʰ SW at the fencing and row of bikes on one side and the bikers smoking on the small back landing across the street. I leaned heavily on my staff that I carried practically everywhere with me. It was as much for my Burner chick aesthetic with its decorative wraps and dangling charms as it was to clobber anyone that decided to make a grab for me.

*I'd learned that lesson...*

I sniffed, my dread lock wig swaying against my back as I looked from one side of the street to the other. With a sigh, I lifted my leather plague doctor mask off my face and perched it on top of my head.

I wish I could say I stood out, but this was Washington. Just outside of Seattle to be exact, and we were right above Georgetown, which was an artsy neighborhood in its own right. The only place I would have been more at home would be Fremont – but I had to avoid Seattle proper now for reasons I didn't feel like getting into.

*Keep that door closed. Locked. Throw away the key.*

I was staying in White Center for that same reason. The *other* reason being that rough as the neighborhood was? It was in the King County Sherriff's jurisdiction, which may or may not afford me some protection. I mean, although I saw Seattle PD cruisers, they stayed on the north side of Roxbury while I most decidedly stayed on the south of it. I mean, I was streetwise enough to know that in the grand scheme of things, it didn't matter.

All cops are bastards. King County wouldn't hesitate to hand me to Seattle, even if I didn't have a warrant. Being *under investigation* was usually enough. What was it cops always liked to say when it came to senseless acts of violence? *She was in the wrong place at the wrong time.* What I had been through? It hadn't been senseless. It had been calculated, and the cops weren't your friend when it was all in the law enforcement family. City, county, or state... it didn't matter. That thin blue line was a towering blue wall when it came to a girl like me.

I was just your average girl who needed to keep her mouth shut. I wasn't just public enemy number one for my protesting and social justice leanings. No, it went deeper than that now, and I was well aware that they could say whatever they wanted about me and the King County Sheriff's Department would just hand me over, no questions asked. The *last* place I wanted or needed to be was within Seattle city limits.

*I'd been warned...*

Hell, they were all buddies. I bet they'd hand me over gift wrapped in a big red fucking bow, which was why I did anything and everything to fly under the radar. Getting involved with The Sacred Hearts in any capacity whatsoever was so not the way to do that.

"What the fuck are you doing, Raven?" I muttered to myself for the thousandth time. Taking in a deep breath, I put my worn-out Doc Marten's I'd scored at a second-hand store for like two bucks into motion over the equally worn-out cracked sidewalk.

I licked my lips, swallowed my fear, and stopped below the two guys smoking on the back landing to their clubhouse and looked up.

"Either of you guys know where I can find Maverick, or Fenris?" I asked.

One of the two scowled down at me, a super hairy guy that looked like a damn neanderthal.

"Depends, who's askin'?" he demanded.

"Does it matter?" I asked, wiping the sweating palm of my hand that didn't grasp my staff on my post-apocalyptic olive-green leggings.

"You're coming to us, so… yeah. Kinda." The other man was eyeing me with mistrust, and I let out a shaky breath, my heart hammering the inside of my ribcage.

"Look, Mace sent me. He was in my bar last night and he got beat up – bad. I helped him, he asked me to—"

The second man who had spoken, the one with the close-cropped dark hair and shadow of a beard just beginning along his jaw, vaulted the railing and landed right next to me. I shied back, but he seized my arm in a crushing grip. I tried to stay calm, fear spiraling through me, coiling in my chest, the panic ready to strike.

"Where is he?" he demanded.

"My apartment."

"Take us," he said.

"Are you Maverick or Fenris?" I asked and he cursed.

"No, I'm the VP, little girl, and you'd better take me to him right fucking now."

"He said to find Maverick or Fenris," I said stubbornly.

"Squatch, get Mav out here pronto."

The hairy one went in the back door of the club, yelling out, "Mav!"

"He dies or something—"

I snorted. "He's not going to, I looked after him myself," I said hotly. That was one thing I wouldn't have called into question. I was a good medic… or had been. I so didn't hang out in the same circles anymore.

"What's the deal?" a new voice interjected, and we both looked up to the newcomer on the back porch of the heavily graffitied back side of the building.

I opened my mouth to answer, but the man who had ahold of my arm went ahead of me. "She says Mace is in a real bad way, won't take us to him."

"That's *not* what I said!" I snapped. "What I said was, Mace told me to bring Maverick or Fenris!"

"Well, I'm Maverick," the man up top on the back porch declared. Vaulting it like the man who was now letting me go, he landed before me and said, "So, lead the way."

Heartened that his name patch on his vest said Maverick like Mace's had said Mace, I nodded.

"This way." I jerked my head and started up the sidewalk. Maverick squinted.

"Where's your car?"

"I don't drive."

"Then we ride," he said.

"No way." I shook my head. "This *way*," I insisted, and I started up the sidewalk.

"Squatch, have DT on standby, Glassjaw, you're with me." He fell into step beside me and pointed up and back at Squatch and called, "I don't call in thirty get ahold of Cipher, he knows what to do!"

"Got it, P!" Squatch was already moving across the street to the front of the motorcycle wrecking yard that was open for business.

"Step it up, girl," Glassjaw growled, and I sighed, lowered my plague doctor mask, and marched at a brisk pace toward home.

It was a good five-to-ten-minute walk, so not bad at all. I'd stabilized Mace myself, so I knew he was okay.

The two men traded a cautious look when I went up the stairs to the second floor and stuck the key in the lock of my apartment door. Reluctantly, they followed, and I let them into my space, leaning my staff against the wall by the door and hanging my mask on the protruding nail from the yellowing plaster beside it.

"Mace?" Glassjaw called.

Mace groaned and called out from the bedroom, the door a straight shot from the front one. "Yeah, Glass, I'm in here."

The two men traded a look and moved practically as one for the bedroom. I just shut my front door and locked it.

"Jesus Christ, what the fuck happened to you, bro?" Glassjaw demanded.

"Jumped by a bunch of pussy-ass frat boys. Where's Raven?"

"Right here," I said gently and appeared in the doorway. I crossed my arms and leaned a shoulder against it, hugging my stomach, crossing my legs at the shin, toe of one boot against the worn plank hardwoods.

"You alright?" Mace asked me and I nodded, keeping my expression cool and measured for the other two men who were staring at me.

"Hold on, buddy. Gonna call in some help," Maverick declared and raised his phone to his ear.

"Thanks," Mace said to me, and I nodded.

"I'll put some tea on, you want anything?" I asked him, and Glassjaw looked up at me.

"Yeah, sounds good... thanks," he said, and his hard looks had been traded for something softer and definitely more polite while Mav fixed me with a look of gratitude and a nod. I nodded back, but he never stopped speaking into his phone, low and insistent.

"Yeah, off sixteenth, toward Roxbury. Above the ice cream shop... Excelsior...Yeah. How long, bro? K."

I went into the kitchen and put the dented kettle on the tiny, ancient, half-sized stove, straining to hear what was being said as I twisted the knob to start it heating.

"No, bro... she saved my ass." I peeked around the kitchen doorway and through my bedroom's door into my bedroom. Mace was lying on one side of my bed, which was really just a queen-sized mattress on the floor decked in mismatched sheets from the second-hand store. Probably the nicest bed I'd ever owned if I was being honest.

"That skinny thing?" Glassjaw asked. "How'd she do that?"

"I don't know, man, I was blackout drunk and beat to shit... gonna have to ask her."

"Not really worried about it, more worried about you and getting you checked out by a real professional."

Mace grunted in agreement and I sighed to myself. Okay, so I wasn't like an EMT or certified or anything, but I was a volunteer medic down at Burning Man every year. I'd taken every CPR and First Aid course and taught myself everything I needed to know about triage and first aid. While I hadn't treated worse than some of the injuries Mace had sustained, I was confident in my ability that I certainly hadn't made anything *worse*. He was as stable as an ambulance crew or hospital could make him. I was certain of that fact.

Maverick made some noises of agreement into his phone and finally said, "Yeah, that'd be great. We'll see you in a couple three hours." He paused as he listened to someone on the other end of the line. "Thanks, bro. We'll owe you one."

He hung up and sighed, lifting his head and meeting my eyes where I was watching from around my little galley kitchen's doorway. His gaze was calculating and decidedly uncomfortable. I ducked back around the corner and away from it, standing in front of the stove waiting for the water in my kettle to come to a boil and hating myself a little bit for it.

I mean, I had all these burly ass bikers in my tiny-ass apartment and for lack of anything better to do I had relegated myself to literally boiling water.

*Don't panic, Raven. Don't panic,* I told myself over and over again, silently in my head. *No one knows they're here, and no one's going to drag you across the city line.*

It was frustrating.

I never used to be like this, but then...

"We owe you one."

I jumped and Maverick chuckled from my kitchen doorway. He wasn't a *big* man, not really. Slender, and not overly tall. Average, really, except for the devastatingly good looks and those deep, dark blue eyes. He peered at me from under his dark hair which was getting in need of a cut and I honestly felt nothing by way of heat or anything else. I mean, he was pretty to look at... so? I'd learned good looks meant nothing in the long run. Most guys that had them just exploited them anyway.

"Sorry," he said with a slight smirk that was surprisingly not off-putting, but actually rather charming. Or it would be if I didn't have my guard up as high as I did.

"It's fine," I said tonelessly, and he looked me over again, curiously this time.

"We'll be out of here as soon as possible," he said. "Got some brothers coming up from the Portland area with medical know-how to check our boy and declare one way or the other what to do."

I nodded and said, "You shouldn't move him. Give him a few days to chill and then he can move. Those ribs need stability and rest."

"You got medical training?" he asked.

"Some," I said. "No super shiny and professional certifications, I don't have an MD after my name, but I know what I'm doing."

He nodded thoughtfully and said, "We don't trust easy."

"Me either," I said quietly. And I didn't. Not anymore.

"We'll be out of here as soon as we can." He pushed off the doorway and turned.

"You said that already, and you know, it's no trouble, honestly," I said at his retreating back. He stopped and turned, coming back to lean in the doorway again. My anxiety spiked a bit at that. There were no windows in this kitchen, only a single doorway in and out of the narrow space.

He seemed to get that I was uncomfortable because he shifted so there was a way to edge around him if I needed to. The water started making noises, ticking and grumbling as it started to heat. It still had a way to go.

"Why do you say that?" he asked. "Everything about you seems to indicate otherwise."

"Some people helped me once," I said, rubbing my lips together thoughtfully. I didn't want to give anything about myself away, but it was true. It was also true that... "Consider this me paying it forward. He just needs a few days of rest and to heal up. I'll take the couch. I mean, I still have to work, but he can just chill. Have him checked out or whatever and we'll go from there."

"That's mighty generous of you..." he trailed off and raised his eyebrows, expecting me to fill in the blank.

"My friends call me Raven," I said and rubbed my sweating palms against my leggings.

He nodded slowly.

"Nice to meet you, Raven. I'm Mav, and the guy over there sitting with Mace is Glassjaw."

I nodded. "Anybody else headed this way?" I asked after his firm handshake.

"A few more of my guys are apt to show up," he said.

I nodded.

"Okay."

"You know where Mace's bike is at?"

"Oh, uh, I hadn't thought about that, but if I had to guess, it's probably still parked outside the bar." I jerked my head in the direction of Shoreman's a block over and two up.

"Which bar would that be?" he asked, a slow smile painting his lips which I think was meant to put me at ease but... yeah... "Rat City is lousy with 'em," he finished.

"Shoreman's," I said, and didn't like telling him where I worked, but... hell. *In for a penny, in for a pound*, I thought to myself. There wasn't really any going back on this one, and I guess there were worse things than being in good with The Sacred Hearts for a minute. At least I wasn't on the outs with them like I seemed to be with so many other factions around these parts. Law enforcement in particular.

"Thanks," he said, and he woke up his phone in his hand and tapped something out.

"Mav, what're you doing?" Glassjaw called.

"Having the prospect pick up Mace's bike from where he left it."

"Oh, got 'cha."

Maverick wandered back in the direction of my bedroom and I felt some of the tension leave my posture, the water starting to boil behind me. I sighed and brought down my teapot and three cups.

It was one of my best possessions, the teapot. A stellar find at a second-hand sale at a church. A genuine Brown Betty. I brought down three of my cracked, but still pretty teacups and spooned in some of my vanilla bourbon rooibos tea into my little brown pot. Pouring the water in after the tea, I dropped the lid on with a satisfying little clatter and set my kitchen timer for a three-minute steep time.

"What're you doing?" I jumped and turned around, eyeing Glassjaw over my shoulder.

"Making tea."

He gave me a sort of crooked grin and asked, "For bikers?"

"Only if it doesn't threaten your fragile masculinity," I answered flippantly, tempering my words with a smile. His smile grew, and he barked a laugh.

"Fair, fair," he said and stuck his hands in his pockets. "Look, about earlier…" He fixed me with a look, and I swallowed hard and stared back. "Took a lot of balls coming up on us cold like that. I appreciate it and I apologize if I scared you."

"Tea?" I asked evenly, and he smiled.

"Not my usual thing, but sure," he said back with a nod.

Cool.

## 3

*M*ace...

It took a couple of hours for the doc to get to Raven's. He was retired out of Vancouver, Washington, right there on the border with Portland. His medical license had been revoked by the state for assisting a terminally ill patient to the other side. That shit was legal just across the border, but his wife had been so bad, and you had to be a resident in Oregon for a year or some shit and, well... he couldn't stand watching her in so much pain. She'd begged him and he'd done his time.

As soon as he'd gotten out, he'd moved across into Portland and tried to rebuild his life. The club had helped; his cousin had brought him in. Now, he was on tap for emergencies like the odd beatdown like mine, or even a non-life-threatening gunshot wound or two.

He was also one of the reasons we were in the illegal prescription drug trade... he was our contact throughout the south and still had his finger on the pulse of where the drugs needed to go. He was also still in touch with old colleagues who knew how fucked the American healthcare system was. They were as fuckin' over it as he had been at the point when he'd given his wife the medication that she'd needed to skirt a lingering death from her inoperable brain tumor.

We filled a much-needed fucking gap, poured some filler in the cracks, and not a goddamn one of us was sorry for it.

"Shit, buddy. You look rough," he said, sliding his soft-sided med kit off his leather-clad shoulder and setting it down next to me.

"Concussion, fractured ribs for sure..." Raven's voice was soft from the doorway. She stood leaning against the doorframe, her arms crossed over her stomach, putting her ample chest on somewhat of display. She wasn't lying about the dreads being some wig. She had them off now, her dishwater blonde hair in a sort of sloppy, looping knot at the base of her skull as she turned her head, not looking at anyone. There was a sort of strange reaction as everyone in the room fixed their attention on her.

"Yeah, well, let's just have a look at 'cha here." Eulogy kneeled down next to me. That was his road name. Although his real name was Jack, a surefire way to get punched in the mouth or get him to hate you would be to call him "Eulogy" to his face.

That was the thing about road names. You didn't get to pick 'em – they were given to you. His was a reminder of the worst time in his life, of the life he took, but when the person you killed was your wife and the act didn't come from a place of angry passion or malice... well, needless to say, sometimes your brothers were fucking dicks and didn't quite know when to quit.

"Tell me what you need me to do, Jack," I muttered and he chuckled.

"Right now? Nothing. I need you to lie there and hold still until I can figure out how bad you are. You look like shit, bro."

I huffed a laugh and immediately winced.

He checked me over, and sat up a little straighter and asked, "You do this?"

Raven stood up straighter from where she slouched tiredly against the doorway now that all eyes were off her and on me. She said, "Yeah."

"I'm impressed," Jack declared, and he sounded it. "There's nothing for me to really do here that hasn't already been done. Her assessment and diagnosis are spot on. You shouldn't move for a few days. Rest, plenty of fluids, some pain relievers and let things set and your body heal."

"What kind of pain relief?" I asked. "Because shit, I could really use some."

"I'll give Mav a list to get outta your chapter stores. Some oxys for the first few days for sure. Canadian Tylenol after that."

"The good shit," Fenris grunted.

"The good shit," Eulogy agreed.

"Thanks for coming up all this way," I said quietly.

"Any time, but let's try and make this the last time if you know what I mean." He raked his hand back through his brown hair which was getting a little long and was going prematurely silver.

"Yeah, I'm with you there," I grunted.

"Talk to you?" he asked Mav, hefting his med pack and Mav nodded. They went for the doorway and Raven turned sideways so they could get out. They stood by the front door to her apartment and spoke in low tones. Mav looked her way and over her considering. I could see the wheels turning and was grateful the swelling had gone down enough I could see again.

"How you hanging in there?" Glassjaw asked from the only chair in the corner.

"Could use something for the pain," I admitted. It'd been grinding on me long enough now that I was *tired*.

"I'll get you some water," Raven murmured, and I heard her shuffle off. She'd made this tea earlier and had Glassjaw help me drink some. While tea wasn't my thing, it'd somehow helped take the edge off. I wondered if it was some sort of hippy-chick homeopathic shit, but I didn't want to be rude and ask.

"Here, man." Fenris came near and put a couple of round pills in my hand.

"You came prepared. Gotta like that." I let him help me sit up and put the pills in my mouth, wincing. Raven came back and pressed a cold glass into my hand, and I chased the tablets down with several cool drinks.

"You shouldn't move if you can avoid it for at least a few days. You can stay here; I don't mind. I just have to go to work. I can sleep on the couch or whatever."

"You sure about that?" Fenris asked her, and she nodded. He gave a nod and looked at me. "It's honestly probably the best thing, bro."

"I don't want to upend your life, sweetheart," I told her, and she smiled.

"Might be nice to have some company," she said glibly. "It gets kind of lonely up here all by myself."

I smiled and fought not to chuckle, coughing a couple of times and wincing which was almost worse.

"Don't make me laugh," I begged, and her expression smoothed.

"Get some rest," she murmured and pulled the thin blankets up a little higher on me.

"I'm going to talk to Mav and Jack." Fenris got to his feet.

I closed my eyes and waited for the damn pills to take effect. Let the grownups sort it out.

~

I SLEPT. I didn't know how long, but when I woke back up, Raven was gone and Fenris was sitting with his back against the wall beside the bed, his legs stretched out in front of him, booted feet crossed at the ankle while he fucked around on his phone.

"Shit, bro, how long you been sitting there?" I asked, groggily.

"Ah, it's been a fuckin' *minute*," he said, stretching.

"What time is it?" I asked. It was dark outside the glimpse of kitchen window that I could see through the bedroom door and in through the kitchen door. The only window in the fuckin' place that I could tell.

"Getting on toward three."

"In the morning?"

He chuckled. "Yeah."

"What the fuck you doing here then? Shouldn't you be home with your lady?"

He put his phone in his jacket pocket and nodded, the long braid of his blond mohawk dragging across the leather of his cut.

"Yeah, I should, but Aspen's cool. She knows what's up and Jack said we shouldn't leave you alone for the first twenty-four or so."

"Got it," I muttered and sighed out, closing my eyes.

"Need anything?" he asked.

"Yeah, help up. I gotta take a leak. Some water maybe."

"I got you," Fen agreed, and he helped leverage me up off the mattress on the floor and into a standing position. My head swam, dizzy from the painkillers or a concussion, I didn't fuckin' know. It throbbed as I staggered into the bathroom and I had to brace myself against the wall over the john like I was drunk as fuck still to get my aim right.

Taking that leak was grim. Pretty sure there was blood, but with the blows to the kidneys I'd taken from those fuckers kicking the shit out of my back, I wasn't really surprised. It'd happened before and I wasn't dead yet, so I wasn't going to fucking worry about it too much.

I went back and laid down again after washing my hands with the bar of herbal smelling raw soap on the edge of the old-school cracked-pedestal sink. I heard Fenris in the kitchen, the tap running. He came in and scoffed.

"This place is a fuckin' dump," he said, and I nodded.

"Yeah, I noticed." What did he expect from an apartment in Rat City?

He sat back down and handed me the glass of water. "Have to run the tap for a while just to get clear water."

"Pipes are old as fuck," I muttered and drank the cold water down greedily.

"Why she would wanna live here is beyond me," he said, looking around at the cracked and water-stained ceiling, the equally cracked and yellowed plaster walls – and I do mean *plaster*. The building was old, like 1940s old and the walls still original. It was all hard original plaster not more modern drywall.

Before my stint in prison, I had worked for one of those contractor places that would come clean up after fire and water damage. It was shitty work, but it paid pretty decent. I wanted to go back, but the boss I had been under was a dick. The evangelical type. Missed the whole point of what it was to be a good Christian.

An actual follower of Christ would have taken me back in a heartbeat. I'd been one of his best employees. This guy, though? Said not only no but hell no. How would it look having a felon on parole working for his company? Like anyone would fuckin' know by looking at me.

Well, maybe they might, but you look at half the fuckin' guys working for him, you would think the same thing. I guess it was the "parole" part he didn't want to deal with.

*Fuckin' jagoff.*

"Same thing about you, bro," Fenris said when I didn't say anything.

"What?" I asked. "What about me?"

"None of us can figure out why the fuck you were at Shoreman's of all places. I mean, what a fuckin' *dive*, man... what's the matter? Free booze at the club not good enough?" His voice held humor, but under it was worry.

"I just needed a break," I mumbled.

"From us?" Fenris asked, and he sounded a little offended.

"No," I muttered. "It's stupid."

"Mace, man, you gotta give me something to work with here, buddy. You almost got beat to fuckin' *death*. We're fuckin' worried about you."

I heaved a sigh. "I'm jealous, alright?" I groused.

"*Jealous?*" he echoed in disbelief.

"Yeah. I get locked up and all y'all out here hooking up in these beautiful *meaningful* relationships and fuck me, *I want that...*"

"Dude, I think everybody wants that," Fen declared, and he sounded a bit shocked. I opened one eye and looked up at him.

"Didn't take me for the type, or what?"

"It's not that, I just... I guess I didn't think it fuckin' bothered you that much being single. I mean, you got plenty of pussy throwing itself at you—"

"Not the same thing," I countered.

"Yeah, I get that," he said. "You didn't let me finish."

He didn't get to, either. Raven came in her front door. I caught sight of her through the bedroom doorway, a straight shot to her front door as she shut it behind her and leaned heavily against it as she threw the long line of bolts.

"You look like hell," Fen commented dryly.

"Tired," she muttered, dragging the strap of her canvas messenger bag over her head, and dropping it with a loud clunk against the worn hardwood floor at her feet.

"The hell was that?" Fen laughed.

"Probably my pistol," she said with a shrug.

"You got a gun in that thing?"

She stooped and dragged it out and Fen started laughing.

"Is that a fucking starter pistol?" he asked and sure as shit, it was. A long-barreled starter pistol, the kind Connery had in that popular old Bond promo shot.

"Shut up," she grumbled, putting it back into her bag. "It got those fuckers off of him, didn't it?"

"Oh, shit. Is that how you did it?" Fen asked and she nodded, tiredly and went over to the couch, falling onto it face-first.

I laughed, it hurt like hell. Fen stopped mid-chuckle to turn a wary eye on me.

"Raven," I called out, but there was no answer. I felt myself soften up. *Was she already out?* "Raven," I tried again.

Fen got up and went over and looked down.

"She is out like a goddamn traffic light," he said, and I nodded.

"Some fuckin' bullshit," I muttered.

"What?" he asked, looking down at her curiously

"Her sleeping on her own damn couch."

He lifted a shoulder in a half-assed shrug and said, "She signed up for it." He was doing that thing he sometimes did without realizing it – staring down at her a little intently, like he was memorizing every line and feature but at the same time wondering what she would look like with her skin off. It was an incredibly creepy and intimate look, and it didn't sit well with me.

Usually, it was kind of fascinating watching him watch somebody like that. It was something that was uniquely fuckin' Fenris – or so I'd thought until I met that one dude from the mother chapter out in Kentucky. *That guy* was a stone-cold fuckin' freak.

It wasn't a sexual thing, that look. It wasn't gendered, or anything you could label. What it was, was nuanced, predatory, a raw curiosity that usually involved blood or ichor if the dude casting that look was given a chance to indulge whatever curiosity he had.

"Fen," I said, and he shook himself a little, as though waking up from some terrible dream. "I can't say I much like the way you're looking at her right now, buddy."

"Not her," he said honestly. "Sorry, bro… I just have my suspicions."

"Yeah?" I asked.

"Yeah."

His blue eyes met my brown ones, and a silent something passed between us. I nodded and he nodded too.

There was something to it. The way she didn't want or like to draw attention. I mean, nobody willingly lived in a dump like this that wasn't hiding from or running from something.

"Help me up, bro."

"Why?"

"So, I can get her in her own bed tonight to sleep. I'll take the couch."

He chuckled and shook his head.

"This bed's big enough for the both of you," he said, kneeling down, and swiping the weird wig thing she had going on off her head. He laid it over the back of the couch and spoke softly. Raven groaned and turned over in her sleep and he said, "Atta girl."

He got his arms under her and leveraged her willowy thin frame up and brought her over. I struggled to sit up and twitched back the blankets on the one side and he set her down. I flicked them over her legs as she turned onto her side toward me and tucked her hands under her cheek.

"Thanks," I said, and he nodded.

"Another round of painkillers?" he asked.

"Yeah."

He got me the pills and some more water. I took the tablets, wincing at the taste they left in my mouth. Fuckers dissolved too quickly.

"Go on, get out of here, bro," I said quietly. "You've got Aspen waiting."

"Doc said to not leave you alone," he tried to argue, and I raised my eyebrows.

"I'm not alone," I declared and jerked my head in Raven's direction.

"Right." He nodded.

"You don't need to watch us both sleep," I said, and he nodded.

"Okay. I'll send the prospect by tomorrow afternoon with your new phone. Cipher is getting all that shit handled."

"Thanks, man."

"No problem."

He let himself out and I didn't bother getting up to lock the door. It was a bad hood, sure, but that was another thing Fen left behind in case I should need it. I glanced at the black nine-millimeter on the floor beside the bed within easy reach and turned my back on it to focus on the girl in the bed beside me.

She was so tired, she even looked exhausted in sleep. I didn't think that had everything to do with me, though... there was another type of world weariness under it all. I closed my eyes and breathed in slow, her rich, earthy, herbal scent filling my nose.

She smelled good. Natural. Like a woman. God, I'd missed that smell...

## 4

*R*aven...

I sucked in a sharp, shuddering breath and stretched, smiling to myself when I met resistance at my back. What could I say? I was an unabashed cuddle slut and while I had *no idea* how I'd managed to get into my bed, as I distinctly remembered crashing on my couch face-first after my shift, I couldn't argue that it was *really nice* to wake up to being held.

A guilty pleasure I shook off entirely too quick as I looked back into Mace's battered face, propped on his hand, and murmured, "Sorry, I don't remember crawling into bed."

"You didn't. I had Fenris put you here."

I blinked, taken aback, and felt my mouth drop open into a little 'o' of surprise.

"Oh," I finally managed, not sure how I felt about that.

"Nothing by it," he said carefully, searching my face, his own expression carefully closed off and... and vulnerable in its own way.

"Couldn't stand the thought of you sleeping on your own couch. It didn't sit well with me."

I gave him a slightly crooked smile and said, "And they say chivalry is dead."

"Not with me, it's not."

He took his hand from my waist and I bit my lips together silently for a moment and finally ventured with, "It's okay. I... I kind of liked it there." Which was another thing I didn't know how to quite feel about.

He smiled slowly and even with all the bruising and the swelling; he was handsome.

"Yeah?" he asked, putting it back.

I smiled carefully. "Yeah."

"Well alright then."

"You need anything?" I asked, forgetting my manners. I mean, *shit*. He was hurt and here I was making it all about *me!*

"No," he said. "You should sleep some more."

I smiled then and said honestly, "I was about to ask if that would be alright with you."

"Guess you have your answer," he murmured with a cheeky grin, and holy hell, my heart almost stopped at that smile. I mean, it damn sure tripped over itself and then started just *pounding*.

"Okay," I said and laid back down. I sighed out and he cuddled me. It felt *so nice*.

"You good with this?" he asked a moment later as I sighed out again.

"Yeah, you?" I asked.

"Yeah, but what was that for?" he asked.

"What?"

"That big sigh."

"Oh, it was nothing," I lied, but I'd always been a bad liar.

He jostled me a tiny bit. "Raven," he said, tone gently chiding.

"It's nice is all… I've um, I've missed this. Just, being held by someone." Which was true. Which had led me down the road to ruin in the first place. A wave of sorrow crested somewhere in the center of my chest and crashed over me.

I could hear his careful smile in his voice when he spoke next.

"Yeah, me too. I mean, I've missed having someone to hold onto."

"How long have you been single?" I asked, curious, though knowing it was probably none of my business.

He snorted. "Too long."

I thought about it and answered, "Yeah, me too."

I closed my eyes and after a few moments of silence figured the conversation was concluded and so I slept some more.

THE NEXT TIME I WOKE, it was to the sound of soft masculine voices and I was alone in my room. I pushed up into a sitting position sharply worried about Mace, and the voices ceased. I looked into my little living room. Mace was seated on my couch, Glassjaw standing over him, both looking in my direction.

"Did we wake you?" Glassjaw asked, and I ignored the question in favor of one of my own.

"What time is it?"

"A little after noon," Mace answered.

"Shit, I overslept," I muttered, and I had. I'd missed the food pantry up at Holy Family. *Shit.*

"Where you gotta be?" Glassjaw asked. "I can give you a ride."

I shook my head.

"Closed now, I missed it."

"Clue us in, Raven," Mace said gently.

"Food pantry up at the Catholic church," I finally relented.

"How much you need?" Glassjaw pulled a wad of cash out of his front pocket and I blinked. I don't think I'd ever seen that much cash in one place at one time and that included counting the till at the bar.

"What?" I asked, as much to buy time as anything.

"Least we can do with you putting me up like this," Mace said, and I frowned slightly and pushed to my feet, giving a long stretch.

"What are you even doing up, anyway?" I asked, changing the subject. "You should be resting."

"I couldn't take lying down anymore." He chuckled and winced.

I rubbed the back of my neck and nodded tiredly, that made sense.

"Anyway, you need anything else?" Glassjaw asked, peeling off some bills and handing them to Mace.

"No?" I asked a little dazed and still waking up.

Both men chuckled and I felt myself turn red. *Of course, he wasn't asking you...*

I lurched into the bathroom and shut the door, bracing myself on the edge of the sink and sighing at my reflection.

I looked wrecked. Like, *damn.*

I ran water in the sink and waited for it to both clear and get warm before scrubbing my face. I needed a shower; some fresh clothes, but I didn't want or need as much of an audience as I had out there for that. I mean, Mace I was comfortable with… Glassjaw could suck it. I was still mistrustful after he tried to strong arm me. First impressions, they were a lasting one.

I used the bathroom, washed my hands again, brushed my teeth, and without anything left to do decided I had better quit stalling and get out there. When I emerged from the bathroom, it was to silence. I peeked around the corner into the living room to find Mace on my couch, alone, a new phone in his hands.

"You got a Wi-Fi password, and what's your network?" he asked.

"I can't afford groceries, and you expect me to have Wi-Fi?" I laughed and he grinned.

"Shit," he muttered, and I chuckled some more, coming into the living room.

"Oh, wow."

There was a small television hooked up to a video game console on the floor across from the couch. I hadn't been at an angle to notice it before.

"I rob the free Wi-Fi from the ice cream shop downstairs. They don't mind," I told him. "Gets sketchy during business hours with everyone connecting to it, but in the evening after hours, it's fine."

"Excelsior exclamation point?" he asked.

"Yeah, that's the network."

"Password?" he asked.

"Here."

He handed me the controller and I entered the password and handed it back.

"Cool, thanks," he said.

"You're welcome."

"Here." He handed me his phone. I blinked at the screen.

"What's this?" I asked.

"Groceries. Order whatever you want or need, stock up, have it delivered."

"Oh, it's alright. I can—"

"Raven." He stopped me with his even tone that brooked no argument. I blinked and held very still, not sure what to make of all of this. "Order whatever you need," he said gently when I said nothing at all.

"Got anything you want in particular?" I asked softly.

"I'm starving, so whatever is quick."

"I, uh… it says it takes up to two hours for delivery. I can run downstairs and up the block to the noodle place. They're cheap and easy."

He held up the cash that Glassjaw had handed him.

"Take it," he ordered and again, it brooked no argument.

I handed back his phone and didn't take it. Not yet anyway.

"Let me grab a two-minute shower and get dressed. I'll run to the noodle shop, come back here and order groceries while we eat."

"Efficient. I like it."

I smiled.

"You don't have to do all of this, you know," I said, turning back from the doorway to my bedroom.

"You saved my life," he said plaintively. "I owe you a fuck of a lot more than just some food."

"I'm uneasy taking anything from—"

"Me? The club?" he asked.

I swallowed hard. "The latter. You do know you all have a reputation."

"Yeah, and it's well earned," he agreed matter-of-factly. "But you're not on the receiving end of the bad. You made yourself a friend of the club for what you did. The club takes care of its friends."

"I don't know what that means."

"It means get your shower, sweetheart. It means, I buy you dinner and groceries for the week and we sit down and either play a game or watch some movies until you have to go to work tonight."

"I don't work tonight. It's my night off."

"Even better." He smiled, and pain edged his expression.

"You need something?" I asked, and he smiled a little bigger.

"Food," he said.

I startled a bit.

"Oh! Right. Sorry."

"No need to apologize," he said to my retreating back as I gathered clean clothes and my towel and went into the bathroom once more.

I tried to keep my shower brief but the hot water against my back was so sweet, it was hard to resist its siren's call. A cloud of steam preceded me out of the bathroom and I sighed, toweling my hair and padding barefoot back into the living room. Mace paused whatever he was playing and looked up.

"Feel better?" he asked.

"Yeah, sorry I took so long."

"You don't have to apologize for that."

"Shouldn't be more than fifteen minutes," I said. "Noodle shop is fast."
I sat down on the floor to put my socks on, and he smirked

"I'm a big boy who's used to taking care of myself," he said.

"What's that supposed to mean?" I asked with a slight laugh.

"Means that when you went in to shower," he held up his phone, "I ordered up the food to be delivered. I just went with the generic stuff."

"Generic?" I asked.

"Yeah, the shit you actually recognize on the menu – beef round eye number one or whatever. Times two."

"Oh!" He'd ordered for me too. "You guessed right," I said. "Thanks."

"Don't mention it," he replied as there was a knock at my door.

I got up and went over, took the food from the driver as Mace called out, "Thanks, man!" and I shut and locked everything up.

"I'm not used to all of this," I said with a nervous laugh as I went past him. He caught my hand. I looked down at him and he up at me and there was something in his brown gaze. Something heavy.

"You did a good thing," he said, and he swallowed hard. Emotion skated behind his gaze and my discomfort eased in the face of it. "You're still doing it by letting me recover here for a couple days. Let me thank you with a meal or two, yeah?"

"Yeah," I said a little startled when he shook my hand when I didn't respond right away. His hand was gentle, and warm where it wrapped around mine lightly and it sent a current of... of *something* through me. Something pleasant. Which was unexpected.

He nodded and let me go. I turned the corner into my little kitchen to fix our soup, my mind a million miles away and racing.

When I returned to the living room, the console was on the menu screen and Mace was looking uncomfortable.

"You okay?" I asked.

"I will be, just need some food in me and maybe some of the good Tylenol."

"You sure you don't need something a little more substantial than Tylenol?" I asked and he took his bowl from me.

"Maybe later when I go to bed. That shit knocks me out and I would rather use it sparingly."

"Makes sense," I said and sat down on the floor, putting my back against the old, worn couch.

"What kind of movies you like?" he asked me, and I lifted a shoulder in a shrug.

"Never really watched a whole lot," I said. "Never really been my thing."

"That's not helpful," he said with a chuckle and I smiled.

"I don't know, thrillers? Mysteries? Drama?"

"You asking me or you telling me?" he asked with a laugh that ended on a groan.

"Shit, sorry."

"Stop apologizing." He rolled his eyes. "You don't have anything to be sorry for."

I blushed and turned toward the television that looked so out of place in my barren living room and said, "Habit, I guess."

He grunted and spooled over to a streaming service, opening it up. He scrolled through and we went back and forth, looking through different selections until we landed on something that looked tolerable to the both of us.

I would be lying if I said it wasn't nice, watching something over noodle soup in the comfort of my own living room.

When I finished my bowl and set it aside, his phone appeared over my shoulder with the grocery app open.

I chuckled and took it, perusing selections, asking what he might like for dinner later. We talked food, and I made some picks and handed his phone back to him. He handed it back to me at least twice telling me to get more than that.

"You got a microwave?" he asked when I handed it back for what I hoped was the last time.

"Yeah, why?" I asked.

"Popcorn," he said, and I smiled.

"Okay."

He made a few additions and put the order through, and I tried not to think about the cost. I'd been trying to ride the line between being conservative with his money and still buying enough that he would be satisfied. I picked up some staples, sure, but had gone a little buck wild in the produce section with fresh fruits and vegetables.

I was relieved he seemed satisfied this last time with what I'd picked. I didn't want to be insulting, but I didn't want to spend his money, either!

It was just another example of how I couldn't win for losing, I guess.

"Hey." I looked up from my vacant staring at the television and back over my shoulder. "You good?" he asked.

"Yeah, I just... I don't feel like I really did anything that anyone else wouldn't do and I don't like taking your money," I said honestly.

"Even after that ass whoopin' of the ages, you still give humanity way more credit than it deserves," he said with a charmed sort of smile.

I rolled my eyes.

"I'd like to believe people are basically good," I muttered with a lift of my shoulders and I would... but an uneasy feeling almost like heartburn rose in the center of my chest because I had been through it, and I knew the truth... people *weren't* basically good anymore. Far from it. Which is why I almost felt like I had to be, to balance some of the scales.

*Do no harm, but take no shit...* It had been my mantra when I first started out but somehow, somewhere along the way, I'd lost sight of that last bit.

I sighed unhappily and got up to take the dishes into the kitchen and to generally clean up. I heard Mace grunt and the springs of my worn couch groan in relief as he heaved himself to his feet.

"You okay?" I called out.

"Ready to lie down, maybe take a nap," he said, and I nodded without looking, washing up bowls and utensils at my sink.

"I don't suppose I could get you to maybe lie down with me," he said and I jumped slightly and turned. He was leaning heavily in the doorway to my kitchen, and he looked... vulnerable. Something in his eyes that wasn't something I could speak on. I mean, it was one of those things that was there, that you knew it when you saw it. That called to your heart and my heart? It answered with an almost longing of its own.

I hadn't realized how lonely I'd gotten.

"You're sure?" I asked softly, hesitating, a moment of my own vulnerability answering his. I was unsure. I wasn't anything to be wanted. I could put on a veneer of awesomeness when I worked, but here in my own apartment, with him standing there battered and bruised looking at me looking at him, asking for...

I didn't really know what he was asking for, to be honest. It definitely wasn't sex. Not in his condition.

"If I wasn't sure, I wouldn't be asking," he said with a crooked smile.

I nodded, and scraped my bottom lip between my teeth, dried my hands on the dish towel, and for no reason at all other than my own nervousness, made sure the drain board was over the lip of the sink, letting the dishes air dry in the little rack.

Mace held out a hand to me and I took it. He gently led me back to bed and I spotted him as he eased himself down onto the mattress on the floor.

"I wish you had a frame for this," he said with a slight chuckle.

I smiled and told him honestly, "Me too. You okay?"

"I'm good, just everything hurts." He laid down on his side with a weary sigh and I went around and laid down too, facing him, several inches of mattress between us as we faced each other.

"Somehow I always pictured myself rescuing some damsel in distress like some white knight," he said and closed his eyes, pain marring his face.

"Yeah?" I asked softly.

"Yeah, never thought I'd be picked up by some warrior queen."

I snorted. "I'm no warrior and I'm certainly no queen," I murmured.

"Don't sell yourself short," he said and fixed me with a look I couldn't quite identify.

I laughed a bit nervously, blushing a bit furiously, unused to and unsure what to do with compliments the likes he was paying me. I would be lying if I said it didn't feel good – it did. I just didn't know how to take a good compliment and always felt so undeserving of them.

He reached out and touched the side of my face, stroking his thumb over the skin of my cheek. He leaned forward and I froze as he pressed his lips lightly to my forehead.

I sucked in a sharp breath and positively *melted* from that warm press of his soft lips against my skin. *Which was so confusing!*

"Thanks for getting involved," he murmured, and his breath was warm and sent tingles along my scalp and down my back.

*God, that felt so nice.*

He pushed some of my hair behind my ear and looked me over, while I looked back. We lay like that silent, just taking each other in until a loud knock at my door made us both jump and him wince.

"Oh! Oh, I'm sorry!"

"It's fine. Groceries," he grunted, and I reluctantly pushed myself to my feet.

"Rest," I told him and went to the door to accept the delivery.

There was a lot more than what I thought I ordered, and it had gotten here super fast! I had no idea what I was going to do with all this food, but I had better figure it out.

## 5

_M_ ace...

I listened to her move, almost whisper quiet, putting things away. She was different here in her home as opposed to how she'd been in the bar. Quiet, reserved, almost tired. It wasn't a physical tired. It was almost a weariness of the soul. I could relate entirely too well. Mine stemmed from loneliness, hers was something different. How, I just couldn't put my finger on yet.

It wasn't a mystery I was in any kind of hurry to unravel. I had time. Nothing _but_ time, really. Prison had done one thing for me; it had instilled an almost superhero-like level of patience. An appreciation that anything and everything could and would come in due time.

I had no desire to go back into the system, and I admit to having similar feelings of frustration as the first time I'd ever been caged or locked up. Except instead of concrete and metal bars, the prison I was in at the moment was a prison of my own body. One of pain, and new limitations imposed by injury.

It rankled me and left me feeling restless with nowhere for that restless energy to go. Add to it, I just couldn't fucking get comfortable, no matter how hard I tried. My mood was swiftly starting to deteriorate.

"Here." I startled and looked back over my shoulder where Raven kneeled behind me. She handed me some pain pills and held onto a glass of water.

"Thanks," I grated, a bit ashamed to admit I needed the drugs.

"You shouldn't wait so long between doses," she chided gently, and I sighed after swallowing the pills down.

"Addiction runs in the family," I told her. "I'd rather not go there."

"Ah." She made a sound of understanding, but it sounded like that understanding ran deep, just from that one syllable alone.

"You got an addict or three in your family tree?" I asked, and she smiled and stuttered a bit of a laugh at my bad poetry.

"Something like that," she confessed.

"Then you know," I said and grunted turning to settle back down.

"I know," she said quietly and rose as noiselessly as she'd arrived and departed the room. She was in a nice pair of athletic leggings and an oversize tee with the neck cut out, so it hung artfully off one shoulder, the cotton midriffed so she was modest, all the important bits covered, but *damn*.

She was lithe, graceful on her feet, and the long shining fall of her light bronze hair begged to have my hands in it. I wanted to revel in her, bring her silky hair to my nose and breathe her in deep. Her scent was something else, too. Rich, deeply herbal, and natural. She was the goddess Persephone, all rich earth and green growing things, and I wanted to know her – but I didn't know how.

Shit, she didn't owe me anything, and me? I owed her everything. *Everything.* She'd saved my ass from being a permanent cripple, or worse – dead. I was well aware of that fact with how deeply everything ached, the bruises feeling like they were bone-fuckin' deep.

I couldn't sleep. I didn't want to, really. Not while she was awake. Instead, I lay with my eyes closed and just listened. Listened to her put things away and listened as she tried to puzzle out *where* to put some things in her tiny-ass kitchen. I smiled to myself. I'd loaded her up on the non-perishable shit. She'd picked a lot of health food stuff – lentils, quinoa, and oatmeal.

She baked her own bread, at least I thought so. She'd ordered a couple different types of flour and yeast. I wasn't sure what the difference was between the dry stuff and the nutritional stuff, but she'd gotten both.

She went fairly liberal on the fruits and veg, and I didn't up her quantities too much with it just being her here. I wouldn't be here any longer than I needed to be, so there wasn't much sense going overboard to feed two for too long.

"Mace?"

I jolted lightly; I'd started to drift without meaning to.

"Yeah?" I asked.

"Your friend is here, with clean clothes," she murmured, and I looked up.

"Hey, Prospect," I muttered.

"Jesus, you look like shit," Sauley said, and I knew it was bad but—

"Thanks, bro." I grunted and sat up.

"Sorry, man. They said it was bad but… I didn't know what to expect."

"You could use a bath or a shower," Raven said gently. "The hot water would help with the stiffness."

I nodded. "Sounds painful," I said.

"Probably, but you'll probably feel better for it. I can help you if you can't." She directed that second "you" at Sauley.

"Ahhh—" Sauley looked taken aback.

"Fuck that, I don't want him seeing me naked," I said, and Raven laughed.

"That leaves me seeing you naked," she said dryly, and I shook my head. "You don't have to, either. I can do it myself."

"You'll need help," she said, gently.

"Naw, fuck that, I've got it," I argued.

"Fine. Bath, not shower. I don't want you to fall," she countered, and she looked like she wasn't about to take any shit.

I snorted.

"Bro, I'd listen to the lady," Sauley said.

I gave him a dirty look. What I wanted to say was *shut the fuck up, prospect. I want your advice; I'll give it to you.*

What I didn't want was Raven to take it wrong. She didn't know our world and the general hazing that went along with signing onto the club charter. Plus, Sauley wasn't trying to be a dick, unlike me. He was just genuinely trying to help. He was a good kid.

"What'd you bring me?" I asked.

He sighed and said, "What the doc ordered. Sweats, loose-fitting clothing. Comfortable." He shrugged. "Sorry it took so long, I had… uh…" he eyed Raven. "Club business," he muttered finally.

I nodded. It probably wasn't too deep of club business, but I caught his drift. Business enough that the citizen between us didn't need to know about it.

"You did good," I told him.

"I'll draw you that bath," Raven said, arching a brow. She went into the bathroom and turned on the tub. I pinched the prospect's cheek and gave it a tight shake between forefinger and thumb when he helped himself to an eyeful of her ass as she bent over the tub.

"Don't get cute," I told him, and he grinned, rubbing out his cheek.

"Sorry, bro. Didn't realize she was off the menu," he said quietly, letting the tub drown him out to her ears.

"Not trying to disturb her life any more than I have, that's all," I said when she looked back our way.

"I told you before, it's no trouble," she said, straightening.

*Ha. That's a straight-up lie.*

In the end, I had Sauley leave what he brought and told him to fuck off – as polite as could be, but he got the picture. When Raven shut the front door, I gasped, reaching over the back of my head was a lesson in agony. I got the shirt halfway up my back and over my head, groaning when light hands touched my arms and Raven's voice insisted, "*Stop!* You're only going to hurt yourself and tire yourself out. Let me help you."

I relented, and let her take my dirty, bloodstained, and torn tee the rest of the way off me. I stopped her hands when she went for my belt.

"Whoa, hey!" She immediately backed off, turning scarlet.

"I'm sorry," she rushed out. "I didn't mean—"

"It's okay," I said quick to cut her off. "Just took me by surprise is all."

She wouldn't look at me and looked like she was close to tears with, if I had to guess, embarrassment.

"It's okay," I soothed. Wincing, I raised my arms and asked, "These wraps need to stay on?"

"No, of course not."

She went for them and gentler than I could have imagined anyone could be, unclipped the Ace bandages and unwound them carefully from around my ribcage. I grunted and winced.

"Didn't realize how much that was doing for me," I confessed with a restrained laugh, and she nodded.

"I know, it's like that," she said.

"Sounds like you speak from experience," I said carefully.

"I do," she confessed, and her sorrow was as palpable as my rage was instantaneous.

"How bad?" I asked carefully.

"Bad enough," she said. "I'd... I'd rather not say more than that."

"No, I get it," I said, and she glanced up at me with steely blue eyes, the outer iris wreathed in an iron gray. Her eyes were stunning. Reminding me of an overcast, storm clouded sky over the churning of Elliot Bay.

"You have really pretty eyes," I said, her gaze apparently taking out my brain-to-mouth filter.

She quickly looked away and said, "Thank you. Can you get up?"

That was a fuckin' misery, but I made it.

"You can get your pants," she said and actually turned around, giving me her back. I chuckled.

"Ain't ashamed of what I got, you don't have to do that," I said.

"It's okay," she said, and her posture was stiff.

I got everything undone, but...

"Fuck." She twitched and I sighed. "I need help getting things off all the way," I said with a sigh.

She nodded and turned around, keeping her eyes resolutely on my face while she did what needed doing. I don't know if it was better or worse, her looking at me like that as she took my pants.

*Worse, definitely worse,* I thought to myself as my cock stirred.

She turned and preceded me into the bathroom and bent to shut off the water. *Fuck* if that view of her ass didn't send me from a twitch in my manhood to half-mast and growing taller by the second.

I covered myself with my hands when she glanced behind herself in my direction and I sniffed.

"I thought you weren't shy..." she said with an almost sly slow-spreading grin.

"It's not that," I confessed and wondered if she could see the creeping blush through the bruising.

The smile evaporated and she looked almost timid when she said, "Oh."

"Sorry. Really, I am, it's just..." I stopped myself before I could embarrass myself further.

"What?" she asked, straightening.

"You're my kind of beautiful," I said, and rushed out, "Shit, that sounded corny, fuck."

She hugged herself across the middle and bit her bottom lip. She didn't smile, but she didn't look displeased, either.

"No, it was nice... thank you," she murmured and turned sideways so I could get past her.

It was some interesting jockeying to get me into the fuckin' tub and it was a little too full for the displacement created by my ass. Still, as old and shabby as the fuckin' thing was, it was clean. She kept her space neat. A real minimalist or whatever.

"You okay?" she asked as I tried to breathe around the pain. The only good thing about it was with as much hurt as I was in? Total boner killer.

"Yeah, yeah I'm good," I said.

She sighed and I could see she was strained, emotionally or whatever, and I felt it too.

"Look, as soon as I can, I'll get out of here. I can't tell you how much I appreciate everything you're doing. Truly. I owe you. A lot more than some fuckin' groceries."

"It's not you," she said around an uncomfortable laugh. "It's not. Really."

"What is it, then?" I asked, capturing her gaze with mine where she sat on the closed lid of the john.

Her lips thinned and she shook her head, remaining resolutely mute on the subject.

"Okay, that's cool with me. We don't have to talk about it or anything at all, really."

"You must think I'm a total basket case," she said with a sigh, putting her face in her hands.

"No," I answered truthfully, even though it hadn't been asked. "I'm not sure what's going on, and it's not my place to judge," I said with a shrug. "If I had to guess, though, I'd say you've maybe been through some rough stuff?"

She nodded, looking away, and said softly, "Yeah."

"You don't have to tell me anything," I said. "But if you want to talk or anything, I'm here."

She smiled and still wouldn't really look at me which was fine. I think she was doing it for my modesty's sake at this point.

"I appreciate it," she murmured.

"Don't mention it," I said.

~

THE NEXT MORNING, I woke in pain to my phone shrilling beside the bed. I answered it, groggy and the woman's voice on the other end of the line was like being doused by a bucket of ice water.

"So, did you just forget you had an appointment with me this morning, Mr. Anderson?"

"Oh, oh, shit no. My phone got broken and the reminder didn't transfer over," I answered honestly. "I'm like two blocks away."

"Uh-huh."

"No, really, I am. Dumb luck that part but it's the God's honest truth, Kim. I'm right around the corner and I'll piss test, I'll do whatever you want. Just please—"

"You have ten minutes, Caleb. Get here," she said curtly, and the line went dead in my ear.

"Fuck," I muttered.

"What is it?" Raven asked thickly from beside me.

"Fucking parole officer. The office is around the corner. I have ten minutes. I've gotta get there."

I groaned and sat up, struggling. Raven sat up too.

"Parole?" she echoed faintly.

"Yeah," I said unhappily. We'd talked a lot, late into the night. She knew I'd been locked up but I hadn't mentioned the whole parole thing. "Can you help me get there?" I asked.

"I can get you close, but—"

"No, that's great. I don't need you to go in with me."

"I just… I just don't have a – you know what? Never mind. I like you. I don't want you to be in trouble. You probably shouldn't be seen with me," she said softly, and she got up and started getting dressed. I pulled my boots on under my straight-legged sweats.

"That's a fucked-up thing to say," I said, coughing and crying out with pain.

"It's the truth, I won't get into it now… just, come on. We should hurry."

She ducked under my arm and helped me up and into my jacket. I left my cut. She shrugged into her coat and resumed her position as my crutch, and we went swiftly. It was raining outside and cold. The chill burned my lungs at first and I fought not to cough. It hurt, every step a grinding painful ache.

Kim, my parole officer, was waiting outside the Washington State Parole Board's storefront office. *Good ol' Rat fucking City*, I thought. There was bail bonds on the corner, fucking parole and probation office in the middle of the street, right next to a King County Sherriff's satellite and community policing office. Guess that tells you what kind of area we were in if nothing else.

"You look like *hell*," Kim remarked dryly, her arms crossed over her chest. She wore her uniform of khaki tactical pants, blue polo with stitched on badge, and blue and yellow windbreaker marked *Parole Board*. "You know, staying out of fights was a condition of your parole, Caleb."

"It wasn't a fight," Raven said before I had the chance to speak.

"She's right, it was a straight-up ass kicking."

"He got his ass handed to him defending me from some jerks in my bar. He was minding his own business. Honest. You… you can look me up," she said. "I have a clean record. You can see for yourself. I'm not lying."

"Both of you, inside now. We'll sort it out at my desk."

Raven looked fucking scared when I glanced at her in wonder but she nodded without looking at either of us. We followed Kim to her cubicle where she pulled a chair up opposite her desk to match the one already there. Raven lowered me into the first seat and took the one beside mine.

"See some ID?" Kim asked and Raven produced hers and handed it over.

"Tanis McGowan," she muttered, and she put her fingers to keys.

I watched Kim's eyes bounce back and forth behind her blocky glasses as she read what was on her screen and then she paused, sitting back a little as Raven shifted nervously in her seat.

Kim fixed her with what could only be described as a sympathetic look.

"He works out of this office sometimes," she said softly. "But not today. You can relax."

Raven looked up sharply and her eyes welled up, but she didn't cry. All she did was nod.

"No way you're lying," Kim said, handing back her ID.

She fixed me with a look and said, "Okay, tell me what happened."

I cringed a bit and said, "Honestly, I was drunk as fuck and don't remember most of it. I was at the bar, Raven – I mean Tanis here was all friendly like and cutting me off and the next thing I know, I'm being stomped into the barroom floor and then the next flash I have after that? I'm being stomped some more into the pavement outside."

"Okay." Kim nodded, running a hand back through her short, iron-gray hair. "Your turn. Fill in the blanks." She looked at Tanis.

"I work the bar at Shoreman's a few blocks over. Mace was having some drinks. Quiet, minding his own business, when these four frat assholes came in and started harassing me. Mace told them to knock it off and leave me alone. He never left his bar stool, just kept telling them to stop. One of them broke a pool cue over him and all four of them jumped him. It was four on one... um..." This is the part where she embellished the story. "Our cook came out of the kitchen as Mace tried to get away from them, going outside. Our cook is a big guy. I threatened to call the cops and they split. I did my best to take care of Mace for standing up for me."

"Uh-huh," Kim was typing into her computer and she looked back at me. "I'm not putting any of this in. No need to jam you up for doing the right thing here." She sighed. "I'm putting you down as having been late due to some honest car trouble and that you did make it, and everything is good – like it has been every visit since you got out." She leaned back. "Still working the goat farm?"

"Yes, ma'am."

"How many days you been here in White Center."

"Three. My employer absolutely knows about it. You can call them. I have the sick leave."

Kim nodded. "We're all good here," she said and she turned her attention to Raven.

"Thanks for bringing him in, Ms. McGowan. I'm sorry that happened to you. I know all about Max." Kim shook her head. "You guys go on and get out of here. I'll see you in two weeks."

"Yes, ma'am." She scribbled a date and time on a reminder card and handed it to me.

"Stay out of trouble, Mr. Anderson."

"Absolutely."

"Sure you shouldn't be telling *me* that?" Raven joked, but it held the flavor of self-deprecation.

"This kind of trouble isn't the kind of trouble we can avoid," Kim said in a moment of what was clearly women's solidarity.

*The mystery deepens,* I thought, looking at Raven beside me who wouldn't look at me. She got up and helped me up.

"Until next time," Kim said with a nod. She was a hard lady. Tough, but fair. I could appreciate that about her.

"Yes, ma'am," I said and let Raven help me out.

The walk back to her place was slower and silent. She was somewhere else. Pensive, a million miles away.

"I have to go to work," she said when she helped me to settle on her couch.

"We going to talk about it?" I asked.

She still wouldn't look at me, and she shook her head.

"Okay," I said gently, and I let her do her thing – shower, get dressed, get ready.

She made me a couple of sandwiches before she went out the door.

"I'll see you when I get home," she said softly before leaving. She locked the line of dead bolts and the knob lock behind her.

I had a feeling when I found out whoever Max was, we were going to have a come to Jesus meeting.

## 6

*R*aven...

*Caleb Anderson...* He didn't look like a Caleb or a Mr. Anderson. I mean, he just didn't. I guess I expected him to have a last name that was like Mason or something.

*Just where did the nickname Mace come from, anyway?*

"Yo, Raven. You good?"

I pulled myself out of my reverie and looked down the bar at one of my barfly regulars, a retired old longshoreman by the name of Whitey.

"Yeah, Whitey. I'm good. Need a refill?" I asked.

"If you don't mind, honey."

"That's my job, babes," I shot back and came down the bar to pull him a fresh beer, taking his old glass and putting it in the washer.

I did a lot of daydreaming on that shift, and it went by surprisingly fast. Still, I was bursting with questions for Mace, but at the same time, cringing inwardly, knowing that he had so many to ask in return. Imagine my surprise when I stepped out of the bar and Sauley, their club's prospect was standing there.

"Oh, hi. Is Mace okay?" I asked.

"Yeah, yeah! He's good. He just sent me to walk you home," he said nervously.

I kind of froze. "Um, what?"

"Uh, I'm here to walk you home?"

I laughed a bit unevenly, not really sure what to make of this.

"You came all the way over here at three in the morning just to walk me two-and-a-half blocks because Mace told you to?" I asked. It was more than a little far out to even consider it.

Sauley grinned. "I'm the club's prospect, which means I'm pretty much their errand boy to utilize however they see fit until I prove myself." His chest puffed out in a bit of pride and I nodded slowly.

"So that's how it works," I said, and he nodded.

"Don't tell anyone I told you so, but it's a pain in the fucking ass."

He laughed and I nodded and said, "Hazing usually is."

"So, let a lowly prospect walk you home?" He stuck out his arm with a cheeky grin and I couldn't help but smile a little more.

"Mace really sent you?" I asked.

"Wanna see the text?" he asked.

"Actually, I kinda do," I answered, blushing.

"K, but don't rat me out."

"Wouldn't dream of it," I said honestly.

He pulled up the text exchange on his phone and I read it.

**Mace: Hey, Sauley. Get on over to Shoreman's before last call and wait on Raven. Walk her home.**

**Sauley: Everything okay?**

**Mace: Just do what I fuckin' tell you and yeah, everything's fine. I just worry about her.**

I felt a warm glow at the words on the screen and I smiled and handed the phone back.

"Thanks," I murmured, and he shrugged one shoulder.

"I live to serve, plus, it isn't exactly a hardship walking a pretty girl a few blocks."

I laughed and asked, "Laying it on a bit thick, aren't you?"

He shook his head, his look stone-cold sober as he said, "Not at all."

I turned my head and smiled, embarrassed, or flattered, or whatever. I couldn't really identify the name of the emotion. It was uncomfortable and yet not in a bad way at all. He winged out his arm and I looped mine through it cautiously.

"Lead the way, m'lady," he said. I nodded and we set off at an easy stroll.

Rat City never really slept. At least not completely. There was distant rap music and the thump and bump coming from cars with rims that cost more than the vehicle itself as they cruised up and down the streets – gangs patrolling their territory. It was a sketchy neighborhood on a good day and there weren't many good days around here despite the efforts made and the creeping gentrification that was slowly taking hold.

Soon this neighborhood would be like Georgetown, or South Park, only perhaps trendier considering it had much more storefront space at its core than either of the aforementioned neighborhoods. The only thing keeping the boutiques out right now was the high potential for their front windows to be shot out or for the place to be robbed in its first week.

"You did a really good thing for Mace," Sauley said about a half a block into our walk.

"Yeah, I know," I murmured, nodding.

"You didn't have to. You could have just let his ass get beat."

I chuckled mirthlessly and shook my head. "No, I couldn't have. It's not my nature," I said.

"That makes you a really good person."

"I don't know," I said honestly. "I'd like to think I did what anyone else would have done."

"They wouldn't," he said with conviction and I paused in my step.

"What makes you say that?" I asked.

"You know why a lot of us guys turn our back on the world and join the club like we do?" he asked. I froze up as a Seattle Police Department cruiser glided by, going up Roxbury. The black-and-white SUV shiny, polished, and new.

I shook my head, letting out a breath I hadn't known I'd been holding as it continued by without stopping.

"Because the world turned its back on us first. People judge and judge harshly. I feel like the internet has just made that shit worse, but at the end of the day? Man." He raked a hand back through his hair. "No." He pursed his lips and shook his head. "People like you who treat us like we're human and not garbage? You're few and far between and I for one appreciate that about you. Mace is *alive* because of you. We all know it. Eulogy even said so. You did us a huge favor."

"Uh… um, you're welcome," I said, for lack of anything better. He met my eyes, his expression solemn and nodded.

We continued walking, and it wasn't lost on me that Sauley made certain he was between me and the street. He was taking his duty very seriously.

When I stuck my key in the lock back at my apartment, Sauley remained at my side like some sort of loyal guard dog. The locks started to click and flip from the other side as Mace undid them. When he opened the door, he looked me over first, then said, "Good job, Prospect. You can go."

"Sure thing, night Raven." Sauley gave a half wave and stuffing his hands in his jean's pockets strolled down the hall and went down the stairs.

"Night!" I called after him and turned back to Mace who was smiling at me warmly.

"You didn't have to send him to walk me home," I declared. "I've been doing it for a long time before all this."

"No, I know. You can take care of yourself," he said, standing aside so I could slip into my place.

I moved past him, lifting my messenger bag over my head and setting it on the floor by the door as he shut it, and threw all the locks and bolts behind me.

It occurred to me, that although tired, I was *comfortable* around Mace. With the days going by and his movements becoming better and his pain diminishing, that comfort level wasn't diminishing at all as he regained his strength.

That was… curious.

"How you doing?" he asked me, backing off and giving me some room to breathe.

"Tired," I said truthfully. "Just want a cup of hot tea to warm up, and bed."

"Sit down," he said. "Let me figure this whole tea thing out. I think I can manage."

I smiled and chuckled lightly and touched his arm softly on my way past to the kitchen.

"You're supposed to be resting," I chided.

"I'm restless. Can't help myself," he said.

"Mm, not used to being sedentary, huh?"

"Nope. Not at all. You?"

I shook my head. "I like to keep busy," I said as I filled the kettle.

He switched on the stove for me as I turned with the kettle in hand. I smiled and set it on the burner.

"Seriously," he said when I sighed. "Go sit down. Let me do something nice for you."

I eyed him and haltingly nodded.

"Okay," I murmured, and I edged past him to go sit down.

"Feel like watching something?" he asked.

"Mm, no." I shook my head and smiled to myself, knowing he couldn't see either from inside the kitchen.

"Just tea and sleep, huh?"

"Pretty much. I lead a boring life, what can I say?"

"I don't know if I would go that far. Seems pretty interesting to me."

"How do you figure?" I asked softly and looked up and over from my seat on the end of the couch to where he leaned in the kitchen doorway.

"You helped me," he said softly. "Not just once, but several times now."

I smiled and said, "I just don't know any other way to be, Mace. I'm just me…"

"I like you," he said and lightly punched the archway into the kitchen, biting his battered bottom lip and looking so unsure of himself. "It's easy to talk to you and… I don't know. I don't want to say I'm *glad* I got the shit kicked out of me, but I can't say it wasn't worth it since it brought you into my life. I mean, more than just some passing banter in your bar. I guess what I'm trying to say is, I'd like to get to know you better, Raven. That is, if you're up for it."

I smiled and dropped my gaze to my hands in my lap, unsure what to say. I mean, I'd been up early and just worked a double, and I knew he was getting better and that he would have to leave but… I wasn't sure I was ready for him to go. Not yet.

"I guess I sort of figured you'd get better and *leave* and that would be it," I confessed. I cleared my throat and swept my wig off my head and tossed it up on the back of the couch.

"Is that what you want?" he asked and sounded as unsure as I felt.

"I don't, no," I confessed, and it was hard to meet his eyes, but I made myself do it anyway. "I feel safe with you around. Is that crazy?"

He smiled and laughed a little and the accompanying wince wasn't as pronounced this time. "Depends on who you ask," he replied honestly. "One of my boys? No, it's not crazy at all. Your average citizen? They'd probably call you certifiable."

"Yeah, well, you're a wolf in wolf's clothing. It's the wolf in sheep's clothing you've got to watch for."

"I know that's right," he agreed.

"I'd like to see you again," I murmured. "When you're better."

He smiled, and it was almost enough to reopen the split in his bottom lip.

"I was hoping you'd say that," he said and ducked back into the kitchen to make my tea.

"Two teaspoons of dried tea in the pot, add hot water, if you want it like I make it, add a half teaspoon of the raw sugar to the cup before you pour," I told him.

"Thanks," he said, and I could hear the smile in his voice. "I was gonna ask."

"I thought you might," I told him with a laugh, knowing he had no idea how I made my tea.

He brought two cups, balanced on saucers, around the corner and lowered one to my raised and waiting hands. I lowered the offering to the top of my leg and wrapped my hands around the cup, sighing in relief as the warmth radiated through the porcelain and into my chilly hands.

"Cold out there?" he asked.

"Very," I answered, sipping carefully. He lowered himself onto the couch next to me.

"Should have gotten in a hot shower."

I shook my head. "In the morning. My hair will never dry all the way and will turn into a hot mess if I try to sleep on it wet."

"Ah. I volunteer as tribute," he said carefully. "Feel free to warm frozen appendages against me."

I laughed. "Are you sure you're from this planet?" I asked.

He grinned and said, "Nah, what was that old book or plan thing or whatever? *Men Are from Mars, Women Are from Venus?*"

"Never heard of it," I said with a shake of my head.

"Oh, ouch." He put a hand to his chest and made a face. "Makes me feel old or some shit."

"Ha," I muttered. I did not picture Mace as *old*, even if he was older than me by some; how much, I couldn't tell. It seemed rude to ask.

"Go ahead," he said.

"What?" I asked and raised my eyebrows.

"Ask."

"Ask what?" I asked.

"Whatever you were just thinking – I'm open. Ask me anything."

"Anything?" I perked up a bit.

"Anything," he said, and his grin was slow and sweet with just the slightest hint of spice.

"Why are you called Mace?"

He laughed and held his ribs when he did it and asked, "Out of all the things you wanna know, that's it?"

"I didn't realize I was limited to one question," I said with a lazy grin.

"Ahhh, I can be tricky. Okay, alright; why am I called Mace? Well, now that's a story…"

He sighed out and bowed his head and looked up at me without raising it. He asked, "You're sure that's what you want to know?"

My smile grew, and I nodded. "Oh yeah."

He groaned, huffed out a breath, and said, "This is going to make me sound like such an *asshole*… Okay, so this was back right before I patched into the club. I was still a prospect, but like the same weekend I earned my colors, so I was on the tail end of it, right?"

"Sure," I said nodding, sipping my tea and smiling behind the rim of my cup. I liked his voice. It was velvety and smooth, rich and decadent all at the same time. I could honestly listen to him talk for hours if he would let me.

"So, the guys had been *up my ass*, like more than usual. Of course, when you get your colors, you don't know it's gonna happen. All those decisions are made behind closed doors. So, I'd been tasked with pretty much all manner of petty-ass fucking *bullshit* for *days* and one of those tasks was to walk the ol' lady of the then VP from the strip club she worked at to the bar the boys – including her ol' man – were at."

"Okay." I nodded my understanding and curled up in the corner of my couch comfortably.

"Right, so we're halfway down the block from the bar and the guys and the VP are all sitting out front in this little gated off patio area. It's summertime, and it's warm for around here. We're almost there and this homeless dude starts hassling my VP's ol' lady for money and I tell him to fuck off. This dude, he gets all belligerent and my VP is getting pissed. I'm shaking my head and telling this guy to fuck off and he opens up his mouth to really start screaming at me... and that's when I pulled the cannister of pepper spray out of my pocket and hosed that motherfucker right down his throat."

I started laughing and I couldn't stop. The look on his face must have been the look on that guy's face and oh! Oh, my, it was priceless.

Mace shrugged and said, "The name stuck. I've been 'Mace' ever since."

I wiped a tear from the corner of my eye and nodded. "See, that was every bit as worth it as I thought it would be."

"Yeah?" he asked and smiled.

"Yeah." I nodded. "I needed that laugh."

"What about you?" he asked.

"Raven?" I asked. He nodded. I shrugged.

"I've always liked them. I got the tattoo," I rounded my shoulder at him, "and like you, it stuck. Some of the other burners started calling me Raven and I've been Raven ever since."

I smiled fondly at some of those memories, but just as swiftly as the smile touched my lips, it turned brittle with what came after... with what happened after that.

"See, now there," he said, and I looked up from the dregs of my teacup.

"What?" I asked.

"Whatever, or should I say *whoever* just wiped that smile off your face."

I bit my lips together and didn't say anything.

"Whoever he is, he'll find his *come to Jesus*. They always do," he said gently.

I swallowed and nodded.

"Someday," I murmured. "Hopefully."

"You hungry?" he asked, and I shook my head. "Warm enough, now?" I smiled slightly and shook my head again and he smiled. "You're definitely tired, though." There was no question about that, and I didn't even try to deny it.

"Come on," he said. "Let's get you to bed and get you warm."

I felt a little guilty, but there was honestly nothing to be guilty about. The comfort Mace offered was freely given and I could tell, there was no expectation of anything in return. Anything sexual... and to be honest, I missed the simple contact of being held through the night, which is what had led me to that dating app in the first place.

He got up, wincing and moving a little slow, but I could already tell he was doing better, and our time was growing short. I went into the corner of my room and unlaced and toed off my boots.

I appreciated he kept his things neatly folded in another corner; that he wasn't a slob. All of my clothes that I owned hung in the closet. I had a few baskets in the bottom for socks and underwear, but the rest I hung on whatever hangers I managed to rustle up from the dollar store on fifteenth.

Mace lowered himself in his sweats and tee to the bed with a grunt and got in while I slipped out of my clothes to my sports bra and underwear. I stuffed my dirty things in the top of an old army duffel. I got it from a surplus store back when I had more money. Those days were long gone, though.

"Come, get in here," Mace complained. "You're freezing."

It was true, the winters here were typically mild, but we were well into it and the clothes I had were the clothes I had and were honestly more suited to the summertime. I was a sun worshipper at heart, and he honestly didn't have to tell me twice. I pulled the deep tan, boat-neck loose-knit sweater over my head. You could honestly see right through but still it was better than nothing. It was soft and fell around me to the hip and I moved my skinny ass to get under the covers. Mace carefully pulled me into his side and said, "There you go."

I smiled and laid my head on his shoulder carefully, his warmth divine.

"Your landlord should be fuckin' shot," Mace said, and I chuckled.

"He's the owner of this building and the building that Shoreman's is in. I rent under the table. This place isn't up to code or suited for habitation. He doesn't tell and I don't tell."

Mace snorted. "Fucking vulture."

"Eh, it works," I murmured. "And it's what I can afford."

He sighed and pressed his lips to my hair. I got the distinct impression he was breathing me in but surprisingly, I didn't mind. I didn't find it creepy coming from him. I found it... I don't know the right word, but it was good. The sensation of his gentle attention leaving a silvery glow in its wake.

I closed my eyes and sort of relished the comfort. It'd been a long time. I'd always been weak for a good snuggle and he was so very good at it.

"Get some sleep," he whispered when I'd been quiet too long and had begun to stir out of a sort of restless feeling that I should be keeping the conversation going or something. Instead, he held me just a little tighter, and I drifted off faster than I had in a while, sound asleep in the hushed quiet of the deepest morning.

# 7

*M*ace...

"Hey, Kim. You gotta minute?"

My parole officer looked up from where she was about to light her cigarette, the slim white paper-wrapped tobacco stick bobbing between her lips as she asked, "Not supposed to see you for another couple of weeks, Caleb. What can I do for you?"

"It's not about me," I said, leaning gingerly back against the wall she was leaning against. She offered me a cig, and I waved her off.

"Quit when I was locked up," I said.

"That's what I like about you," she said with a smile around her cig as she took the time to flick her Bic and light it. She took a long drag, held it, and plucking the cig from between her lips said, breath held, "You took your time inside to actually better yourself." She blew out a plume of smoke that caught in the breeze and came my way. I seriously wondered how I could have ever smoked those things.

"So, to what do I owe this pleasure?" she asked and took another drag.

"The girl I was with yesterday... something happened to her, yeah? Something that showed up on your screen?"

Kim raised her dark eyebrows and nodded as she took a third hit off her cigarette and plucking it from between her lips exhaled, she said, "Yeah. You didn't talk about it?"

I turned my head and smiled a little sadly and said, "Some things you just don't ask a girl, now do you?"

She eyed me speculatively with her brown eyes from behind her glasses, the expression on her round, face curious and calculating.

"What do you want to know?" she asked.

"How bad are we talking and who's Max?" I asked low.

"You going to do something stupid?" she asked me.

"Nope," I said honestly.

"Too bad," she muttered, dropping her cigarette on the ground and grinding it out with the round toe of her state-issued tactical boot. "Sometimes, an ex-con is just what you need in the interest of justice."

She jerked her head, and I followed her inside to her desk. She clacked some keys and swung the monitor on its arm in my direction then gave me a pointed look.

"Now, you stay right there while I get your paperwork for your piss test, and I don't want to hear it," she said.

I nodded and gave her a two-fingered half-assed salute as she got up and fucked off, turning my attention to the monitor and the complaint listed there.

*Ms. Tanis McGowan said that she met WA State Parole Ofc. Massimiliano "Max" Bianchi on the dating app Tinder. She said after several days of interacting with Ofc. Bianchi that she agreed to a date. She states that in the course of the date, Ofc. Bianchi became aggressive, and when she tried to turn down his advances, he then raped her.*

Fucking son of a bitch.

*After interviewing Ms. McGowan at length, she wished to pursue charges, however, after some time to think about it, she phoned the district attorney's office and requested those charges be dropped, stating she was mistaken, the sex was consensual but rough and that she just wanted to put it behind her.*

Yeah.

I'll just bet that's how that fucking happened. Maybe after ol' Max paid her another visit or had some of his boys in blue, do it for him. Fucking animals.

I sighed.

No wonder she was hiding out. Scanning through, it looked like Max lived in Seattle and the attack happened inside the city limits. I bet the city pigs had something to do with her recanting. It would damn sure explain why Sauley had texted me and let me know the Seattle police driving by had spooked the hell out of her.

I felt a cold anger grip me and I nodded, sitting back in my seat, the address listed for good ol' Max firmly burned into my brain. The old address they had on file for Raven was somewhere in the Fremont or Phinney Ridge neighborhood, maybe even as far as Greenlake. I was betting there were roommates. She could barely afford the shithole she was in now. There was no fucking way she could afford those neighborhoods without a gang of fucking roommates.

I wondered if any of them knew. I wondered if any of them cared enough about her, missed her, was worried about her.

I would find out.

She'd saved my life. It was time to give her back hers.

I pissed in the cup and told Kim it would pop positive for opioid painkillers. She nodded and without breaking eye contact, ditched the cup and her rubber gloves in the trashcan under her desk.

"You quit doing what you're doing, and I won't have to keep hassling you like this," she said with a wink.

"Yes, ma'am," I said and stood, looking over the cubicle farm to the glass-fronted lobby.

"Go on, get out of here," she said and back to the keys of her computer her fingers went. I got the fuck out of there. No sense overstaying my welcome. I'd gotten more than I'd bargained for, honestly.

I thought about Raven, her soft skin, her warm herbal scent, and her soothing rich teas on the walk back to the club.

I missed her already, but I was no good to her like this. She didn't have a phone, but I knew just how I was going to keep in touch.

Call me the romantic type.

# 8

*R*aven...

I woke by myself, and when I had turned my head to Mace's empty place in my bed, it was to a torn piece of paper bag on his pillow. Scrawled in thick black pen on its plain surface was *I'll be in touch. -Mace*

I'd groaned and sighed out. That had been several *days* ago and as I wiped down the empty bar at Shoreman's, I couldn't tell you the soul-deep disappointment that took root in my chest at the prospect of going home to an empty apartment again tonight.

It'd only been like three days, but it had, for all its life-or-death drama in the beginning, been a *nice* three days of company. I had to admit, Mace was easy to talk to and even easier to listen to. I wondered if he would indeed be in touch as his hastily scrawled note had said, or if it was just an easy let down.

If I really would ever see or hear from him again.

The thought of not was surprisingly a painful one.

*Was I really that starved for close personal contact?* I wondered. *Or was the experience something real?*

I knew the answer, I was just afraid to admit it to myself.

There was just something about Mace.

"Hey, yeah, sorry, bro. Last call was a while ago. We're closed. We just ain't got the door."

I looked up at Manuk's voice. He was our cook. A big Hawaiian dude who was as easy going as they came – until he wasn't. I'd seen him grab a belligerent drunk by the *face* and march him out the front door to toss him in the gutter. Manuk was slow to anger, but when you got him there, he was like King fucking Kong. All brute strength and scary as hell.

"Sorry, ah, Raven, I'm here to walk you home. Mace's orders… I'll wait outside."

I blinked slowly at Sauley who was standing there, an envelope in one hand and flowers in the other, looking decidedly uncomfortable.

I smiled and shook my head. "He's okay, Manuk. Let him wait inside?"

"Sure thing, girly. Have a seat, brotha. You want a soda?" Manuk lumbered back around the bar with me and picked up a glass.

"Ah, no, I'm good – I mean, no, thank you. Just here to walk the lady home."

"I like that," Manuk said, and I rolled my eyes.

"I'm perfectly capable," I said and Manuk grinned.

"Ain't nobody say you weren't. I just nevah liked the idea of it, you out there this late – even just a couple blocks."

I smiled and shook my head.

"I can take care of myself," I said and Manuk held up his hands in surrender. He knew better than to argue with me.

I sighed and looked to Sauley. With and arched brow, I asked him, "And what's all this?"

"From Mace. I don't know. I don't ask questions. I just do what I'm told," he said with a grin.

I went over and he held up the card. I plucked it from his hand. I smelled the flowers – a hastily bought bouquet of pink and white lilies with pink roses that was fragrant and beautiful –but still had the Safeway grocer's price sticker on them and I grinned.

"He pick these out or did you?" I asked.

"Uh, I did. Do they suck?"

"No." I laughed. "They don't suck; but maybe take the price tag off next time," I whispered loudly and then hid my mouth behind my hand and giggled as he cursed and went to work trying to peel the sticker off the floral department cellophane.

I opened the card while he struggled with that. The front was a cartoon bunny on its stomach holding a flower and under it was written, *Need a Hug?*

I frowned and opened the card, its message was, *Thought so! I've been missing you, too. Hope we'll be hugging soon.*

I smiled. The handwriting above it was extensive and I didn't want to make Sauley wait too long so I decided to read it at home.

"Gimme two secs to grab my hoodie and we can go," I said, and he nodded, still scraping at the damn sticker on the flowers I was going to unwrap, trim, and stick in a quart Mason jar as soon as I got home.

"You out, sistah?" Manuk asked from the kitchen.

"Unless you got anything else for me," I called back.

"Nah! See you tomorrow."

"See you tomorrow!" I called back and gathered my sweater and my bag from under the bar. Sauley stood up and got the door for me. I locked up behind me so Manuk didn't have to come out and do it.

"You really don't have to keep doing this," I said casually, and he laughed dubiously.

"Mace would have my ass," he said, and I twisted my lips thoughtfully.

"Not even sure why he cares," I said with a one-shouldered shrug. "I mean, he just left."

"Yeah, I get it," he said and sounded a little rueful. He handed me my flowers, and I smiled. It was hard to be hurt or whatever with the blossom's heavenly scent wafting up into my face.

"You guys want your TV and game system back?" I asked. "He sort of left that too."

"Oh, uh, I'll ask," he said.

Our noses started to run from the cold, and when we reached my place, I asked for politeness' sake, "Did you want some hot tea and to warm up before you go?"

"Ah, nah. Thanks for asking. I'm just going to head back to the club."

"Okay," I said. "Be safe."

"Thanks, ain't got no problem with that," he said and shot me a wink. He was handsome in his own right; young, a devilish glint in his blue eyes and a slight unkempt scruff on his cheeks, his hair a medium brown and kept short. He was attractive alright, probably tattooed but with the cold, I hadn't seen much to indicate it other than he seemed the type – and I would know considering how much ink rode underneath *my* skin.

I let myself into the downstairs and he waited, watching as I took them to my apartment door. I glimpsed him still standing out there when I slipped inside my cozy if shabby space and I sighed, throwing the locks and bolts behind me, securing myself as best I could from the outside world.

I closed my eyes and rested my forehead against the painted wood and breathed slowly for a moment, letting the emotions wash over and through me; surprised a bit that *relief* was at the fore.

Relief that he had been as good as his words left on the torn piece of paper bag that rested beside my bed. The paper that I held in front of my face and read over and over, trying to divine more meaning than what was there out of the printed words.

I went into my kitchen, used the cheap dollar store sheers I had to trim my flowers and arranged them in some water. The quart Mason jar I had was just big enough to contain them. That done, I went into my room, lifted off my bag and slid the card in its envelope from it. I sat on my mattress, flowers by my feet, and slipped the card out and opened it to read what *he* had written.

*Hey Raven,*

*I told you I would be in touch. I wish this were in person but soon... I want to heal up completely before I come see you. I hope you don't mind I'm sending Sauley as my messenger boy. It's a lot kinder than some of the other shit he could be doing. I'm going to send him to walk you home every chance I get. Feel free to pass messages through him. Either written or verbal is fine. I'll send more with him. I figure if I don't hear something back this time you waited to read this.*

*I know it's only been a few days or whatever, but I miss talking to you already. Gonna heal up the rest of the way, get caught up around here on the farm, and then I'll be seein' you. You don't feel the same or you don't want to see me, you just say so. I'll get my ass gone and stay that way.*

*Sleep tight, I hope you're warm enough. Save me a cup of that tea? It's nice. I miss that too.*

*Mace*

I lowered the card to my lap and looked down at the piece of brown paper bag, the corner of it trapped under the Mason jar. I smiled to myself and sighed. A sort of weight lifted. Maybe I mattered to someone after all. I set the card on top of that large piece of brown paper and got ready for bed.

I needed to write him something back, but I didn't even know where to begin.

Thinking about it kept me awake past dawn.

# 9

*M*ace...

"She give you anything?" I asked when I answered the phone.

Sauley laughed nervously and said, "No, man. I think she read the card part but not whatever you wrote. She looked at it too fast."

I grunted, a little disappointed.

"You go back tomorrow night," I said.

"Oh, man..." He sucked in a breath between his teeth like he didn't wanna say whatever was coming and I felt my forehead crush down into a frown.

"What?" I demanded.

"I'm supposed to do something for Mav tomorrow night, and I don't know how long it'll run."

"Fuck," I muttered. "Mav comes first, you know that, kid. Let me know."

"Yeah! Yeah! For sure, for sure. Walking Raven home is kind of nice. I don't think she has any friends."

I didn't know about that. Not yet. I couldn't ride yet to go find out. I was barely making it around the fucking farm, feeding goats and mucking barn stalls and that shit wasn't that hard, honestly. I mean, they were fucking goats not horses, and I wasn't getting into the pens with them. Not yet. If one of the little bastards head butted me right now, it might break my ribs the rest of the way so Fen had me keep my ass on the *outside* of the fence.

"Yeah, I don't know," I said. "Good lookin' out. Thanks for doing that for me," I said.

"Yeah, no problem," he said.

I hung up and blew out a breath at the ceiling of my corner of the barn loft.

That was another thing. I didn't exactly have a whole lot of room to fuckin' bitch about her apartment and surroundings when I lived in a literal fucking *barn* behind racks and shelves of Fenris' woman's pottery.

I gave one long and slow blink and rocked my head back, rolling my eyes to scan the rows of shelves over my head in the dim moonlight coming through the window by my bed.

*I wonder if Aspen would make her something... a nice tea set. Matching shit that isn't chipped, cracked, or broken.*

I already knew the answer. Of course, she would. All I had to do was ask.

"God fucking damnit," I heard down below.

"Yeah, Fen!" I called out. "What's up?"

"Ginger had a stillbirth."

"Aw fuck, you need my help?" I asked.

84

"No…" he sighed. "Yeah, maybe."

"I'm already up," I said groaning.

"Gahhhh!" He made a noise of frustration and I hustled.

"What's up, bro?"

"Here comes another one," he said as I came down the bottom of the stairs. I nodded and went to work, helping him out.

When we were finishing up, we sadly had two stillborn baby goats to bury. It was sad, but that was life. We didn't always get a happy ending. The good guys rarely, if ever, came out on top, and there were a lot of wolves among the sheep just waiting to power trip and take advantage.

I stared down at the hole Fenris was digging at the edge of the property and I was restless. I wanted to be doing something. I wanted to get my facts straight, do my research, and take the time with Raven to earn her trust. I wanted the full story before I did anything, but I already knew this particular story wasn't going to have a happy ending.

"Man, what's the matter with you?" Fen asked, looking up at me. "You look like somebody shot your fuckin' dog."

I grunted and said, "Let you know when I know more."

He straightened and drove the spade into the ground at his feet, the sun rising and the cold morning filling with mist. He crossed his arms atop the shaft of the shovel handle and fixed me with a hard, blank look that said we weren't budging or finishing until I spilled the beans.

"Fuck," I muttered and sighed. "I keep thinking about Raven," I confessed.

He scowled. "She seems nice. Brave but timid at the same time. What's up?"

85

"I don't know, I mean, I *do know* now, but it's complicated and I don't want to be talking out of turn without having all the facts and hearing it from the horse's mouth so to speak."

"It ain't like you, being cagey, brother. You've always been one of the more direct of us."

I nodded. "I know, but I'd like to keep my ass out of prison. I'd like to think I learned my lesson in patience and not going off half-cocked." I cracked my knuckles and flexed my hands.

Fenris studied my face and finally nodded, working the shovel back and forth, his eyes on his work. He finally looked up at me and said, "When you get it figured out, come talk to me."

I nodded solemnly.

"I fuckin' planned on it. For sure," I said. After what'd happened with Fen and his sister? He was going to have a fuckin' field day with this.

THE NEXT TIME I sent Sauley to Raven, I wasn't disappointed. He came back with a sealed envelope; white, business sized, and fairly thick – enough for several pages. I thanked him and told him "off, you fuck" and gave him a carefully packed crate of a teapot and cups for him to figure out how to take with him on his bike.

"How the fuck am I supposed to do this?" he demanded when I handed it to him.

I shrugged and told him, "Figure it out, and you better not break the fuckin' contents."

"Fuck, alright!" he said and with a gusty sigh, I left him at his bike to sort himself out.

I felt like fucking Gollum with his fucking precious with that letter tucked in my inside pocket. I headed across the grass to the outside set of steps up to my space in the barn loft. Hell, I needed to sort *myself* out and get my living situation under control.

This was no place to bring a woman, not even one as organic and down to earth as Raven.

I dropped down onto the full-sized mattress, covered in a thick layer of sleeping bags and took the envelope out of my pocket and slid my knife off my hip, flicking it open and working it under the flap. I sliced it cleanly along the top and took care to put my knife back where it belonged before I pulled the contents out.

It was a few pieces of paper and folded in among them a dried bit of curling fern. I wondered at that and turned my eyes to the flowing script on the page.

*Dear Mace,*

*You weren't lying when you said you would be in touch. I must admit, this wasn't exactly what I had in mind, but it was nice. I keep staring at your flowers. They're beautiful and smell wonderful. You're always welcome at my door for a cup of tea and it is quite cold, isn't it?*

*I'm not sure what else to write. Everything seems so superficial and trite, to be honest. I was surprised to find I miss having you here. I enjoyed our talks and listening to you and the apartment. I don't know, it was never really vibrant to begin with, but it seems even less so after you've been and gone. Colder and emptier... that also might be because my heat broke last night, and I may just be projecting or something.*

*Don't worry. The landlord swears that problem will be fixed straight away. I admit I'm almost afraid to see what he comes up with, but it will likely be fixed before you get this. At least, I hope so.*

*Fuck. This all feels so small... so I don't know. I don't know that I'm strong enough to commit some of my deepest darkest secrets to paper, but I feel like you would be the last person to judge me on any of it and that's nice. I'm afraid I'm a little low on trust. I have reasons for that, good ones, I promise, but that's hardly fair to you, is it?*

*I so desperately want to talk to someone, need to, but you... I feel like I would be taking advantage. You don't owe me anything. You really don't. I would have done what I did for anyone. Really. I'm sorry it happened to you. You're not at all what you seem, and it boggles the mind somewhat.*

*I guess I'm confused about a lot of things, but I don't want to be rude and I'm already afraid I sound judgmental.*

*Your flowers are so beautiful.*

*I took a walk this summer and picked this fern, pressing it between the pages of the notebook I went to get this paper out of. It's dry, and brittle and a little broken, like me. I thought maybe it would be a fair trade and a decent reminder.*

*I think about you too. A lot. I miss having someone to come home to – and I know that sounds more than a little intense, and crazy, but it's true.*

*I guess I hadn't realized how lonely I'd gotten.*

*Anyway, I hope you're healing is going well. Please take care.*

*Raven*

I sighed, thinking, reading, and re-reading every word to wring every bit of nuance and subtext I could out of them.

What I saw in her looping handwriting was a girl who'd once been extroverted, a people person, likely even a people pleaser until that dickhead had come along and low sided her, like I'd been low sided in her fucking bar by those frat boys.

She was no shrinking violet, or hadn't been until something so bad, so heinous, had come along and made her afraid and dulled her shine.

That sparkle was still in there, though. Underneath. I'd glimpsed it a few times with her sharp wit and humor. She'd put me back together, and like fuck I didn't owe her. It was just going to take some serious tender-loving care to fit her broken pieces together. Like that pottery thing Aspen had shown me. Where you mended the broken pieces with silver or gold. The piece was never the same, but there was a new wild beauty in the cracks and breaks to it.

I could see that for Raven, but this wasn't a sprint. This wasn't some wrapped ribs and healed bones. This was something else entirely, and I had to move carefully. I didn't want to end up doing more harm than good. I already felt guilty as fuck going to Kim. Like I was sneaking around behind Raven's back. I mean, I *was,* and it was a shitty fucking thing to do, but was it shittier than opening up wounds barely healed in her soul? Pouring in the salt of memory and watching her mind burn?

I'd been around for guys melting the fuck down over less and it wasn't pretty. She was something else, an iron core that one.

I sat up and turned on the lantern on the overturned crate next to me, pulling the spiral notebook and pen I'd bought to scratch things down and giving it some new life.

*Dear Raven,*

*Stop. Just breathe, woman. Before you read the rest of this, go take yourself a hot shower and let the water beat on your back for a while. Find your most comfortable house clothes, make a hot cup of tea, and get cozy. Do that for me and then settle in.*

*I'm here to listen to or read whatever you want to tell me. I like listening to you. Could do it for hours, actually. I feel like I can tell you anything – everything. You're a comfortable presence, whether at my side or in my mind. Soothing like. I don't get that feeling nearly often enough.*

*I learned some things when I was locked up. Patience, for one thing, and that me getting pissed off and shit wasn't hurting anyone but me. Me and the club. Kind of fucked them over, me being locked up for a couple years like that.*

*You know why I was in your bar that night?*

*I was jealous. Of my brothers. A lot of them are finding good women, starting to settle. Jobs becoming careers and leading the life I always wanted for myself. I fucked that up, and I was in your bar, drowning my fuckin' sorrows over it.*

*I could have just as easily had a drink at the club for free, but I just... I'm surrounded by the guys and their girls and I've never felt more alone – until I woke up half drunk, beat to fuck on your couch. I don't know, maybe you were my guardian angel that night. Maybe my guardian angel led me to you.*

*Whatever it was, you were what I needed in that moment and I'd really like to be whatever you need right now. Friend? Lover? Something less, something more, something in between? I don't care.*

*Whatever it is you need, I'm here for it.*

*A confessional for your sins, I'd happily eat them and bear the consequences. Just someone to talk to, someone to hear what no one else is willing to listen to... I can do that.*

*If you want to vent, to rage, to just talk about the weather or chat about memories or even the simple things like your favorite color or flavor of ice cream, I'm here for it.*

*Truth, your letter was a nice way to pass the time after a day of chorin' around the farm. I'm listening to the goats out there and under the floor I'm lying on. It's quiet, and peaceful out this way. I think you'd like it, but truth be told, I'd rather pull myself up by the bootstraps some before I brought you around.*

*I know I cast more than a few stones about your apartment, but I'm damn sure living in a glass house. My current residence is a mattress on the floor of the loft of this barn. Most of the loft is storage for Fenris' lady's pottery business. I've carved out a quiet little corner for myself, though.*

*The house on the property is impressive, and I could totally stay in it if I wanted, but I'm a bit of an introvert by nature and I like my own space at the end of the day. The quiet.*

*That was something I liked about my time with you. You didn't feel the need to always fill the silence. You let me be me. No expectations or anything. It was nice.*

"Mace!"

"Yeah!" I called back. Sauley opened the door to the loft and came in. I lifted my chin. "What's up?"

"I'm leavin', got it figured out."

"Good deal, two seconds and you can take this with you."

I finished my thoughts, wrapping up quick.

*Anyway, Sauley is here. He's bringing you something. Something I think you'll like. Please accept it.*

*I want to hear more about you. Whatever you want to tell me.*

*Mace*

I pulled the pages from the notebook and folded them in, half tucking them into a half-sized manila envelope. I'd found a bunch in a random box.

"Here, deliver this along with what I already gave you."

"Sure thing." He took the freshly sealed envelope and tapped it against the fingertips of his opposite hand.

"Should have seen her face when she opened that card," he said. I raised an eyebrow but didn't speak. He looked uncomfortable for a moment but said, "She looked... relieved. I don't know. I know she misses you. Like for real, no lie."

I nodded and braced my forearms on my knees.

"What's the point of this whole story?" I asked.

He shook his head and said, "Isn't one, I guess."

I nodded, and he raised the envelope and gave a nod, tapping it one last time against his fingers. When he turned to go, I called out, "Sauley?" He turned, and I said, "Thanks for doing this for me."

He considered me for a moment and said, "It's actually my pleasure. No better feeling than being the bearer of whatever makes a sad girl look happy again. Even if it is just for a few moments."

I nodded and said, "Just wish these damn ribs would heal up faster so I could see it for myself."

Sauley nodded and looked thoughtful a second.

"I've got you, bro," he said and with that, he turned and left the barn.

I chuckled and shook my head. He was a good kid. I had no doubts he was going to make it and be one of us. Still, everyone had to pay their dues.

I lay back, hands under my head and stared at the raw wood ceiling of the barn loft and wondered idly if I'd paid mine yet or if there was more flesh and blood to be extracted still.

When I closed my eyes, Raven's face is the thing I saw, and it made me ache. Ache to hold her, ache to kiss her for real, and ache to love her into a state of pure sweet bliss.

I really hoped I would get the chance to do those things and show her that not every man out here was a douchelord. I wasn't entirely sure how bad Max had hurt her, but when I found out, I could tell you one thing; he was going to hurt ten times worse.

## 10

*R*aven...

"Here, I think you're supposed to read this first before I let you know what's in the box." Sauley handed me a smaller manila envelope.

"Oh, um, okay." I laughed slightly and slid into the booth he occupied, an old brown apple crate with a nest of cardboard shred – like packing material overflowing from it sitting on the table.

I leaned forward in the dim but serviceable bar light hanging over the center of the table, plucking the envelope from the top of the mess in the crate and bringing it to the light to see what I was doing as I opened it up. I unfolded the pages and smiled softly at the handwriting on them.

I went through a range of emotions as I read through the pages, and finally smiled. Setting them down, I looked up to Sauley grinning on his phone. The sound of a message being swept into the ether of the internet emanating from the device.

"What'd you just do?" I asked.

"Sent him a picture. Hope you don't mind."

I felt myself blush and thought of Mace looking at my photo and blushed even more. I wondered what he would think. I rolled my lips together and took a deep breath.

"I mean, I don't know exactly what it is, but I do know it's pottery of some kind. Maybe I shouldn't have read the letter first."

"Nah," Sauley said. "I think you definitely were."

I narrowed my eyes at him in suspicion and stood so I could see down into the crate. Reaching my hands in, I found multiple paper-wrapped hard pieces.

"Oh! There's a lot in here!"

"Yeah, might want to wait until you're home. Whenever you're ready. I'll carry it for you."

"You're too sweet," I told him with a smile, and I think it was his turn to blush.

He walked me home and insisted on carrying the crate up to the apartment which honestly jangled my nerves. I was polite but firm at the bottom of the stairs.

"I'd really rather do it myself," I said, and he acquiesced, inclining his head, and handing over the crate.

"You got it?" he asked.

"I think I've got it," I said, and he let me have it.

"Here, let me hold this door."

"Goodnight, Sauley. Thank you once again. You really don't have to do this every night."

"I won't be able to," he said. "But I will until Mace feels up to it himself. You have a good night."

"Thank you. Um, I'll have a letter for him next time. Is that okay?"

"Absolutely. Anything I should tell him?"

"Sorry I didn't have a chance to write him one this time?" I winced slightly.

"It's no problem. I'm sure he gets it."

"You guys really are too sweet," I said, stepping into the tiny square of broken tile in front of the stairs. Sauley smiled, winked, and shut the door tightly, waiting it seemed until I was up the stairs and inside my apartment.

I sighed and set the crate down, turning and flipping on lights so I could really see what was inside. I sat down on the couch and dragged it over. I lifted the biggest paper-wrapped package out from the center, undoing it and gasping at the rich emerald-green-and-black glazed teapot in my hands.

"This is so beautiful," I murmured.

It had a lid and five matching teacups and saucers. I had never owned anything both so functional and so beautiful at the same time.

"Mace," I whispered quietly. "This is just too much..."

I sighed, and I think my heart gave a twist in my chest, a deep pang of longing flowing out from it.

"God, I miss you," I said with a tsk at how ridiculous I knew it had to sound, even though no one was listening.

I half thought about racing down the stairs. Of chasing Sauley halfway up the block back to where he was parked at the bar and begging him to take me wherever Mace was, but those sorts of grand romantic gestures were only done in the movies. Do them in real life and you were a pathetic, crazy, sad sack, which to be fair I felt like I was all of those things.

I did as the letter suggested. I took my new teapot and cups into the kitchen and washed them at my sink. I prepared the tea and set the kettle on the stove, but I didn't turn it on yet.

First, I took a shower, then I found my comfiest house clothes that were fresh and clean from my excursion to the laundromat on my *other* day off the day before. I found my notebook and pens, went back to the kitchen, and made myself a brew.

Back to the couch, I opened the notebook and balanced it on my knee.

*Dear Mace,*

*I love my new tea set. I can't thank you enough for it, but you have to stop spoiling me!*

*I have to confess, I don't play or watch anything on the console or TV, but I do listen to music. I missed having music in my life. It's the one thing I missed the most after smashing my phone.*

I hesitated. Did I want to get into this? It had the potential to ruin so many things. I chickened out and didn't say anything more about *why* I had smashed my phone. The threatening messages, the phone calls… No, I didn't get into any of that. I just wanted to enjoy things just a little longer.

I turned some music on and took my pen and book back up.

*One of my favorite things that I used to do was fire spinning. Yes, I was one of those crazy people with the fireballs on chains, except they're called poi balls. Not to be confused with the Hawaiian dish, poi. Manuk and I had a laugh over that one once. He was really confused when I said I missed spinning my poi. He thought I splattered fermented taro root paste everywhere. Anyway, the music makes me want to get back into that. I'd need to start with some training wheels, so to speak. I'm probably quite a bit rusty now.*

*For reasons I don't want to get into, I left a lot of my things back at the house I used to live in. I don't know what my old roommates did with it. If they got rid of it or kept it.*

*One of my favorite things in the world was gathering at Gas Works with my fellow fire performers on summer nights, all of us taking turns, getting live practice in. It's been a while.*

*What about you? What are some of your favorite things? You talked a lot about the things you did to pass the time in prison, and about what put you in prison, but you never really said much about the good things. How long has it been since you indulged in anything good?*

*You have me here, hot shower, favorite comfy clothes, drinking my favorite tea out of my beautiful new tea set – what do you do to relax?*

*What's your passion? What sparks your curiosity?*

*What makes you happy?*

*I love the elements, myself. Walking in the woods, touching the trees. Spinning fire, and walking along the beach, my feet in the water. I feel the most grounded when I'm connected to the four basic elements. I always have, I guess.*

*I don't know that I'm necessarily religious at all, but I'm certainly spiritual. I guess Pagan would be the closest fit, but I wouldn't call myself a Wiccan or a witch.*

*I just am. I love existing in nature and revel in just being... or I used to.*

*I guess I know something of existing in both the light and dark the world has to offer. Don't we all in our own ways?*

I sighed and closed my eyes, the deep wellspring of emotion opening up beneath me and swallowing me whole, the hopelessness, the helplessness of my situation closing over my head.

I wondered to myself, and not for the first time, how one person could do this to another and not only get away with it, but were aided by the very people sworn to protect. It was sick, and it hurt. Also, and not for the first time, I wondered… what did I do to deserve this?

I closed the notebook. Maybe I would finish writing Mace later… maybe I should stop. After all, he was sweet, and it'd already been proven he was far from invulnerable.

I hugged my knees and finished my tea, drowning in the depths of my sorrow and memories that just would not be put to bed.

## 11

*M*ace...

It'd been something like three weeks since I'd left Raven's and I was almost back to one hundred percent. I was definitely back enough that I could start to manage some things. The letters went back and forth two or three a week. Some of the other guys started getting invested in what was up, and when Sauley couldn't go, occasionally one of the other guys would.

I appreciated it. Appreciated even more when they came around the farm for whatever reason, they asked questions.

Things were pretty much handled around here, so I went over to the main house and let myself in to the kitchen to see if Vyking would let me borrow his truck.

"Hey, whoa, how's it going?" he asked when we nearly crashed into each other.

"Good, good, man."

"You need something?" he asked.

"Uh, yeah. I was gonna ask to borrow your truck," I said, blowing into my chilled hands.

"Aw, yeah? What for?"

"Was gonna run up into the Phinney Ridge and Fremont areas. That girl I'm trying to see had to clear out of her place in a hurry and she left some stuff. Was going to see if her old roomies had any of it and if so, reclaim it."

"Ah-huh." He looked at me over his glasses and asked, "She know about this master plan of yours?"

I chewed my bottom lip and shook my head, sniffed and said, "No, man, there are some serious complications surrounding everything. I don't think she left her roomies on *bad* terms but she did leave suddenly and with only what she could carry."

He scowled. "What's she into?"

"Nothing that can get your truck fucked up," I said. "Scout's honor."

He grunted and nodded, fishing the keys out of his hip pocket.

"Good luck, son."

"Thanks, man."

I caught the keys he tossed at me out of midair and ducked back out into the damp winter cold.

THE DRIVE to Raven's old neighborhood was sort of stressful through the tunnel. Fuckin' yuppie tech sector scum around here didn't know how to fuckin' drive! Made me glad I was in Vyking's truck and that I wasn't on my bike. I would have ended up back in fuckin' prison for the same damn thing I'd gone up for in the first place.

The streets in this part of the outer edge of the city were tight, and parking was a fucking joke, but I found something a few doors down that would be serviceable if I hurried my ass the fuck up.

I got out the truck, shrugged into my cut and went down the cracked sidewalk and stopped in front of the place. It was a two story and clean on the outside, the small yard more of a vegetable garden than anything else. Boy was I out of place in this type of hood. I let myself in the low front gate of the white picket fence and went up onto the big wrap-around porch. The front door opened before I got halfway up the steps painted a brick red.

"Can I help you?" The man was skinny, probably vegan, and the woman that peered around him was tiny and just as granola.

"I'm a friend of Raven's," I said. "I was hoping to talk to you."

"Oh, my God! Is she okay?" The woman darted around the man in front who tried to keep her back.

"She's okay," I said, nodding.

"Where is she?" the little girl demanded.

I shook my head. "I'm not about all that," I said. The man frowned.

"She doesn't know you're here."

I shook my head. "No. She did me a solid close to a month back and I'm trying to get a handle on her situation. Can we sit out here and talk?"

The pair exchanged a worried look and finally, the guy raked his hands back through his long hair and settled his hands on top of his head, letting out an explosive breath.

"Sure," he relented, and the girl gestured at me to have a seat. We migrated away from the front door and they both took a seat on the porch swing while I settled on the low wall railing thing.

"Where is she?" the girl asked and her face was pinched.

I said, "First thing's first. I'm Mace."

"Angelica," she said.

"Robert," the guy said, and I shook the man's hand.

"I can't answer your question, exactly. She's hiding."

"Son of a bitch," the dude muttered.

"What happened?" I asked.

"She went on a date with some guy," Angelica said. "She came back way late. Her clothes were ripped, and she wouldn't talk about it."

"Then a couple weeks later, we were at the park," Robert said.

"Fire practice," Angelica said.

"Some cops came, arrested her."

"We couldn't find her. We called everywhere. It was late." Her voice was laden with something like guilt.

"When the rest of the Burners left, they found her out by the street."

"She was beaten really bad. They brought her here. She wouldn't let us take her to the hospital. Some of the Burner medics helped us do what we could."

"As soon as she was able, she left. We found her phone smashed on her bedroom floor, some of her clothes gone, but that was it," Robert said.

"She never came back…" Angelica looked hurt.

I shook my head.

"She couldn't," I told them.

"She's safe?" Robert asked.

"Yeah, she's about to get safer if I can help it," I said.

"She's a really good person, private though. Please tell me we didn't make a huge mistake telling you any of this." Angelica looked up at me and I pulled my proof out of my pocket, an envelope with my name on it in Raven's writing. The letter I held in reserve and would only use it if I had to.

She told me things, a lot of things, private things that I didn't want to share. Some of it skirted the big bad that haunted her. I was still trying to fill in the gaps.

"That's your name, and that's her writing," Robert confirmed, looking over Angelica's shoulder.

Angelica sniffed and tossed her dyed black dreads over her shoulder. She looked up at me, face pale, blue eyes glittering with tears as she handed me back the envelope. I cued up the video Sauley had taken of Raven reading one of my letters on my phone and handed that to Angelica. She covered her mouth with her hand and bit back a sound, starting to cry, studying every nuanced expression of Raven's face as I had probably a thousand times before.

"You uh, happen to keep any of her stuff?" I asked, taking my phone back while Robert hugged what I presumed was his girlfriend.

"Yeah, we uh kept all of it. Boxed it all up in totes and put it in the basement."

"I brought my truck; you trust me to take it to her?"

They exchanged a look. "Can we go with you?" Angelica asked.

I shook my head. "You want to write her a letter or something, I'll make sure she gets it."

"What happened to her?" Robert demanded and the fury in his dark eyes was one I harbored myself.

"That date didn't go well," I said. "I think you already know that. As far as the rest of it, Raven was right to get the fuck out of here. The less you know, the better off you are, but hey; I'm going to get it taken care of," I vowed.

"How are you—" Robert gripped Angelica's shoulder, and she looked up at him. He looked down at her and shook his head. Smart man.

"Your man's right. Best not to ask any more questions," I said. "I can't say more."

"I'll give you a couple of totes of her favorite things," Robert said. "If she wants the rest, she can come get them."

"Robert!" Angelica protested. "She left money to keep us going until we could find a new roommate. She doesn't owe us anything," Angelica argued.

Robert gripped Angelica's arm and towed her in the direction of the front door, and I shook my head. "See now, Bobby, that's no way to treat your lady," I said.

"Robert," he said affronted, and I raised my eyebrows.

"Don't give a fuck, let her go."

He dropped her arm immediately.

"I'll bring you Raven's things," Angelica said. "The stuff I can carry."

"Alright, thanks. I hear any problems, I'll come and help," I said, giving her a pointed look.

Bobby, excuse me, *Robert*, slammed his way into the house like a petulant child.

"Sorry, he's usually not like this," Angelica said. "He's upset."

"A man knows when and how to control himself," I replied and yeah, I know, I needed to learn to take my own lessons to heart.

In the end, I took two big totes – the things Angelica knew she had loved best and had left behind. The sentimental things. I could hear her and Bobby argue it out and I couldn't fault him too much. He was worried. I gathered that clear enough.

I was worried too, only difference was, I was fixing to do something about it. Of course, I couldn't fault him on that either. Most citizens didn't have the know-how to fix something like this, and if they did, they damn sure didn't have the balls. I had both – in spades – and I would use them.

I slid the first tote into the back of Vyking's truck and turned. Bobby handed me the second one, and he'd earned points. For as upset as he was, he wouldn't hear of making little Angelica carry the heavy thing up the block.

He handed it to me, and I said, "Hey, I know you're upset and pissed off, believe me, I get it... but stop and think a minute. If you showed up in front of Raven like this right now, would it be the best thing for her?"

He stopped and thought about it as I slid the second tote into the truck. When I turned back, Angelica held out a note to me. I took it and tucked it into the inside pocket of my jacket.

"We miss her," she said and sighed, stuffing her hands back into her pockets.

"Yeah." Bobby nodded.

"She did what she thought was best, bro, you gotta believe her on that."

"Yeah, well, a little low on trust."

"Aren't we all, brother?" I asked him. He looked me over and nodded.

"She doesn't know you're here, does she?" Angelica asked. I shook my head and they both sort of reeled.

"How did you even know she lived here?" Robert asked, brow rumpling in confusion.

"I got my ways," I said, and he nodded.

"Just tell her we send our love," Angelica said, and I nodded.

"That I will do," I answered and put up the tailgate on the truck.

Tonight, I would be picking her up from work.

It was time for the big talk.

## 12

*R*aven...

Sauley was standing outside again, his back to the door, waiting. I went to it, unlocked it, and said, "How many times do I have to tell you just—"

Mace turned around and I couldn't help myself; I yipped out a shout of glee and threw my arms around him. He caught me and grunted, and I immediately tried to pull away saying, "Sorry! Are you oka—" but I didn't get to finish because his lips met mine.

I froze, speechless, and just as quickly as he'd kissed me, it was over and he was leaning back to search my face.

I blinked up at him stupidly for a second then brought my mouth to his, pressing my lips against his once more, timid yet intrepid. He kissed me back, slowly, an almost chaste kiss, his cold fingers brushing against my cheek as he cradled me with his other arm and I sighed out, pulling away slightly.

He closed his eyes and rested his forehead against mine as the blood raced through my veins.

I shivered, and it had nothing to do with the cold.

"Come on, let's get you inside," he murmured and pulled back to smile at me.

I nodded mutely, and he walked me backwards through the front door of the bar and into its warmth.

"You good?" he asked, and God, I'd missed his voice.

I closed my eyes and nodded. "I'm better than good," I whispered and just soaked up his being here.

"Finish up, babe. I'll walk you home."

I smiled and comfortable, asked, "You spending the night?"

"Absolutely," he responded and let me go.

I was tickled pink and almost felt *normal* again for the moment as I went to finish closing.

He waited for me, and we kept trading looks and laughing at each other. Finally, the chores around the bar done, I called out to Manuk that I was leaving.

"Aloha!" he called back, and he waved at Mace. Mace raised a hand back and pushed out the front door. I locked up behind us.

Mace took my hand, and I smiled up at him. He grinned back and dipped his head, hesitating, making sure it was alright, and my smile only grew. I closed the gap and kissed him softly and he kissed me back. Still chaste, still no tongue, although I wouldn't be opposed, I was still shy.

"Come on," he said, voice husky and breath pluming the early morning air. "Let's get you home."

We walked briskly and when we arrived, there was his motorcycle parked at the curb. I blinked and said, "You rode here, in *this?*" He went to it and got a backpack out of one of the hard-sided cases on the side near the back tire.

"I ride year-round," he said as I unlocked the downstairs door.

"That's crazy," I said. "It's so *cold* and *wet*."

"That's why they make cold weather gear and Gore-Tex," he said. His eyes and smile were laughing at me even if there was no sound.

I shook my head and held the door open, but he indicated I should go first. I slipped through and he made sure it was secure behind us, trailing me up the stairs to my apartment door. I let us in, and he stilled my hand on the last lock.

"Pro tip, only lock one or two of these when you're not home. It's taking you too long to unlock them all to get inside. Once you're in, definitely secure them all."

I stared at him for several heartbeats as what he'd told me sank in and then I felt stupid for a moment.

"Of course," I murmured. "Thank you."

He nodded and I let us in. No need to worry with him standing there, sheltering me.

Mace was quite a bit more imposing sober and healed than he had been drunk or injured, only my comfort level with him hadn't diminished in the slightest.

He shut the door behind us and meticulously threw all the locks like I liked, turning and smiling at me as I stood in the middle of my tiny living room and watched him.

"Why don't you put some of your music on?" he asked.

"Yeah?"

"Yeah, I like it."

I frowned and asked, "How do you even know what I like? I don't remember ever telling you."

His grin grew, and he said, "You're using my music account. It syncs across all the devices I have it logged into."

"Oh." I scrunched my face in embarrassment. "Right."

"Go make us some of that tea?" he asked.

"Only if you'll make yourself comfortable," I countered.

"I'd planned on it." He winked at me.

I disappeared into my kitchen and set to making a pot of tea. Music filtered in from the television a few moments later and then I heard him go into my room.

When I came back out, the water ticking in its kettle on the stove as it slowly heated, he had come out of my room, jacket and vest gone, his boots left behind too.

"Hey," I said lamely, softly, and he reached out, taking my hand in his to lead me to the couch. He sat down and practically drew me into his lap. I sat beside him and toed off my own boots which I hadn't laced properly earlier for the aesthetic.

I stiffened, and things got a bit awkward as he tried to move me, and I couldn't quite anticipate what he wanted. Finally, I laughed somewhat nervously and just asked, "What do you want me to do?"

"Turn around, put your back to me, and just lie back," he said.

"What, like with my head in your lap?"

"Exactly. Only if you want. No pressure." He held up his hands and the look in his eyes, says he meant it. It eased my nervousness and made it an easy choice. I lay back and put my head in his lap. He put a hand to the top of my head, smoothing some of my hair back from my fore-head. I had it in a messy half-loop bun.

"You ditched the wig," he said.

"It was getting sad," I replied. "I was thinking about dying my hair."

His gaze drifted up from my eyes to my hair and he grunted, an almost sound of disapproval, and said, "Please don't."

I smiled and asked, "Why not?"

"Because it's beautiful – *you're* beautiful, just the way you are."

I think my mouth went a little dry.

"No one's ever said that about me," I whispered.

"Fuckin' idiots. All of them," he said back, his eyebrows raised as though to dare me to argue.

I loved the smoldering look in his liquid brown eyes and how it set my heart to racing. I smiled, reaching up to cup his lightly stubbled cheek, and he closed his eyes and leaned into the touch like there was no place he would rather be in the whole world right now.

"I come with a lot of baggage," I warned him softly, swallowing hard around the sudden lump in my throat.

"Don't we all?" he asked, opening his eyes. He stared down at me and slicked his fingertips along my hair and sent a tingling rush over my scalp. "You accepted me and my sordid past, baby. Not a lot of people would have helped me, let alone would have seen it through to the end the moment they found out I was an ex-con."

"There are a lot of people in prison for things they didn't do," I said.

Before he let me finish, he shook his head and said, "But I *did* do—"

"No, I know that," I said. "What I was going to say, was there are even more in there that don't deserve to be based on the circumstances... I know that you did it," I said. "I also know that I would have done the same thing."

He smirked then and chuckled, shaking his head. "You wouldn't have," he said. "You're too good for that."

I looked away. "I'm not," I declared, knowing that if I could hurt or kill my rapist, I wouldn't hesitate. I would hurt him, murder him, in a heartbeat. Not just for me, but for anyone else he had done this to. For anyone else that he was going to do this to in the future.

I closed my eyes as the emotions welled up from the deepest, darkest parts of me and filled the space behind my eyelids.

I trembled finely and covered my face with my hands, the trembling turning to quivering, and then to shaking.

"Shhh, let it go," Mace soothed and brushed a hand over my hair, and I did, because for the first time in a long time, I felt *safe* when not alone.

Thankfully, the crying jag was swift and over by the time the kettle started to scream.

We drank our tea and talked of other things – lighter things to balance out the dark and to chase the shadows away. I needed that, and I think Mace knew I needed that. For someone with such a rough exterior, he was, at least to me, incredibly generous and kind. I couldn't say it was because of what I'd done. I think he was always this way. I just don't think anyone from the "citizen world" as he liked to call it, had ever given him the chance to be soft around them.

I understood that, somewhat. As a Pagan, as an outlier and outcast, I guess I'd chosen a gentler path. Something akin to the lone wolf howling at the moon until the rest of my Burner tribe had howled back.

"I found a place among them, but I guess I hadn't wanted to or wasn't necessarily ready to completely give up on the rest of the world," I murmured to Mace. I sat curled on the opposite end of the couch, my knees up, cup cradled in my hands as we talked over our tea.

"You don't have to tell me if you don't want to; if you're not ready," he said and put his big warm hand atop my foot, rubbing over it, pressing slightly with his thumb. I jumped slightly at the initial contact, and closed my eyes, sinking into that touch, fathoms deep and sighing in a mix of frustration and relief.

"No, I do…" I said. "I really do."

"Why you think?" he asked, and I sighed again at the monumental task of climbing this particular mountain.

"Because I need you to know it's not you," I answered.

"I know that, beautiful."

He sounded so sure, but it wasn't cocky or anything. I couldn't tell you what it was, but it wasn't that.

"I haven't been with anyone, like *that*, since…" I averted my gaze and felt my cheeks color. I'd never been embarrassed by talking about sex before. This was new and uncomfortable, and I didn't like it.

"Nothing has to happen tonight," he said, tapping the top of my foot. I looked at him and met the sincerity in his gaze. "We can just go to bed, and I can hold you, and call it good. I'm good with that."

"You actually mean that, don't you?" I asked, slightly stunned.

"You bet your ass, I do. I like my women willing and to enjoy it. I'm not down for anything else. We do anything? We do it at your pace, your way."

It was a completely foreign concept.

"I'm not used to men acting that way," I murmured.

"For all that they call *us* the barbarians…" he muttered, but he didn't need to finish. I caught his meaning perfectly, and he was right.

"I'm afraid I've never been good at initiating things," I whispered.

"That's okay, I can do that, but you have to promise me if you aren't ready, that you'll tell me," he said.

I nodded.

"You say 'stop' and everything stops," he said.

I nodded again, and he smiled, looking over my face.

"What?" I asked.

He shook his head slowly. "Just like looking at 'cha."

I blushed and bit my bottom lip to keep from giggling and his smile bloomed into a grin.

"I don't think that's ever going to get old," he said and caressed my calf through my leggings.

We talked more, and eventually with my every other sentence being punctuated by a yawn, he got up and took my cup. I looked up at him and with a soft smile he said, "Be right back," and took the two cups into the kitchen. I heard him deposit them carefully with a slight clack into the bottom of the sink and then he came back around.

He reached down and took my hands and said, "Come on, up you go!" He hoisted me into the circle of his arms and cocked his head, looking at me for several long heartbeats before asking softly, "Ready for bed?"

I nodded mutely, and he nodded with me before pressing his lips to my forehead. My eyes fluttered shut, and I melted beneath that kiss, the safety and security I felt with this man enveloping me tightly even as he kept his touch light.

He let me go and turned, leading me to my bed by the hand and stopping beside the low mattress, gripping the hem of my oversized, tan, post-apocalyptic sweater.

"Arms up," he murmured, and I obediently raised them. He swept the soft garment over my head and dropped it to the floor beside us.

"Again," he whispered, and I hesitated for only a moment, raising my arms so he could sweep off the dusky olive-green cami that clung to me underneath the sweater. He peeled it up and off from over my head and I crossed my arms over my chest. He didn't go for the black sports bra. Instead, he dropped to his knees in front of me and pulled his tee and the waffle pattern thermal shirt he had on beneath it up over the back of his head, turning the sleeves inside out as he stripped it from his body.

He looked up at me, the question of permission in his eyes as he brushed the waistband of my leggings with gentle fingertips. I nodded carefully and he hooked fingers into the waistband and peeled the fawn-colored, thick second skin off my pale legs. God, I was grateful I'd shaved them earlier in the day on a whim.

He left my black cotton bikini panties in place, helped me to step out of the leggings then reared up on his denim-clad knees, tracing light fingertips up the backs of my legs from my Achilles over my calves, eliciting a light giggle out of me when he tickled the backs of my knees, and a gasp when he touched the backs of my thighs.

I closed my eyes, relishing that light touch, and ever the gentleman, he skipped touching my ass altogether, and instead put hands to my hips, drawing me forward a hitching half step to press his lips above the line of my panties but below my belly button, turning his head to put his ear to my stomach and to gently cuddle into me. He nuzzled me softly, his arms twining around my waist and simply holding on.

My arms lowered along with my defenses and I ran my hands through his short hair. God, it was softer than it looked. He looked up at me, and the depths to that look, like staring into still waters, the surface placid and impassive, he really meant it. He would be satisfied with simply going to sleep, nothing else... and for whatever reason, that turned me on, so, so, much.

"Come up here," I whispered, and he got to his feet. I stepped into him and raised my lips. He smiled and lowered his mouth to mine.

I pressed against him and he gathered me up, his hands on my lower back, hands daring to slip lower on my hips, but still restrained. I opened my mouth beneath his and he moaned into it, his tongue flicking against mine lightly, mine meeting his, a careful dance, feeling each other out, groping in the shadowy dark for lines and boundaries that were quickly dissolving and becoming as insubstantial as a soap bubble with the fires lit by this passion, and these *needs* I felt. A need to be close to someone, a need to feel something other than this ugly and deep *shame*.

Mace made me feel things other than bad. He made me feel beautiful, made me feel *wanted* and not just as a prime piece of meat. He made me feel like it was my very soul he wanted. Like claiming my body wasn't enough, that my heart and mind were what mattered, and I was so... so *grateful* for that.

I clung to him, pressing my body into his warm and inviting one and he tore his mouth from mine, looked into my eyes, and asked, "Yeah?"

I nodded, breathless, and answered him, "Yeah."

"Protection?" he asked.

"Please."

"Mm." He returned his mouth to mine and slid his hands to my front, letting me go to work at his belt, unbuttoning, unzipping, sliding his hands inside the waistband of his jeans and shucking them off his hips, letting the weight of his wallet and chains drag them past his knees, stepping on the cuffs and dragging his legs out of them, all while he kept his lips firmly melded to mine.

He pulled me against him once more, the second he was free of his pants and socks and I was less shy about things, pressing myself tight, letting my own hands wander over his heated skin, desperate to touch as much as *be* touched.

He slid fingers up my back, tucking them under the bottom band of my bra, sliding them around to my sides.

"Arms up?" he asked against my mouth and I whimpered, knowing it would pull his lips from mine but complying with the request. He pulled the restrictive garment up over my head and took the time to look at me, groaning as his gaze swept over my chest, my nipples tightening in the chill of my apartment.

He lowered his mouth to the hollow of my throat and pressed a kiss there that was chaste at first, flickering his tongue against my skin, dragging it down before tucking it back between his lips and gently scraping me between my breasts with his teeth in a delightful nip that made me throw back my head and shiver in delight as I let out my breath on a throaty little, *"Oh!"*

I dropped my head and looked at him, meeting his gaze that was rolled up to mine as he took the majority of my left breast into his mouth, teasing the point of my nipple with his velvet tongue, sending whole body shivers through me, his arms locked around me, holding me tight, holding me *up* as my knees threatened to buckle.

"Mace!" I gasped in warning as they did, but he had me, taking his mouth from me and lowering me carefully to my bed.

"I've gotcha baby," he breathed, and I believed him. He climbed over me, kissing his way back to my mouth, settling between my thighs, grinding softly against me, showing me how hard he was, grunting at the contact, closing his eyes and turning his head slightly as though listening to the sweetest music he had ever heard, and in truth, perhaps he had... whatever music his own body made for him at my touch.

I lay back, and he kissed me, one arm delving behind my shoulder and back, his hand cradling my head lovingly. The other, drifting over my skin, grabbing my hip, holding me as he rolled his hips against mine and groaned. I watched his handsome face, his strong features smooth

out in bliss and I felt something I don't think I've ever felt before…
*cherished, special.*

I wrapped my legs around him tight and dragged his mouth to mine
and kissed him fiercely. I let go of my false apprehensions. I knew real
when I saw it, and this was something so very real, so tangible, the
emotions shimmering between us almost something I could touch if I
wanted to.

He reached down between us and slid his boxers off. God, he was
beautiful. Long, not overly thick, and cut, the head of his cock a deep
red and richly engorged, throbbing in time with what I could only
assume was his heartbeat. I gazed at his body, hungry to have it
against mine, positively *starving* to have him fill me; to feel him inside
of me.

"Oh, fuck…" he whispered, and I looked up. The raw need and heat in
his gaze made my body respond in ways I couldn't even imagine.
Without hesitation, I slipped my fingers into the waistband of my
panties at either hip and took them down.

He helped me whisk them down and off my legs the rest of the way
and with a light-fingered touch gazed upon me, letting his eyes feast
on me the way mine had feasted on his only moments before. He
groped off the side of the mattress that I had long thought of as 'his'
ever since his stay here and pulled a box from the top of his backpack.
He tore it open, ripping a condom from the line of them and tearing
open the package with his teeth.

He took the slippery rolled rubber disc and made himself ready for
me, asking me as I watched him slide the condom on, "You sure?"

"Yeah," I breathed, nodding.

"I don't care if I'm mid-stroke," he said, dropping back down over the
top of me, brushing the loose hair off the side of my face, gazing deep
into my eyes. "You tell me to stop, I'm going to stop," he whispered
and swallowed hard. I swallowed hard myself and nodded.

"I mean it, baby. You tell me to stop, I stop," he whispered.

I nodded and feeling like he needed to hear it, hear *something* from me by way of understanding I whispered, "Got it."

He swept his eyes over my face, and kissed me gently, sweetly, turning the heat back up between us until I was wriggling beneath him, silently begging for more.

He reached between us, his other arm back beneath me, cradling my head in his hand, massaging my scalp some, hand buried in my tresses as he met my eyes with his and breathing heavy, asked me, "Yeah?"

I nodded, whispering, "Yeah."

He smiled at me and pressed the head of his cock into my wet and waiting pussy slowly.

I gave myself over to surrender and tipped my head back, moaning, breaths short, body arching lightly into his as he filled me. He let himself go, bringing his other arm up to brace himself, staring down at me, eyes passionate burning embers, his gaze a warm, almost physical touch all its own where it swept over me.

He was careful with his thrusts at first, his cock feeling so good, pressing out against my walls, setting off all manner of sweet sensation inside me as he put a little twist into his hips as he worked himself inside me.

I bit my bottom lip and panted, holding onto him tightly, pulling him down over the top of me. He let out this almost groan of gratitude and let himself go just a little bit more, his pace quickening, his body finding a secret rhythm that sought to unlock all of my secrets.

He felt so good, so wonderful, and my body came so *alive* under his touch. I tensed, tightening around him and he brought his head up to gaze down at me once more.

"Yeah?" he asked, and I knew he was asking if I was feeling good.

I smiled up into his kind face and whispered back, "Oh, God, *yeah*." He smiled, bowing his head, chuckling and picking up his pace. I gasped as he slid over just the right spot inside me and the gate of what could only be described as paradise opened before me.

*Dear God, he was good... so good.*

## 13

*M*ace...

Handling a broken woman is like riding a bike with shot brakes. You don't go too fast. Bad brakes or no, I was going to take her for a ride, but all I had to do was take it easy. That was alright, I wanted to ride her, but I didn't want to do that in a parking lot burnout, we had all the time in the world, for a night.

She was sweeter than I expected.

It was like getting an old bike, one that has had miles thrown on it, but had been waiting all its life to end up under you. Raven reminded me of that sort of bike, one that had been treated like shit by its last owner, paint scratched, chrome chipped, spark plugs burned to hell and back.

The joy there was bringing it back.

Bringing a nearly dead bike back from the scrapyard was nothing but joy.

Raven was that broken bike – misused, abused, and then discarded.

Maybe there was something wrong with me, maybe those frat jack-asses knocked something loose in my head with whatever they low sided me with. Balls deep in a crazy Burner girl, one that was stirring serious feelings in me, and I was thinking about pipes and cracked seats.

She groaned, and it brought me back around, back to Earth.

I wrapped her up in my arms, sliding one beneath her, cradling her head in the palm of my hand, her sleek bronze hair winding around it, trapped between my fingers and the feel of it was something luxurious. The way she looked up at me, her storm-swept eyes heavily lidded with the pleasure I instilled in her... it was marvelous. She was breathtaking. Limbs that I found so statuesque twining around my body; her touch lighter than falling leaves drifting on eddies of wind.

She showed a gentleness and a care that... *fuck*... I doubted no consideration like it had ever been given to her and I wanted to be that man which was seriously different territory for me. I was used to breaking people when the occasion called for it. Not for putting them back together – not that Raven seemed to need it much. She was something wild and fierce. A woman who seemed to have it figured out, she just needed a little help along the way.

She moaned, eyes closing, head thrown back, her back arching, pussy tightening around me and I smiled. She was close, really close, I could tell, and I just wanted to drag it out and make it last as long as possible. I wanted to keep her in that place where it all felt good and everything that wasn't that feel good sensation just fell away. That was the difference between the men and the boys. A boy would thrust away until he was spent, not realizing that the fun wasn't the destination, it was the ride.

I wanted to ride her as long as I could.

Run her through her gears, take her up and down the hills, feel her tighten around me, shudder, and swoon.

Then again.

How many times could I get her over those hills, how many of the bad things in her life could I make her forget with what I had between my legs?

Several times it would seem.

She looked into my eyes, her cheeks flushed, and her legs trembling. When I couldn't ease her over another hill, I kissed her as I came. I held her for a moment, and then we both eased down onto the mattress. One of the very few compliments I could give to a condom was that they were certainly tidy. There was no mess that required attention or a towel.

We were a tangle of limbs and soft kisses for a long time; I didn't even care about how much my ribs burned from the effort.

"I was lonely," she intoned after a tremulous breath, and I stilled for a moment, putting my hand that had been tracing patterns on her back, flat to it. I said nothing, waiting for her to continue her story.

"So, I signed up on one of those dating apps on my phone and matched up with this guy named Max," she said. "We talked, for a long time, a few weeks maybe? Then he asked to meet for coffee, and I agreed because he seemed really nice and was a gentleman, you know? Not crude, no dick pics, and sure he was in law enforcement so it would be fine, right?"

I held her a little tighter when her voice cracked. She cleared her throat, sighed, and said, "He talked about his Italian mother, wore a gold crucifix, and seemed like he had a great respect for women. Told me all about it, right?"

My first thought was if a dude had to tell you something like that, sell you on the idea, it should honestly be your first red flag. Dudes that respected women just did. They didn't have to sell you on the idea that they did. Actions speaking louder than words and all, but I wasn't about to say any of that. There was no point. All it would serve to do would be to make her feel like somehow any of this was her fault when it wasn't. It was this Max guy's fault.

Raven was too sweet, maybe a little naïve, but I couldn't picture her doing anything to cause anyone any kind of upset. It just wasn't her. She was a pleaser by nature – a healer, a fixer, and a radiant light.

"I'm listening," I assured her when she fell quiet.

"We walked for a long time around the park, and he invited me back to his place for a glass of wine. He seemed genuine, but he wasn't and when he kissed me it," she shuddered, "it felt off and I wasn't okay with going further so I got up to leave and—" She huddled in on herself and shuddered against me. I held her tight, kissing the top of her head.

"You don't have to tell me anymore," I said.

She sniffed and said, "He raped me, then put me in the back of a ride share to take me home. I begged the driver to take me to the hospital instead. They called the police who didn't seem to really want to take my report. They kept twisting my words and… and I feel like it was a miracle at all that I got through that and to the prosecutor."

"They get him?" I asked, feigning innocence of any knowledge of how this shit turned out.

"No," she said hollowly. "The police came, two men in uniforms, to fire spinning practice. They arrested me, wouldn't tell me what for, and took me away but not to jail. They drove me to the bottom of a parking garage, threw me on the ground and Max was there. The three of them kicked me halfway to death. That's how I knew what to do about your ribs. They told me to drop the charges or they would tear my life apart, make me disappear. I was so scared. They knew where I lived, they could hurt my tribe. I didn't know what else to do so I called and refused to cooperate and then the messages started coming, telling me to keep my mouth shut. I got rid of my phone, packed what I could, and ran."

She sobbed a little, a bubble of misery choking off her words and I held her. This fucking guy... I'd never killed a man before. Came close but had never sealed the deal. I aimed to make sure this fucker could never do this to another woman.

"All I can see when I dream is that goddamn gold crucifix swinging on its chain in front of my face as I waited for him to be done with me. I was so scared that with anyone else that would be all I would ever see... but you... thank you," she murmured thickly.

*Yep. I was gonna fucking kill him...*

"HEY, FEN, YOU BUSY?" I asked, striding across the field. Several goats brayed.

"Depends on what you want," he said, in the process of pouring feed into pans.

"It's your specialty," I said.

"I only have two specialties, and since you aren't pretty enough for the first, then it's gotta be settling a score," he said, shoving one of the more demanding goats away with a boot.

"Yeah," I said. "I know you've gotten used to handling these goats, but I have a pig that needs to be dealt with."

"You know I love fresh ham, bacon." He grinned savagely and pushed another goat away. "Fuck, now I want breakfast."

"We can take care of that, but I found out a few things. Pig fucked Raven over, and I want to fix it," I said.

"What kind of payback we talking about? You gotta be careful when taking a pig to market."

"Oh, that's what I was hoping you would say." I grinned. "This guy raped her, then when she filed a complaint, they put the boots to her, medium style."

"Medium style, huh?"

"Medium style, enough to send someone to the hospital, but not enough to kill 'em. You know, enough to send a message and make sure it stuck – in her case drop the charges and keep your mouth shut."

"No shit?" he asked. "That's why she's *skittish*, eh?" He looked thoughtful and angry. I could tell, he didn't need any winning over.

"Yeah, that's why she's skittish. That's also why she's living in Rat City, in an off-the-grid apartment, and walks everywhere. The pigs have her blackballed."

"And taking this one to market will fix it?" Fenris asked.

"I think so. You know how these jagoffs are, they rally around their own, but you take that one out, they go back to covering their own asses." I growled and crossed my arms.

"You're still on parole, that's playing with fire," he said.

"Raven was a fire spinner, it seems fitting?" I shrugged. "And besides, it could be a public service, something nice to do for her, sure, but the rest of humanity will surely benefit, too."

He nodded and poured the last grain bucket. "She's weird. I like her," he said. "And yeah, I'll take care of it, just tell me who this walking bag of pork rinds is and consider it done."

"No, not like that. I'm not asking you to take care of it, I'm asking you to help me with this. I want to take this guy out, with my own hands."

"Oh, that sounds like the old Mace, and fuck yes. Count me in. What about the club?" he asked.

"I don't want to bring the boys in on this. If things go sideways, that would put them at odds with an entire police force. They don't need that hassle, not on my account," I said. "Maybe the prospect, though. Yeah. He could use some real experience here."

"The nervous kid, oh Thor's hammer, yes, the prospect should be involved." Fen laughed. He took a slow breath and closed his eyes. I took a small step back. Fen took some of this stuff really serious, and when he opened his eyes again, he almost seemed like a different person, like maybe not even human. "You know what, Mace, no. We'll leave Sauley out of this, unless you need someone to babysit Raven. You know what you are asking to do?"

"Yeah, get rid of a pig," I said.

"No, Mace. This isn't getting rid of a pig, it's murder. You are going to take another human being out of this world, and you're going to do it right," he said. "You're going to look into his eyes when he dies, and it is going to change you. The prospect isn't ready to even be near that happening."

"This guy is a rapist, and his cop buddies have covered his ass," I said. "I'm not worried about getting rid of him."

"He's a human being, and you are going to end his life, and after that, you'll be like me," he said. "Like DT."

"No one is like you, Fen," I said. "No one's like DT, either. You think we should involve him."

"You'll be a killer, then, like us." He smiled with something that could only be described as grim glee. "And no, DT would spill it to Mav. I know where his loyalties lay, and it will always be club first. This is definitely beg forgiveness over ask permission. Plausible deniability."

He looked far away and thoughtful. I had to guess he already had this half figured out.

"You can be a scary motherfucker, Fen," I said as the creepy and insidious smile grew on his face. It was half way a man looked when he was on the way to a boner. Seriously creepy in this context.

"I know it," he said, and rounded the gate, closing it up behind him. "Come on, there are things to consider."

# 14

*R*aven...

"I want to take you somewhere," he said, and I smiled, leaning forward on my hands across my bar. Mace smiled and gave me the kiss I was looking for and I backed off, a happy girl.

"Oh, yeah?" I asked, popping the top on his preferred beer and setting it on a coaster. He took it up and put the lip of the bottle against his lips. I tried not to outwardly shudder at the thought of what it felt like to have those lips against my skin.

One night with Mace, and I swear to God, it was like my switch had been flipped or something. Sex with him was suddenly all I could think about. I was craving him like he was some sort of drug – addicted to his kiss, to his touch, like nothing else I had ever had the occasion to desire before.

"Yeah," he said with a wink. "You think you could get a whole weekend off from this place?" he asked.

"Depends," I said, pulling the pencil from behind my ear and the pad of paper from my apron pocket. "What dates are we talking here?"

We talked weekend plans, and I wrote some dates down then asked, "Where you planning on taking me?"

"You trust me?" he asked softly, picking up my hand and pressing a kiss to my palm.

"Of course, I do..." I said, some of the tension leaving me at the sincereness in his deep brown eyes.

"Enough to let me keep it a surprise and still be comfortable?" he asked, and I hesitated.

"Am I really that bad?" I asked and winced.

"Not at all, babe," he promised me. "I just don't want to do anything that puts you ill at ease. You've been through enough."

I bit my lips together and nodded thoughtfully. He ducked his head, and the movement brought my eyes back to his.

"You okay?" he asked, and I nodded.

"Yeah, just thinking about what you asked." I took a deep breath and let it out in a rush. "You can keep it a surprise," I said, and he grinned.

"Yeah?" he asked, making sure.

"Yeah," I nodded once, resolutely.

"Alright then." He took another pull off of his beer and followed me with his eyes as I drifted up the bar – one of my regulars beckoned.

It was going to be my night off the next night, and Mace had agreed to take me to his place. He kept warning me that it was far worse than mine and I couldn't fathom. When he'd told me that he was living in the loft of a barn, I just had to see for myself. It sounded like quite the adventure.

"You're sure about this, now?" he asked me later, when he held the passenger door of a pickup open for me. I climbed in without hesitation and said, "If I can trust you for this, I can certainly trust you for a whole weekend away, can't I?" I'd shot back. He grinned, stepped up on the truck's runner and smacked a kiss to my lips before shutting me in to come around to the driver's side.

The late night/early morning drive to this goat farm he lived on was uneventful and traffic was light. It *was* the middle of the week, so I hadn't expected much. What surprised me was the three people still up, sitting on the covered back porch of the house across from the big old barn.

Fenris, I recognized, the woman and the older man I did not.

"You seriously gonna take a lady up to that old pallet in a barn loft? Boy, ain't you got no class?" the older man called out as Mace rounded the front of the truck and I slid to the ground from the passenger seat.

"It was good enough to conceive you!" Mace called back, winking at me.

Fenris laughed and the old man chuckled as we walked up.

"Vyking, Aspen, meet Raven. Raven, this is Vyking, Fenris' dad. Fenris you know, and Aspen here is Fen's lady."

"Hi, it's nice to meet you," Aspen said cordially and held out her hand to me. I took a big step forward and shook it.

"Nice to meet you, too," I said.

"Aspen made your tea set," Mace said, and I smiled really big.

"Oh, it's just beautiful. Thank you so much," I crowed.

"I'm so glad you liked it!" Aspen said. "Thank *you* for what you did for Mace!"

I looked over to Mace and felt like my smile was ridiculously cheesy with how much I cared for him by this point. I felt like every time we were together; he gave another lost piece of me back. Like a crow gifting shiny things to a human that'd helped. Except the shiny bright pieces that he gave me were invaluable, an incalculable gift.

"What are y'all still doing up?" Mace asked.

"Oh, you know, shootin' the shit," Vyking declared, and I bit my lips together to keep from giggling.

"Being fucking nosey," Fenris corrected him, and I did laugh then.

"Can you blame us?" Aspen asked. "It's always Raven this and Raven that," she said looking at Mace who, by God, was turning red in the overhead porch light.

"Right, you need to use the restroom?" he asked me, changing the subject.

"Ah, sure," I said.

"This way." He led me into the house. "We can use this one down here." He flipped on the light for me. "Back door is always unlocked so we have access."

"That's the door we just came through?" I asked, leaning a shoulder against the doorframe from inside the bathroom.

"Yep."

"K." I smiled, and he grinned back.

"Feels weird having you here."

"Weird bad, or weird good?" I asked softly.

His smile grew as he leaned forward slowly. "Weird good," he whispered against my lips. "Weird *definitely* good." He kissed me and I melted all the way down to my toes.

"I'll hurry up," I whispered against his lips and he drew back.

"K."

I rushed through freshening up and he was waiting for me on the back porch with everyone else. They seemed to be giving him a hard time but lightly.

"Alright, you two. Sleep tight," Vyking declared with a chuckle.

"Goodnight," I bid them, and Mace led me across the grass to the stairs on the back side of the barn leading to the second floor.

"It's cold out here, but look at those *stars*," I murmured, and he stopped with me to look up. "So many of them."

"Yeah, you don't get as much in the city."

I breathed out the cold and cleansing air in a plume.

"It's warmer inside. Not by much, but it is," he murmured, taking my large macrame tote from me and hoisting it up on his shoulder.

"K," I said, drifting after him to the stairs, soaking in a last glimpse of those stars in the sky.

He shut the door behind me to the big loft and I blinked letting my eyes adjust to the even darker gloom. There were rows and rows of shelves holding pottery in various stages of completion.

"Stay right there," he said. "I'll get the lantern lit."

I waited as he moved through his familiar space, through the shelves to the front of the barn under what appeared to be a bank of windows. There was a hiss, and then a soft *wuff* and the glow that permeated the loft was one that resembled a captive star, all fierce white radiance that could only be a camp lantern.

I picked my way carefully around the shelves to find him.

His space was as sparse as mine, just a mattress on the floor and a row of crates on their side to use as shelves, holding his clothes and other miscellaneous things.

I smiled.

"I could get used to this," I declared. I loved it.

"If I have anything to say about it, you won't have to, babe. It's fun for a night or two, but for months? Not so much."

He stood up and turned, resting his hands on my hips lightly.

"Well, I like it. It appeals to me greatly."

He smiled and stepped a bit closer. "I can appreciate a woman who likes the simple things," he said.

"Yeah?" I asked, softly.

"Yeah," he said with certainty. He kissed me then, and I swooned into him, my arms going around his waist as he gathered me close.

"You up for an orgasm or two?" he asked me, and I hesitated.

"It was a long day," I murmured, deciding that while I was up for sex, I also needed to see…

"Hey, that's okay," he said without missing a beat. He kissed my forehead and caressed my cheek with his thumb, and I felt myself go lax with relief. An end to an anxiety I hadn't even known was riding me. "Let's get you undressed and into bed, yeah? I want to hold you," he murmured.

I smiled and nodded and that's what we did. Got into what passed for PJs for the both of us and cuddled close in the nest of sleeping bags he used for blankets.

"I ask you something?" he asked softly when we'd been settled for a time after he'd doused the light. I lay, my head on his chest, staring at the deep, dark blue sky out the dusty window and the smattering of stars across its surface.

"You can ask me anything," I murmured.

"You know I don't want you to think badly of me," he said, and I tore my eyes from the sky outside and tipped my head to look up at him.

He rearranged his to look down at me and I blinked and said, "Why would I ever?"

"That's what I wanted to ask you," he said solemnly. "This... this Max guy."

My breath stilled in my chest.

"What about him?" I asked uneasily.

"You want I should take care of him?" he asked.

I swallowed hard and cuddled into his side and said, "He's too powerful, too connected. I would be afraid for you," I said.

"Nothing to be afraid of here," he said, and stroked my hair. I closed my eyes.

"I wish he were dead," I told him honestly. "I don't want to be afraid anymore, and I really don't want him to do this to anyone else."

I shuddered and Mace held me close, making a soothing, "Shhh" that ruffled my hair.

"He won't," he said. "I promise."

"Don't make promises you can't keep, baby," I said to him. "They're the worst kind. The kind to break the heart the most."

He was quiet for a time and finally said, "Okay."

He held me and my mind raced for a good long while. Finally, I asked, "Could you really do it?"

He chuckled and kissed my hair.

"Go to sleep, Raven. This conversation?"

"Yeah?"

"It never happened."

I nodded against him.

"Okay."

"You're safe, you know," he said. "As long as I'm around, as long as the club's around… you're safe now."

I closed my eyes.

I so desperately wanted to believe that.

## 15

*M*ace...

Fenris was all business. We didn't leave the farm until all the animals were fed, their water troughs seen to, and he checked on several of the fattest nanny goats, close to bursting with their kids. It was odd to see him like this, concerned about the animals.

We left the farm on our bikes and went to a place that I didn't expect Fen to even know existed, a public library. The place was small and rough looking, and inside the terminals were scuffed and dated, but that wasn't what we had come for. The woman working the desk had the same look as he did, blond hair, shaved on the sides, and she had a massive double-headed eagle tattoo piece across her chest. They spoke, and in a few minutes, she had more information on Parole Officer Massimiliano "Max" Bianchi than I could have found in a month. She also said strings of words I couldn't follow, like tor, and dark web, doxing, and blockchain data.

It didn't matter how, but I had the fucker's home address, thanks to Kim, and the rest came later via Cipher. We had his phone number, home and cell, and even shit like his blood type and uniform measurements.

"We case the joint, but we do it quiet like. Looks like it is a nicer neighborhood, so we can't wear colors or ride the bikes. We'll stick out," Fen said as we walked back to the bikes.

"So, what, we use the truck?" I asked.

"Nah, even that sticks out," he said.

"We call an Uber to drive us through the neighborhood?"

"I was thinking about walking, but that might work too." He laughed.

"Split the diff, take an Uber to the neighborhood, then walk the alley, check the place out like that?"

"Good plan, and we do it at dark," he said.

"Because we won't be noticed?"

"Because people aren't as on guard, in their homes, when the sun goes down," Fen said. "They think they are safe." The way he smiled when he said it made my blood cold.

A VERY NERVOUS man showed up and drove us from a popular night spot back to a house a few blocks from Bianchi's house. The kid was really glad to have us out of his Maxima, but Fen gave him a good tip and a smile as he all but did a burnout leaving. Even without our jackets, the two of us were a pair of scary looking motherfuckers.

We walked a short distance from the house we had been dropped off at. The alley afforded darkness and a lack of attention, plus this place was absolutely the sort of place that hated us, and everything about it. Cookie cutter houses sat on postage stamp lawns, but each jagoff had an oversized riding mower, SUVs in driveways, and everything reeked of fake wealth.

These assholes were over their heads in bank loans and mortgages.

Fen followed a few turns and then stopped at a backyard. "This is the one."

"Follow your nose?" I asked.

"GPS, man, get in the twenty-first century." He tapped his phone.

"Well fuck me, then," I said, and pulled myself up to look over the fence. Bianchi had a clean-cut backyard, but it was mostly empty. No toys, no bikes, no shit like that. That was good, no sign of kids. "Does this asshole have a wife or anything?"

"You don't know?" Fen asked.

"No, man, I don't."

"You saw it all as good as I did. He isn't married. Divorced, no kids, ex lives down in Fresno," he growled. "So no, we don't have to worry about women or children being here."

"Or we do." I gestured toward the sliding glass doors on the back of the house. I finally got my first look at Bianchi himself. He was what I expected, an average looking white guy, on the thin side, but in a decade or so he would hit the middle age spread and turn into one of those potbellied cops who nursed a coffee cup and a donut every-where they went, shotgunning whiskey and blood pressure pills. Right now, he was probably still running miles in the morning, and spending time at the shooting range.

He wasn't alone.

There was a woman with him, a bottle blond, fake tits, a little on the heavy side.

"Looks like he has company," I said. "We aren't ready, anyway."

"Who said we aren't ready?" Fen asked. He pulled a long-bladed knife from the top of his boot. The light caught on the blade, and there were Celtic knots etched in the steel.

"That's all you brought?" I asked.

"Gun crime does real time," Fen said. "Besides, when it comes to something like this, I would want to use just my hands."

"Oh," I said.

"Guns are for war, knives are for lovers, and bare hands are for your worst enemies." I could almost feel the gleam in his eye. I could certainly hear it in his voice. "As long as no one comes down the alley, we wait."

"For what?" I asked.

"When the time is right, you'll know."

"And if I don't?"

"If you keep asking fucking questions, I'll send you to go get some frozen yogurt and some hair ties, since you're being a little girl about this," he said. It would have been less intimidating if he had raised his voice or spoken harshly, but this was just matter of fact. Fenris was hunting, and I had to stop asking so many questions if I was going to go through with this.

It would be a lot easier to just let him handle it, just let the berserker loose, and then head back to the farm, and Raven.

Jesus, being back at the farm and railing Raven again would be better than this. But I couldn't. How could I make the promise to her to get rid of this shitstain on her soul, and then chicken out at the last minute, just let Fen go in? If things went sideways, there would be no mercy for Fenris from the police. They would put him away for a long time, and that's only if he survived to be arrested.

The boys in blue were good about making sure attempted cop killers committed suicide, overdosed, or were just suddenly armed and they were justified in filling a man with lead. If there were two of us, then it would work. Fen knew how to do this, he had killed. I had to do this for Raven, for myself, and it would go better if he was watching my back.

"I only have one question," I asked.

"Sure," Fen said.

"What if he has a gun?"

"Of course, he has a gun, but he's a fucking coward, ain't he?"

"I would say yes just because of the badge," I replied.

"He rapes a woman, then has her beaten. He's a coward because nine times out of ten, a single man can take on a woman in a fight. Most women can't fight for shit. Most men can't either, but they are at least the same size as the coward with a gun. A cocksucker who needs a bunch of his brothers to boot stomp a woman, he's a fucking coward. He will be scared. If he goes for the gun, his aim will be shit. He probably won't go for the gun. I'm betting bullets to goat shit that this cop is more likely to offer to suck your dick than to pull iron on you."

I grunted a response. I had said one question, so it would be smart to keep it to just one question.

The cop and the blonde drank some wine. They talked.

They made out.

He sat on the couch, and she vanished. I realized that their conversation had turned to her sucking him off. Then they fucked.

Then she was near the back door, fake tits out. He bent her over the couch and went back to pounding her.

"Oh, this is putting me in a mood," Fen says. "Aspen might have a right nice evening when this is over." I didn't respond other than giving him a short laugh. This felt weird. If we had a rifle or something, it would be done and over.

Instead, we kept a vigil over the fence, asses planted on a dumpster, watching this asshole give it to this blonde. They went at it for a while, and at one point, I barked a laugh.

"What?" Fen asked.

"She checked her watch," I said.

"Either she's bored, or she's billing hours." Fen laughed. "Plastic tits and cheap hair, I'm betting the second." There were a few words between them, and then she was on her knees and he was giving it his best 90s porn guy pose. Thirty seconds after he was done, she was up and out of the room, leaving him leaning against the back window, obviously winded and sweating.

"Definitely the second," I said.

"We won't do anything until she leaves," Fen said. I nodded in agreement. No reason for whoever she was to get drawn up in Max's fate.

The next couple of hours seemed to never fucking end. She cleaned herself up. They talked. There was coffee. They talked more.

They might have had an argument.

They made up and talked some more.

She eventually left.

Max fucked around in his house for a bit longer, took a shower.

Dicked around, watched some television.

Then, thank fuck, finally turned out his lights and went to bed.

"How do you have the patience for this?" I asked.

"I slept." Fen shrugged. "After he finished his business, I closed my eyes. I knew nothing interesting was going to happen."

"You could have told me," I said.

"Figure it out, Mace," he said. "We'll move when the moon is directly above that tree." He pointed at the tallest tree in the neighborhood.

I leaned back against the dumpster and thought about getting some sleep myself. I wasn't sure how to sleep, my nerves were all jangled up, and I didn't know how this was going to go down. We had one knife, no guns. This guy was a cop, and I would so rather be with Raven right now. Next thing I realized, Fenris was shaking me awake.

"C'mon, Cinderella, it's go time." When he stood, he seemed like some sort of ancient Norse god, or a wolf that had come to levy judgment. "You still remember how to pop a sliding glass door?"

"Of course, I do." I looked toward the house. The work I had done, construction and shit, of course I knew about doors and windows. I never imagined that remodeling would be a useful skill in dealing with a bad cop.

We hopped the fence and stole across the backyard in a low run. Max didn't have any sort of personal security, no cameras, no flood lights. Fenris looked at the door when we eased up next to it. I could see the look in his eyes, smash the glass and go right through. There were two things though, some of these doors weren't glass, they were energy saving sandwiches of composite materials, and more often than not...

I slid the door open.

They were left unlocked.

I gestured for quiet, and he nodded. I saw a flash of teeth, and then the flash of the crazy Norse knife he was carrying.

"What's the plan, Jesus," I hissed.

"You're going to jump him, and beat the shit out him," Fen said. "Then, we're going to kill him, slow like."

"Just beat his ass?"

"Yes, beat his ass, then we are going to kill him, because this is what you wanted to do."

I nodded and clenched my fists. Fen had my back; he had that knife. Fuck, Fen didn't need my help to do this, he was fucking babysitting me.

It took three doors to find the bedroom.

I flicked on the light, and Bianchi sat up, groggy and confused. He looked less confused when I put a fist in the middle of his mouth. Then he looked at the ceiling and fell out of the bed. I shook my hand for a second, that hurt. Teeth are hard.

I went over the bed and landed on top of him, throwing a few more punches so he knew what was going on. There was a bit of shouting, some blood, and something crunched. I hoped like shit it was his nose, and not something attached to me, like any of my fingers.

"Get him!" Fen shouted.

I pounded his face a few more times. I was panting, and Max wasn't doing anything but laying on the ground, bleeding.

"Atta boy!" Fen said, coming around the bed himself. He jerked the top sheet of the bed, wrapped it around Max's arm and head, and used it to drag him out of the bedroom. Max screamed and kicked, knocking a lamp over and then he grabbed at the doorframe. Fen gave him an encouraging kick in the ribs to get him to let go.

Fenris dragged him into his own living room and then hauled him up into one of his own dining room chairs.

"Who, who the fuck are you guys?" Bianchi spat out a mouthful of blood. "What do you want?"

"Do you remember a woman named Raven?" I asked.

"Who? No!" he said, leaning forward. He drooled a ribbon of blood on the floor.

144

"Her name is Tanis McGowen, that familiar?" I asked.

"I haven't seen her in a long time," he said. I rocked his head back with a knuckle duster right in the cheek.

"Do you recall the finer details of your date?" I asked.

"Think really hard," Fenris said. "I don't like wrong answers."

"I took her on a date, that was it," he said. I caught him on the side of the jaw with my off hand.

"Easy with the fists, you're going to break your fingers on his skull," Fen said. "That's why we have the seax." That caught Max's fragmented attention. He looked up at us, and then the blade that Fen had drawn.

"Who are you guys? I never did anything to you."

"You didn't do anything to me, but you might recall putting your dick in a woman who wasn't real keen on that, and when she turned your ass in, you and your boys arrested her, and beat the ever-loving fuck out of her? Is that ringing any bells?"

"None of that is true. She was just a trashy piece, and she gave me a fucking STD," he spat. Fen caught my wrist before I punched Bianchi in the face again. "If you're up in those guts, you better get checked."

"Cut him," Fen said, and handed me the knife.

"What, where?"

"Get creative, just don't stab him," Fen said.

"What the fuck, are you a fucking amateur?" Bianchi asked.

"Cut him like a billy goat." Fen laughed. "Give his balls a tug."

"Look, I'll give you whatever you want. I have cash. Other stuff," he said.

"No, I think my friend has a good idea," I said, taking the blade from Fen and gesturing for him to hold Bianchi. The man immediately started struggling, but Fen jerked him up into a submission hold. Bianchi started to scream but Fen's forearm cut off his air supply.

He kicked, but it didn't stop me from doing something that I never thought I would ever do – I grabbed another man by his tackle. I steeled myself and remembered that this piece of shit was a cop, one of the people who was supposed to be a good guy, someone who was supposed to protect people.

And that he was a rapist, and that when she had tried to stand up to him, he made sure she went down in a heap of blood and broken bones. I slashed with the seax and Bianchi shuddered. I was holding a wad of flesh and my hand was drenched in blood.

He pissed all over himself.

"Brutal." Fenris laughed.

Bianchi let out a sob.

"This is for Raven," I said, and put the ruined handful of his own flesh in his hand.

"I bet she wasn't the only one, was she?" Fen asked. Bianchi was silent, except for his shoulders shaking.

Fen smiled as he watched what I did to that man. The blade was incredibly sharp, and it parted skin and muscle easily.

While I was figuring out the dance, Fenris kept telling Bianchi what he would have done if he was the one with the knife and I was the one holding him. He did offer some praise for the full business castration, and that the only downside of that cut was after the initial cut, there wasn't pain, just a terrible feeling of loss, and numbness where once his manhood had dangled.

"I'm sorry." He let out a wet sob, and then threw up.

"You'll have to speak up," Fen said.

"I'm sorry for what I did to Tanis, or whatever you said her name was," Max said. "It wasn't anything personal, she was just pretty, that's all."

"That was all I needed to hear," I said. I gestured for Fen to move, and then I stepped behind Max. Given the amount of blood on the floor, there wasn't much fight left in him. He wasn't going to come up out of that chair fighting. I grabbed a fistful of his hair and pulled his head back. Fenris threw his head back and howled.

I drew the blade across his throat and released a pulsing river of blood.

He convulsed, kicked, and gurgled.

Then he shit himself and went limp.

I felt my hand shaking, and I thought I was going to vomit.

"There is more blood than I expected," I said.

"Oh yeah, people are fucking full of blood," he said, pushing Bianchi's corpse off of the chair. It hit the floor and jerked. "They'll jerk and fart for a good while after you kill 'em too."

"We should probably go," I said, feeling a tremor in my hands.

"Let's make sure there isn't anything we need first," he said. "Like does this sack of shit have any good booze? Then, we torch the place, no evidence."

"I should take something more than his booze," I said, looking down at the gold cross necklace laying on his chest. "I'll keep this, for Raven."

We each found a bottle of high-end booze and used the rest to start a fire. Bianchi and his sheet were the center, and we stood in the back-yard long enough to make sure that the fire really took off. We walked a few blocks and downed the bottles.

"What did you think?" Fen asked.

"Well, it's not my favorite thing in the world. Probably the worst thing I've ever done."

"I'll ask you again in a week, and we'll see how you're doing. Maybe wait a few days before you give that trophy to your girl and wash the blood off of it. Most girls don't like being handed a bloody present."

*Fuck.*

I did vomit. Fen pushed me off balance and laughed at me, shaking his head.

"This is why it's DT and me for this shit, bro," he said, shaking his head and his expression sobered.

"Maybe just stick to beating the fuckin' brakes off a motherfucker and leave the killing to me from now on. It's not for everybody, man."

I nodded and spit, doubled over, my hands on my knees.

"I had to see it through," I said, and he took a pull from his bottle.

"You did good for bein' fuckin' amateur hour."

"Thanks," I muttered. "I think."

"You're welcome." He lifted his head as sirens split the night air. "Come on, keep walking. They're singing our song."

"Yeah, let's get out of here."

We fell into step and made strides until Fen deemed it safe to order up a ride.

## 16

*R*aven...

"Where *are* they?" I wondered out loud. It was *late*, the darkest dark outside Aspen's shop windows.

She sighed and looked at me with something like pity and said, "When the guys say club business, it's none of our business. I've seen it where Fen's been gone a couple of *days*. No explanation and definitely no questions asked. It's difficult sometimes, but it's how they are," she said with a bit of a shrug.

I smiled and thought about it and nodded.

"That's... that's a lot," I said and sucked in a deep breath. "But in all fairness, my schedule can get pretty weird too."

She smiled at me and nodded. "It can be a lot sometimes, but I wouldn't trade Fen for the world. It's just a part of him, you know?"

I nodded slowly and said, "Yeah, I might have some idea."

It was true, I did. Burners led an artistic and nomadic lifestyle for the most part. I know I had certainly been guilty of following my heart and my creative purpose to the detriment of a relationship or two. It would be hypocritical of me to expect or demand anything from Mace when it came down to it.

He had his life, and I had mine. They would either fit or—

"Wait!" I looked back over my shoulder at Aspen who was working some clay on her wheel. "Don't go out there. Let them settle down and get showers or do whatever. They'll come find us when they're ready."

"You act like they were doing something illegal," I said jokingly but the look on her face said I had hit the nail right on the head. She looked away.

"Club business is none of *our* business. Is it patriarchal and kind of bull?" she asked. "Yes, but it's also *practical*. You learn to look the other way, or things won't last long."

I wandered back over to my seat and dropped into it a little heavily.

"And is that worth the trade-off?" I asked softly.

She smiled at me then and it was a genuine one as she pushed an escaped blond curl from her ponytail off her forehead.

"It's absolutely worth it," she said. "Do I worry? Yes, but I've also developed an understanding."

She worked the mound of clay before her into the beginning of a mug shape. She'd actually been working on them for hours and just about every available surface in her workshop had one on it drying.

"What do you think they do?" I asked curiously, staring out her little shop's window at the back of the house where the men had disappeared.

"Oh, eventually, you're around long enough, you get some ideas," she said and sighed. "Nothing's ever confirmed, but you'll know."

"I've been in situations like that before," I said a bit grimly. Drugs were a thing in Burning Man circles. Some more insidious than others. Most for recreational purposes. Still, addiction was pretty rampant.

"I shouldn't say anymore," she said kindly and smiled. "I'm afraid I'm giving you the wrong ideas."

I shook my head slightly and said, "If anything were to give me the wrong idea, it's their already established reputations," I murmured. "They're very confusing in that regard."

Aspen laughed and nodded. "Yes, they are!" she agreed with gusto. "Despite all appearances, and rough exteriors, their world makes more sense in a lot of ways. It's simpler, somehow."

I nodded. "So simple it gets complicated," I said, thinking about some of the activist circles I ran in.

Aspen nodded. "Yeah, that sounds right."

"A lot of drama then?" I asked, and she shook her head.

"Oh, no! Not like most places and with most people," she said. "Usually, a quick fistfight and it's quashed." I chuckled and nodded, and she went on, "They're passionate." A small smile touched her lips. "You'll never be loved as fiercely as they will love you, and the family ties with them run deeper than any blood relative tie I've ever had. There's a lot more that's good than bad in this life and I wouldn't trade it for the world."

I smiled then and said, "Now *that's* definitely something I know something about."

"What's that?" she asked.

"Chosen family being better and more supportive than the family you're born into. Everyone needs to find their own tribe and each tribe is going to be different. This is no exception," I mused. She nodded and her smile said that she was relieved that maybe I did understand. I think it had maybe taken some serious getting used to for Aspen at first.

I understood that. She was a nice woman, but she was also very... what had Mace called us? *Citizen*. She was normal, not that it was a bad thing. I could appreciate her deep connection to and general earthiness. She was kind, and sweet and while I couldn't fathom what she was doing with a big Pagan like Fenris, who was admittedly pretty damn scary – I couldn't deny what I'd seen between them as the real deal.

He loved her every bit as fiercely as she claimed and she, I think, sort of balanced him in some hidden way. Her earthiness brought him back to Earth, grounded him. It was absolutely undeniable looking at them that they were each other's missing pieces.

I couldn't tell you how I'd longed for the same thing in my own life. How I had pined for it to the point I'd been blind to my vulnerability. I had no desire to ever be prey ever again. Not like that. But my heart was a soft thing, and I also had no desire to let what happened to me make me hard. I didn't want to be ensconced in a bitterness as to be blind to possibility and goddess, I couldn't tell you how hard and fine the line was to walk, but when the door to Aspen's shop opened behind me and I turned to meet Mace's solemn gaze?

It suddenly felt effortless. It suddenly didn't feel like a tightrope act at all. All my anxiety and misgivings melted away when his expression softened as he looked me over and found me well. I could suddenly *breathe* again.

"Hey, you!" Aspen called as Fenris edged in behind and around Mace. I heard the man grunt and the sound of a kiss being exchanged behind me, but I couldn't look. My attention was firmly captured by Mace.

"Doing okay in here?" he asked mildly, and I smiled.

"Am now," I declared, getting up from my seat. Without even thinking about it, he reached for me and tugged me into the circle of his arms. I hugged him and a fine tremor went through him as he held me tight.

"You alright?" I asked carefully, whispering in his ear.

"I will be," he said. "You ready to go? Or you want to hang with Aspen a little more?" I appreciated that he asked. I turned to look and giggled. Fenris had captured her mouth with his and slid his hand into the neckline of her blouse. He was massaging one of her breasts while the mug she'd been shaping between her hands had turned to a mass of ruin. She certainly didn't seem to care and to be honest, were I her and Fen, Mace? I don't think I would care either.

"I don't think we'll be missed," I murmured. Mace huffed a slight laugh and walked me outside, closing the door behind us.

"You sure you're alright?" I asked him carefully.

He nodded and murmured, "Just tired and missed you."

"Mm, I wished you hadn't had to go," I whispered, cuddling closer to him in the damp chill of your typical Pacific Northwest winter.

"Club business," he said softly, letting his gaze roam my face, the slight smile on his lips fracturing my heart with want.

*God and Goddess, he looks at me the way I've always wished for,* I thought to myself and on the heels of that thought, I darted my head forward and kissed him.

He hummed in pleasure and captured my face between his hands, putting his arms around me and pulling me in closer still.

"I'm sorry it went so late," he murmured against my lips, pecking the tip of my nose as the clouds rolled overhead in the stiff breeze.

"I'm a night owl," I whispered. "All is not lost."

"Did you have a good dinner with Aspen and Vyking?" he asked, and I smiled and nodded.

"I did, I'm sorry you had to miss it."

"Me too." He turned and arm over my shoulders and hugging me into his side, we made for the stairs on the back side of the barn to the loft.

"Did you at least get something to eat?" I asked.

He nodded. "We did. Had a couple of drinks."

"I'm glad you're here," I confessed. "I was a little nervous about staying here without you."

"I'm really sorry, babe. It happens sometimes. I hope it wasn't too bad?"

"No." I shook my head. "Aspen is great, I'm just a big ol' scaredy cat."

He stopped on the landing, hand on the door to the loft and faced me. "You have every reason to be. You feel whatever you need to feel. I get it if it's going to take some serious heavy lifting on my part. You don't have to trust me but thank you for doing it anyway today." He pressed his lips against my forehead, and I leaned into him.

"Don't suppose you're up for giving out a free cock ride right now," I said, biting my bottom lip to keep from grinning too stupidly.

He grinned and laughed. Nodding, he said, "I think that can be arranged," as he opened the door for me. I slipped inside, trailing my hand down his chest, skipping it over air to land it in his palm to draw him in after me.

I wanted him, wanted *this*, so much...

## 17

*M*ace...

Laying eyes on Raven made the horror of the last few hours, and the long stint of boredom before it completely worth it. The light in her face, and the way she bit her lip, I felt a thrill run through me when she asked me to give her a cock ride.

This woman was magical.

I would kill a dozen more men for this woman. I smiled to myself.

Maybe then Fen wouldn't give me shit about being amateur hour.

The loft above the barn wasn't the most romantic place, but when Aspen had her kilns fired up, it wasn't cold. Add the lack of light, the moon shining in the window over my bed, it was romantic, not just fucking dark. I put my arms around her and kissed her. "I'll give you a cock ride, woman, but I'm not just gonna jump on you and ride you down to the strip and back. I want to ride you all," I kissed her, "night," I pushed my hips into hers, "long."

Raven groaned and pushed back against me. Something certainly had her in the mood, and I really wanted to be in the mood, but it was going to take a bit for me to get over what I had just done. Killing a man didn't have my dick hard and ready to tear her up. Just thinking about what I had done actually seemed to take me out of the mood.

That was okay, there was totally an answer for this, and it was going to put a fuckton of gold stars next to my name. Motherfucking foreplay.

I kissed her, where could I go? Earlobes, she liked that. Neck? There wasn't a woman alive who didn't like her neck being kissed.

Then I thought of Bianchi, how easily the flesh and blood of his throat had parted under Fen's blade, and for a second, I pressed my lips against her skin and breathed out.

I was not going to fucking puke again.

*Fuck that.*

When everything seemed to settle down, I looped back, lips to lips, my hands in her hair, her real hair.

The wig still bothered me, but it wasn't here.

I pulled her shirt down low so that I could put my lips against her collarbone. There was something about that I liked. There was nothing sexual about her collarbone, or that little gap between them at the base of her neck. I kissed it, and let my hands wander a bit, grabbing her ass, and grinding against her. She seemed to be a little surprised that I hadn't just gone right for the treat in the middle, but she didn't know what I had done.

I was getting warmer, closer to being in that mood.

I started pulling her shirt up, and she was more than willing to pull it off more expertly than I was able to. Her tits were fantastic, and I took them in my hands and then buried my face in them.

I found something there that I didn't expect, relief.

It was absolutely dumb, but with my face buried in her chest, her scent filling my nose, I forgot all the horror and the blood, and I learned the meaning of one of the words from English class that I never really got. *Sublime.* This was sublime.

Maybe subtle? I fucking sucked at English.

Didn't matter.

Her nipple in my mouth was exquisite. Her hands were in my hair, and the more she raked her nails across my scalp, the less I cared about anything. It was beautiful and if I were a softer person, I might have shed a tear, maybe a few.

She let out a breathy "oh fuck yes" when I let myself ease down to my knees, dragging my lips down her stomach to the elastic band of her black panties.

Did she own any other color?

Didn't matter, either. It was the wrapping paper on the gift. And like the wrapping on a gift, it didn't stay on long. Panties were easier to pull down than getting a shirt off.

It wasn't the first time I had seen the reveal, and not even the first time I had seen Raven's reveal. The dark strip of hair seemed like an arrow pointing down to where I should pay attention. There was a hint of pink, the shape of her lips, and the hint of what was concealed between those.

I kissed her hips and eased the panties all the way off her. She kicked her pants and the rest away and backed to the mattress, dropping back onto it.

"I never thought anything like this would ever happen to me." She sighed.

"What, go down on you?" I asked.

"No, I mean make me feel things, in my heart, not just down there," she said, running her fingers through my hair.

"I want to make you feel things all over," I said, grinning at her.

I felt my cock twitch. *Finally.*

She leaned back on the mattress and slowly parted her legs for me. It was glory, nothing but glory. There was that perfect moment where her lips clung together and then parted, showing me her world. I sighed out and kissed the top of her pussy, letting my tongue search for her clit. She groaned. I went down on her like I was drowning, and her thighs were my life preserver.

God help me. I could have died right there.

There was a moment when I tasted her, the scent of her filling my head, and her flavor on my tongue, I felt contentment, as sharp as her taste, fill me.

"Raven." I whispered her name and buried my face in her. I felt her moan, and her hands were rough against my head. She groaned and rolled her hips so that what she wanted me to lick was pressed against my face. I was never one to deny a beautiful woman's pleasure.

I undid my belt and dropped my pants. It was more awkward than I wanted, but I was determined to not part myself from her sweet pussy until my cock was hard and free. I couldn't go down on her and fuck her at the same time, I was nowhere near that flexible.

"Oh God, Mace," she said huskily as I pulled away from her. I knew my face was wet with her juices, and my cock was throbbing. I moved to enter her but didn't immediately penetrate her. I wanted to savor the feeling, how wet she was, and how I could feel how hot she was. There was also an almost religious reverence, making a moment of prayer, giving thanks to whatever god looked down on me, for her.

The first few strokes didn't enter her, but instead I was just grinding myself against the furiously pink lips between her legs. I groaned, excited, anticipating the moment. Then I pushed the head of my cock into her. She made a sound that I couldn't describe, and there was nothing but desire as I buried myself inside her.

"Raven..." I gasped.

"Yes," she said, her hands pulling my face to hers, to kiss her.

Our strokes were slow, measured, sweet. I wanted to lose myself inside her.

And I did.

For a long time, that was all we did, devouring kisses from her lips and laying them on her neck, and shoulder. I groaned and tried to thrust like I could put more of myself into her than just my cock. The way she moved under me, if I could have, she would have taken every-thing I could have given.

She changed positions on me, pushing me back with a foot so she could turn over onto her knees, instead of her back. Her arched back and presented bottom invited me back to my task. The way she glis-tened in the dim light told me that she was happy with the slow pace I was keeping. How easy would it have been to forget patience, and hammer away for a few brief moments and then blow my load inside her?

I took her from behind and she went from just enjoying the ride to picking where we were going, and how we were going to get there. I could feel her getting closer and closer to her first orgasm. I went quicker, grabbing her by the hips, and pushing her through it.

The goats were probably bothered by the noise we made.

I felt when it happened; she tightened up around me. I held her tight and kept going until she was overcome and fell forward, away from me. I followed her down, but rather than plunge back into her, ride her again, I pushed her legs apart and went down on her again. It was different, but hotter, and wetter, and she recovered quickly enough to push herself back against my face and howled with ecstasy.

Our positions changed, and I found new ones I had never tried before. I wasn't sure if these were entirely new things I had stumbled upon, or if Raven, in her years attending Burning Man, and whatever happened there, was teaching me new ones.

I held her leg, my face pressed against the bottom of her foot. She was laid out on the mattress, as I thrust into her. I found myself increasingly caught up in the excitement, not just the feel of her, the scent of her, but all the thoughts of her just being with me.

I managed to pull out, because in our haste, there had been no thought of condoms on either of our parts. She grabbed me by my balls, and then it was over. I grunted and felt everything come spurting out of me. I looked down to see her pulling on my shaft until there was nothing but a few drops running down her wrist, and the rest spread across the inside of her thigh and spattered across her pussy.

I groaned and started to lean forward.

The other direction would be falling off the mattress onto the loft floor. She caught my shaft and as I pitched forward, I plunged back inside her.

It was like finding that Heaven had another place that it considered Heaven and then burying myself in it.

I shuddered and was still.

Raven held me, and we kissed a few more times, but we were both breathless and sweaty.

"My God." I laughed, when after a few minutes I felt myself finally slide out of her.

"Yes," she purred. "You are." Then she laughed, and it was the freest I'd ever heard her.

# 18

*R*aven...

"Tell me something no one else knows," he murmured, and I laughed a little. I bit my bottom lip, looking away, hoping it appeared coy to him and not like I was afraid he would glimpse my secrets in my eyes – which is what I was absurdly afraid of.

He didn't let me get away with it. Instead, he touched my face lightly, a gentle stroke along my cheek, threatening to tip my chin. I looked up, tracing patterns against his chest in the dark, a swath of bright moonlight cutting across us from the window over the mattress we used as the bed. The sleeping bags we had tucked over and around us did a good job of keeping out the cold, but I was beginning to miss the amenities of my apartment.

"Babe," he murmured, and his voice was edged in humor, slightly chiding.

"I'm thinking..." and it was true, I was. He'd sort of caught me off guard with that one. It wasn't that I didn't hold any secrets, if anything I held too many, but like with most things the second he asked, I just sort of blanked and couldn't think of a single one off the top of my head.

I laughed nervously and tried to explain my predicament and he smiled down at me and said, "I got all night, baby, but I want to know something."

"What?" I asked stupidly.

He grinned. "Anything. Just something you've never told anyone else."

"Oh." I squeezed my eyes shut and laid my head back down. He placed his hand over mine, pressing the palm of my hand to his chest, ceasing the nervous patterns I had been thoughtlessly tracing over the same spot. I sighed and settled in, closing my eyes, and tried to think. When the answer came to me, it was a bittersweet one.

"Not to sound like a total whore," I said, nervousness creeping into my voice, "but of any man I've ever been with I…" I faltered and he was still, and though I didn't look at him, I knew he hung on my every word. "I've never felt the way that I do when I'm with you and I know, it sounds cliché—"

"Don't worry about any of that, it's just window dressing," he soothed. "Tell me how you feel."

"Loved," I said quickly, rushing it out before I lost my nerve, swallowing hard right on the heels of that one little word, tears threatening to spring to my eyes. "I've never felt that before, from anyone, until you," I said, looking up into his eyes, startled to realize they were smiling.

"Good," he said evenly and nodded slowly and slightly awkwardly. I kind of froze, blushing, glad for the dark and that it likely hid the color in my cheeks.

*Did he just—? Did he just* agree *with me? Was he saying he loved me?*

Holy shit.

My eyes did well then and his smile which had been small, grew just a little and he twisted his head on his neck and pressed his lips squarely to my forehead. I melted from that touch. That gesture that made me feel so small and so safe and so... *loved*. If only he knew what it did to me. That every time he did it, I lost just that little bit more of my heart to his capable hands.

"You make me so weak," I confessed softly, and he chuckled.

"Impossible," he whispered. "You're incredibly strong, one of the strongest people I think I've ever known."

I shook my head against him, and he laughed outright at that and said, "Going to have to agree to disagree on that one, darlin'." He cuddled me just a little bit tighter.

We lay in silence for a time and the burning urgency of just needing to *know*, of wanting to hear it but also being terrified to hear the answer might be *no* was just ravaging me, forcing me to look up at him, prompting him to look down at me.

"What?" he asked, and a lump formed in my throat.

"Do you?" I squeaked, so afraid the answer would be 'no' and yet not knowing what to do if the answer was 'yes.'

"Love you?" he asked me evenly, and his face was steely, unreadable. I couldn't trust my voice and simply nodded dumbly.

"Not sure how you couldn't know by now, but yes. I love you. I wouldn't do half the things I've done for and with someone I didn't." He rolled, half taking me with him and I went with it, giving no resistance when he nudged my knees apart with one of his own as he held himself over me; pressing down on top of me. It wasn't *oppressive*, the way he held himself above me. It was wonderful. *Safe*, sweet, and protective.

I stared up at him in wonder as he stroked the side of my face, his other arm buried behind me, holding me lovingly as he looked over my face.

"Just look at you," he murmured softly and the wonder in his eyes. *Gods above and below*, I felt so beautiful with the way he looked at me. This man, he looked at me with the reverence you reserved for such works of art as the *Mona Lisa*. Not for some poor as fuck Burner chick from the fringe.

Of course, maybe that's why we fit. Broken in some similar ways, both of us from the fringe; from the outskirts of a society that didn't care, that overlooked us until we were a problem, that thought nothing of us unless we were squarely in their way.

"I love you, too," I whispered, emotion welling hot and fresh, overwhelmingly so. I put my arms around him, and he crushed my mouth with his. Hungry, as though he were devouring my words, swallowing my love whole, and he acted as though it would be enough to sustain him for the *centuries* to come.

I wrapped my arms around him and pulled him down even closer. He folded elegantly, like an origami crane, all sharp points and angles, perched above me protectively, ready to slash with sharp wit any and all who came near wishing any sort of harm.

I don't think I had ever had any occasion to feel so safe and at once so afraid. I knew Mace could be a dangerous man, and it was like I lay here, maybe not with a paper crane but rather a paper tiger or some other big cat in my lap, softly purring in that big cat way that was difficult to differentiate whether it was indeed a purr or a growl... but it didn't matter. He wouldn't hurt me.

No, the predatory sheen that cloaked him, rippling through his musculature beneath my palms had nothing to do with *harm*. His hunger was carnal in nature, sure, but it was an appetite for pleasure and he wasn't so much about his own as he was mine. He'd proven that time and time again, and though I was positively exhausted, there was no way I could resist. I wanted, *needed* him inside of me just as much as he wanted and needed to be there.

He was slow, the connection between us fathoms deeper than anything I had ever known with anyone else as he slid his hard length against me looking for purchase. We both threw our heads back and sighed, shuddering in sweet surrender and tandem as he slipped inside of me, filling me gently, pressing out against my walls which ached to have him there, trembling finely around him and through me at his presence as though he was coming *home*, even though we'd just been doing this very same thing less than an hour before.

This was different. The connection raw and unveiled, like each of us were a live wire, touching, sparking fire, the heat building to a rosy glow between us. A glow that felt and for the longest time was sustainable with no end in sight.

His deep brown eyes looked deep into mine, soul deep and even deeper still to the fragment of stardust at the center of my being that I felt we were all made of imbuing it and me with the magic that only truth and love possessed.

I had no doubt in my mind, heart, or soul that Mace spoke his heart and it was something I needed so badly, so desperately to heal the cracks and fissures in mine.

I pulled his mouth to mine and poured everything that I was and everything that I wished I could be into the kiss that I gave him. He made it taste like anything was possible and for more than a brief shining moment it was and a moment after that, I knew that it was everything I had ever wanted. For the first time in my life, rather than resist it, I melded into the moment and allowed it to happen and I *trusted* with my everything in what could be.

I loved him so much for the gift he bestowed on me… the gift of him loving me.

## 19

*M*ace...

Getting out of Rat City for a while seemed like a really good idea. Taking Raven somewhere on my bike seemed like an even better one. There wasn't anything good for her in Rat City, and she needed to have a smile on her face for something better than a societal outcast, a dirty biker if you will, saying that he loved her.

She deserved better than that.

There were plenty of places to go, I just didn't know where would be a good start. I mean, the ride was gonna be cold as fuck since it was damn near the dead of winter. It would be a couple three weeks yet before spring would appear and that was only if this wasn't going to be a year where we had a fuckin' June-uary. That's when the Pacific Northwest's winter weather – cold and wet – literally dragged on through June and sometimes into July.

I sighed and waited for her to come back out into the kitchen from the bathroom where the shower had quit what felt like forever ago. I wanted to take her for a ride, let my elemental woman really feel what wind felt like as we took some of the sweeping curves around here. I also wanted to take her to breakfast. It was an easy decision when I put just an ounce of brain power into it. The Black Diamond Bakery and Café was a local spot that was almost a hidden gem – touristy to an extent, and old as fuck.

It haled back to when Black Diamond, Washington was a coal mining town and first opened up in like, 1902. The place made legendary fresh baked bread and over the years, a café serving a mighty fine breakfast had gone in next to the bakery with a real country diner kind of vibe. The kind of place that a lot of local church-going folks hit up right after service on Sunday.

In other words, it would be busy, but she would be with me and that meant anyone that could or would try to give her shit, would have to go through me first so it would be alright. She would be just fine.

"So," she started, sliding onto the kitchen stool beside mine, leaning her arms against the counter and stretching like a cat. I admired the smooth, lean, lengthening of her muscles underneath her skintight olive-and-charcoal post-apocalyptic fashion choice for the day and put my hand on her back. I couldn't help but touch her. I could never get enough of touching her.

"What's the plan?" she asked, smiling over at me and I felt a slow grin overtake my lips.

"How about breakfast?" I asked.

"Oh, God, yeah. I'm starving!" she nodded emphatically, and I laughed.

"Cool, let's take a ride."

She perked up a bit. "What, like on your bike?" she asked.

I nodded. "Figured I'd introduce you to the wind."

She smiled at that and some of her apprehension sloughed off.

"I hadn't thought of it like that," she murmured.

"Scared?" I asked.

"A little," she confessed, then laughed at the look on my face and asked, "What, is that stupid?"

"No." I shook my head. "I would never say that about you," I said, and it was true. "It's just, I guess I'm confused. You swing things around that are *on fire* and you're afraid of riding on a motorcycle?"

"Hey, to be fair, I'm in control of the fire as much as is possible when it comes to fire."

I grinned and gently teased her, "You saying you don't trust me to keep you safe?"

"No!" she cried. "I would never say that about you." Her voice gentled, and she sounded vaguely hurt. I pulled her into my arms and held her tight.

"Relax, baby. I'm just teasing," I said. She looked at me, searched my face for a second and nodded, deciding I was telling the truth.

I loved that about her – she was in a lot of ways tough as nails and capable but that didn't negate the fact that she was a soft thing, sensitive and caring. It was an interesting dichotomy. One I didn't think I would ever get tired of.

"So where are we going?" she asked, and I smiled. Watching her resolve galvanize real time was a treat.

"Ever been to the Black Diamond Bakery?" I asked her. She shook her head. "Then it's my treat."

I loaned her an old jacket of mine that was way too big on her but would protect her well enough. She looked trepidatious as we approached the bike, and I had to smirk.

"What's the matter?" I asked. "Scared?"

Bold as brass and honest as fuck, she answered, "Yes."

I laughed a little, my plan out the window. I was hoping by challenging her on it that she would buck up a little in denial. I guess we were well past the phase where she would feel the need to.

"Look," I said. "Is it dangerous? Sure. But is it any more dangerous than you spinning fire around you?"

"It's not that," she protested, shaking her head.

I eased up and searched her face. "It's that you have to trust me, isn't it?" I asked.

She bit her lips together and nodded, and had the grace to look borderline ashamed, but there wasn't a need. I got it. She'd been handed an awful lot of raw deals over her lifetime. It left a mark. Trust was hard to come by in that instance and that was something I for sure understood. I think all of us in the club did.

"C'mere." I drew her into my arms and wound hers around my waist, gathering her face between my hands and pressing my lips to her forehead. I felt the tension ease out of her.

"I've got you," I promised, looking her in the eyes. "I won't let anything bad happen to you. Look me in the eye and tell me if I'm lying."

Her steel blues searched my face right back, and she shook her head slightly. "No, I know you won't," she breathed.

I smiled and nodded. "Okay, this is all I need you to do…" I murmured and told her all the things I wanted and needed from a passenger. By the time I'd finished, she looked less spooked, a little more grounded, and all around curious.

We got on the bike and she snuggled herself close up against my back and God, that felt good.

"Stick your hands in my pockets if they get cold," I told her, and she nodded. "Hang on," I reminded her and fired my bike up. She jumped at the growl and held on a little tighter and I smiled.

"And away we go," I called, and put us in motion. She looked around as we headed through the trees and I thought to myself, *the hardest part of the ride was going to be keeping my eyes on the road ahead and off her lovely face in the rearview mirror.*

## 20

*R*aven...

The rush of the pavement beneath me was almost as intoxicating as the wind in my face. I know it was stupid, but I almost wished I could take off the helmet to feel it in my hair. I held onto Mace's lean, hard form through his leather jacket and after a few minutes and one or two sweeping curves took his invitation and stuffed my frozen hands into his pockets.

He called back to me once or twice, slowing to check on me and I grinned and hugged him a little tighter and he would accelerate. I lost myself in the exhilaration of the ride all over again.

How I could have ever been afraid of this was beyond me! This? This was wonderful. I didn't even know how to explain it. It was like... like being part of the world in a bigger sense. When he carefully pulled us up over the scattered gravel in the street outside the bakery, I was almost sad it was over.

"So, what 'cha think?" he asked when we got off the bike. I threw my arms around his neck and kissed him soundly as he made this chuckling purr of happy satisfaction into my mouth.

"That... that was..."

He laughed. "A lot different living the scenery versus just watching it go by in a cage, huh?

"*Yes*," I agreed. And that was *exactly* it. It was the difference between watching a movie and being a part of the production.

He held out his hand to me and I grasped it. We went inside to put our names on the waiting list.

I closed my eyes and breathed in the scent of freshly baking things at the bakery counter, of flour and yeast, and from the café side of things, rich maple syrup and frying bacon, and over and under it all, the decadent and robust scent of coffee. It was an assault on the senses in here, loud, the burble of countless conversations reverberating off of the old wooden walls. The crowd, while it could have been over-whelming, it wasn't. Instead, it was... cozy.

Mace hooked his arm over my shoulders as we perused the bakery menu and leaned in, his lips soft against my temple, his breath warm against my ear as he murmured, "Get whatever you want for the week, babe. My treat."

"I don't know what's good," I mused, and I could hear his smile. My gaze wandered the hand-drawn lettering on the chalkboard menu over the shelves of bread. There were already several empty slots among the shelves and things crossed out on the board. One or two shelves only held one or two loaves.

"The Crystal Mountain Loaf is always good," he said, pointing.

"Is there enough room, being on the bike and all?" I asked.

He shrugged. "Be amazed at how much fits in the saddlebags, and I've got a backpack in one of them. You could buy one of everything and it'd be a challenge, but we'd make it," he said. I giggled.

"I doubt I need *that* many carbs in my life," I said.

"But they're *so good*," he said, and I laughed.

"It's true. I think I'll go for one of those Crystal Mountain loaves and one of those giant cinnamon rolls for tomorrow night when I get up."

"You got it," he said and stepped up to the counter to place our order. I smiled and admired the fit of the seat of his jeans as he leaned forward to be heard over the low din by the counter's attendant.

He ordered some things for his household and with a few pink bakery boxes in a paper bag with handles, the plump round loaf of bread in its plastic bag on top, we headed to the back of the narrow lobby in front of the bakery counter to listen for our name to be called.

Breakfast was everything Mace had sworn it would be – rustic, flavorful, and all-natural ingredients. I happily filled myself with steel cut oatmeal and munched on a side of thick-cut bacon that was the perfect marriage of crispy and chewy.

It was a perfect time spent with Mace, who I couldn't deny I was falling deeply in love with. I hoped, and not so secretly, that this was just the beginning to a long life together. After everything... damnit, I deserved to be happy.

"HEY, YOU!" I called out to Sauley as he stepped into my bar.

"Hey!" he called back. "You are cordially invited." He gave a sweeping bow and handed over an envelope and I smiled.

"What's this?" I asked, as he shook his hair out of his eyes. The guys had decided a few weeks back that he didn't need to cut his hair anymore, and it was in that awful in-between phase of growing out, where it was too short to pull back and too long to keep it out of his face.

It was driving him nuts. I could tell.

"A little something something from Mace," he said, slipping up onto a vacant bar stool. I got him a beer.

"Let's see here," I said, tearing open the card.

It was smaller than a greeting card and was indeed an invitation. Golden no less. I laughed.

*You're invited!* was emblazoned on the front.

I opened the card, and the pertinent info was filled out on the form.

*Time: Tonight*

*Place: The Club*

*Dress: Casual*

On the three lines meant for the personalized details, Mace had written, *Come Party With Us!*

I smiled and said, "I would love to."

"Yeah?" Sauley grinned.

"Absolutely!"

He chugged the rest of his beer and set it down. After a belch that could only be described as adorable, he said, "Rock on, we'll see you then."

"Alright, be safe!" I called after him and he waved over his shoulder.

The invitation was some sort of wicked curse. By delivering it, Sauley had unleashed it onto my world, and it made the clock positively *drag*. The needle scooting arduously around the clockface until the appointed hour when I could get the fuck up out of here. When I waved and called out my goodbye to Manuk and turned for the door, there was my Mace, waiting for me just outside, his phone to his ear and his bike at the curb.

He swiftly got off the line when he saw me coming, shoving his phone away in a pocket.

"Hey, there's my girl," he called out when I shoved out the front entrance to the bar. God, he looked delicious in all that rugged denim and leather. I smiled and went to him and he pulled me close. His lips were cold against mine and he smelled of wind and the outdoors – beneath it all like clean man and there was nothing better.

"Hey, you," I said softly, and he grinned. "You ready?"

"Absolutely."

He led me to his bike, and we took the short ride to the club. It was *loud*, the music blaring from inside, out the open back door as he had me jump off so he could back the bike into the line of them outside the club's motorcycle junkyard.

He came to me, waiting on the sidewalk, and took my hand in his, swinging our arms between us happily as we made our way across the street to the back door of the club. There were a few of his brothers on the small square landing, smoking, beers in hand, laughing and talking.

"Heeeeeey, there she is!" Sauley crowed, more than a little sauced by this point, saluting us with his beer as we made our way across the worn and sad blacktop of 15th Ave SW in his direction.

I nodded politely at the brothers on the landing with him and one of them, a tall ebony man with dreadlocks, nodded back as he blew out a cloud of fragrant smoke of what was probably some of the highest quality green the Pacific Northwest had to offer.

Damn, I kind of wanted a hit. It would go a long way toward mellowing me out with all of the meeting and greeting I probably had ahead of me. I wasn't always so shy and on edge, I just really wanted to make a good impression, you know? I didn't exactly know how to do that with this particular crowd. It wasn't exactly my niche.

I think the dude toking up caught me looking because he held it out to me. "I'm Major. Welcome to the party."

"Hi, Major. I'm Raven." I introduced myself and availed myself of the spliff, taking a decent hit off it.

Major grinned at me and gave a lift of his chin to Mace. "She's alright!" he said, and I laughed without letting go of any of the smoke as I held it in for as long as possible to let it do its thing.

The other dude on the back porch I'd already sort of met, a guy by the name of Squatch – which it wasn't hard to imagine where he'd come by that name. Dude was *hairy* and looked like a straight-up neanderthal out of a children's book, except, you know, clothed.

Inside, we found Maverick, Glassjaw, and Fenris- those were the ones I knew. The rest consisted of a giant of a man that went by Dump Truck, which he was certainly as big as one, but I don't think that's where he got the name. Then there was Nine, Cipher, Derry, and the rest were sort of a blur after that. I think that had more to do with the combination of whatever weed Major had going on – it was some good shit – and the shots the guys lined up for me to catch up on the bar.

The bartender happened to be a woman. A bigger lady in an animal print kaftan, the boys all called Ms. Momma Kat with a sort of strange deference in their tone. She didn't appear to be with any of them which I know it sounds judgy but that would have been slightly awkward given she seemed significantly older than most of the guys, but they rather treated her almost like a surrogate mother figure or something.

Then there were the women... what can I say about those? Well, other than they were most definitely divided into two camps. The respected and revered and the... not. It was kind of misogynistic and douchey but there was a definite hierarchy to it. The women who were kept and sort of immediately pulled me into their circle and welcomed me, and the scantily clad other women that Maverick's woman, Marisol, seemed openly hostile toward – calling them ho's and telling a couple who stopped and looked in our direction to "fuck off." Which, they did, to my surprise, moving to hang on a brother named Cipher and Glassjaw.

The revered women, for lack of anything better to call it at the moment, consisted of Aspen, who I knew, Marisol, and a woman everyone called Little Bird, and a glam doll bombshell that somehow managed to straddle the line between named Dahlia. I couldn't decide if that was her *actual* name or just another nickname, but I definitely wasn't going to ask her. She was cold, cold, fire that one – the type to send a shiver down your spine with her deeply cutting remarks without you even realizing how deeply you'd just been burned.

"So, Raven, how come it's taken you so long to come around?" Dahlia asked and I sort of stuttered, not sure how to answer. I mean, she gave off the kind of vibe that the question, though innocuous enough, could very well be a trap, and I didn't want to misstep in any way.

"Raven likes to keep to herself. She's shy and slow to warm up to folks. Took me the better part of the day at the farm to get to learn anything about her," Aspen declared and smiled at me.

"Yeah," I agreed. Blushing, I nodded.

"I know the feeling." Little Bird gave me a tight smile, and I returned it.

"You the bartender that patched Mace up a couple months back?" Marisol asked, and I nodded.

"Oh! Okay, that's right." She shook her head. "My little brother has been a handful lately and I'm more than sort of out of the loop." She gave a gusty sigh.

"Who's watching him?" Dahlia asked.

"Prospect from Oregon," Marisol said with a lift of one shoulder. "I don't like it, but Mav insisted. Said I needed a break and some adult time."

"He's not wrong, you know." Little Bird hid behind her glass and took a drink.

"I know," Marisol said, and it was almost dejectedly. "I just worry."

"You're a good big sister," Dahlia soothed, and I felt completely out of the loop when it came to the conversation. With a mighty urge to pee, I stood up.

"Where you going?" Aspen asked cheerfully.

"Break the seal," I said with a shrug.

"Ah." Marisol nodded. "If the bathroom down here is locked, there are like three upstairs.

"Don't mind the mess, they haven't finished the building up there," Little Bird added.

I smiled and nodded and went for the water closet down here. Occupied. I drifted to the open doorway I'd glimpsed stairs through in the hallway just past the bar and went up.

There were heavy sounds of making out in the darkened corners up here, and I ignored those. A girl came out of one of the bathrooms as I was trying to decide which door might be a bathroom and I nodded to her and went in.

I did my business, washed my hands, and fuck... out of paper towels. She could have warned me, but she didn't. Not sure if it was because I was with the "Old Ladies" as they called themselves, or not – but whatever.

There were several boxes and random totes out here in the upstairs and far be it from me to go snooping, but they may have a resupply I could put up in the bathroom. I popped the top off a gray tote in the middle of the room and felt my brow crush down.

It was a lot of random stuff, nothing paper towel or even towel-like to be seen and I went to put the lid back on it but froze. On top of everything, there was a white envelope, and through the glare of streetlight that just happened to make it through one of the paper-covered windows up here where the paper had drooped, I caught my name in bold, black, and familiar script across the face of said envelope.

I slowly half kneeled to set the lid aside, out of the way and wiped my hands somewhat dry on the seat of my leggings. Fingers trembling, I reached for the envelope and tore it open, turning the single sheet of handmade paper into the light.

*Raven –*

*Please come see us. We aren't mad or upset. We're scared for you. Your friend*
*Mace came to see us; he sort of explained without any details what happened.*
*We're here for you and we want to hear those details from you – or not, it's*
*up to your discretion. Please come home.*

*Angelica*

The shock of emotion was so profound I didn't even feel it at first. It was sort of like going numb, like being dropped like a magnet into a pile of kinetic goo, the glob seeping up around the edges and pulling it down, slowly devouring it. The burn of betrayal was a nasty one as it crept across my skin and up my neck and face in a heated flush of... of... I don't even know what to call it. Embarrassment? Anger? Humiliation?

That I trusted Mace. That I believed him when he said all of those things, those things about protecting me, about having my best interest at heart, about... about...

I lowered the paper, the wave of hurt crashing over me and momentarily dousing the fire. I kneeled and put the lid back on the tote and took a deep breath.

Confrontation wasn't my favorite thing, but I recognized a time and a place for it, and this was definitely one of those times if it wasn't exactly the place.

I found Mace, beer in one hand, pool cue in the other talking to some brothers from the Eastern Washington and Western Oregon chapters. I sidled up to him and tugged on his jacket sleeve and asked, "Can I talk to you?"

He smiled at me, but there must have been something on my face, in my expression, because his easy smile faded into something far more serious when he said, "Yeah. Lead the way, babe."

I took it outside, away from prying eyes and curious ears... at least I hoped so.

When I thought we were sufficiently alone, my emotions boiled over and I turned on him, holding out Angelica's note and demanding in a clipped tone, "What is this?"

"Aw, shit... babe, I've been meaning to talk to you about it." He at least had the grace to look embarrassed, which I wanted it to be something but...

"Mace, this is a *huge* invasion of privacy!" I cried and the feelings of fear at my discovery swirled in my breast. I mean, *talk about red flags!*

"Oh, hey... I didn't approach it from that place at all!" he cried, as though his intentions made the result somehow okay.

I shook my head. "And the boxes of my stuff?"

He stuffed his hands in his pockets and hung his head.

"I was trying to bring them to you, make your life a little easier. I don't know."

"Why didn't you just *ask me?* Talk to *me?* Communicate *with me?*" I cried. "Do they know where I am?"

He shook his head. "No. I wouldn't do that to you. I just offered to deliver the note. Seriously, Raven, I didn't want to ask you. I didn't want to hurt you."

"Mace!" I cried and waved the note and envelope between us. "*This?* It hurts! This *scares me!* I mean… Jesus, fuck! Who *are* you?"

He hung his head and stuck his tongue into the side of his cheek like an errant little boy who'd been caught sneaking cookies and not like the grown man standing in front of me who'd gone rifling through my past that I had tried so valiantly to leave behind to protect the people I was leaving behind in it.

The same people those cops and Max had threatened to hurt next if I didn't keep my mouth shut and disappear.

My leg bounced with anxiety the more upset I became and all he did was stand there and look at me, hand to his mouth as his dark eyes glittered in the streetlights and he looked me up and down, waiting for I didn't know what.

"I'm sorry," he said finally. "I fucked up."

I sort of jerked back in surprise. I mean, that wasn't exactly what I'd expected to come out of his mouth. I don't know… I guess I expected excuses, but he didn't give me any. Just looked at me plaintively, guiltily, and shrugged his shoulders.

A sort of helplessness flooded me, and I shook my head.

"I want my shit and I want to go home," I said hollowly, and he nodded slowly.

"I can make that happen," he said carefully.

"And I think we need to take a break," I said. That's when he deflated a little, but he agreed.

"If that's what you need, you got it," he said and sighed. He looked like he was getting a little emotional, which wasn't that a bit rich?

"Let me grab Sauley and we'll walk you back to your place with your stuff," he said, and I hugged myself and nodded.

"You want to wait here?" he asked after a moment of hesitation and I nodded again, not trusting my voice.

"Okay," he murmured, and he was gone, striding back across the cracked asphalt to the club's back door.

"No going back, Raven. Only look ahead," I told myself quietly and let out an unsettled breath.

I mean, what was I hoping he would do? Fight me on this?

# 21

*M*ace...

I insisted on carrying her shit all the way to her door, Sauley on my six as I watched Raven's perfectly toned ass in front of me as we made our way up. I was afraid it would be the last time I got to enjoy the view, and that gutted me.

I'd fucked up in my order of operations. There wasn't any question about that, and here I was paying for it. The price looked to be a damn heavy one.

I'd rather be looking at going back to prison than this.

"Thank you," she murmured as Sauley set the tote he'd carried at the top of the stairs.

"Give us a minute, man," I muttered, and he nodded, jammed his hands in his back pockets and with a sweep of his too-long hair getting into his eyes, he backed down the stairs. When I heard the door at the bottom shut, I raised my eyes to my girl's.

I didn't like the pain I saw in them. Pain that I'd caused.

"You know where to find me," I said, and she nodded. God, those steely blue eyes were too wide, glassy with unshed tears that I could tell she was fighting back.

"I know I don't have a right to ask," I said, taking in a shuddering breath. "But can I get one last kiss for the road?"

Her lips thinned and I could see the wheels turning and finally, she nodded, tipping her face up slightly in permission.

I stepped into her, cupping her face between my hands and brought my lips to hers.

That kiss, the fact that it could be our final one… shit. It low sided me harder and more swiftly than I could have imagined.

She sobbed slightly beneath my mouth and quickly tamped it down as she returned my love, hers a suddenly timid thing – reserved, like weak sunlight filtered through heavy clouds whereas before I could bask in it all day long and feel warmed all the way through.

I'd fucked up. Hurt her. Broke her trust… and it was that kiss that told me just how deeply I'd fucked this. My only consolation prize was that she was *safe*. From Max, at least.

"I love you," I whispered fiercely against her lips as I drew back.

"I love you, too," she murmured, and she sounded absolutely shattered. "Which is why this hurts so much."

I backed off and gave her some space.

"I'm sorry," I told her. "You take as long as you need to either forgive me or hate me," I said. "I'll be waiting."

I turned then, abruptly, so I didn't have to see her cry – but it was too late. I'd seen the crystalline tears of her pain slip down her cheeks, and it gutted me, worse than what I'd done to that pig in her name.

"You alright, man?" Sauley asked at the bottom of the stairs as the door shut behind me.

"No, man. No, I'm not," I growled, and he nodded.

"I'm sorry," he said. I swallowed hard and nodded.

"Yeah, me too."

I went back to the club, Sauley walking silent as my shadow beside me and when I got there? I got good and fucking loaded.

"GET UP!" Someone kicked my booted foot that was hanging off the end of the couch or chair or whatever the fuck I'd passed the fuck out in.

"Fuck off," I growled to a track of masculine chuckles.

"Now is that any way to talk to your president?" Mav demanded.

I groaned and cracked my eyelids. Regret in the form of the dim club lights lanced through them into my skull and set shit *off* into pounding.

"Fuck me," I rasped and closed them again, tight, colored starbursts going off behind my eyelids.

"Oh, I know what that's like," I heard Glass say, laughing.

It felt like my brain was sloshing around, banging into the inside of my skull as I went to sit up. Nausea rolled through me and I stopped moving, gritting my teeth, waiting for shit to fucking settle.

"This fucking sucks," I grated.

"Yeah, well that's what your ass gets for hittin' the bottle like that, homey," Glass declared.

I glared up at him and he just laughed at me.

"That's not what we need to talk about," Mav said with an unhappy sigh. "It's what you *said* after hitting the bottle that hard."

He gave me a plaintive look, and I felt my stomach drop like a motherfucker.

"What'd I say?" I asked. Glass and Mav exchanged a look.

"You're fuckin' lucky you didn't have shit to say in mixed company," Glassjaw told me.

"Just us brothers," Mav agreed.

I laughed a little and tried to ineptly cover my ass when I glibly said, "Y'all act like I confessed to murder or something."

Mav's expression turned even grimmer if that were possible.

*Shit. I totally fucking had... I was so fucked.*

Mav sat down across from me and Glass kept to his perch on the arm of the couch I'd racked out on.

"I'm going to let you confess your sins and then Glass and I are going to confer whether this shit needs to go to full council for a vote," Maverick declared.

*Fuck me...*

I spilled my guts. All of it. Except I wouldn't give up Fen. No fucking way. This was my deal and not his. He didn't need to go down with me.

"And you want us to believe you did this shit all by yourself? Solo? First time and all?" Glass Jaw demanded, scratching amidst the raw stubble on one cheek.

"Damn right," I said. "That's my story and I'm sticking to it," I said grimly.

Mav shook his head.

"Fen helped, we already know he did, but mad props for not throwing a brother under a bus to save your own ass."

"Mav, I'm loyal to this fucking club. Raven's mine, for all that she broke it off with me last night, I couldn't let what that pig did to her stand without consequence even if it did happen before we fuckin' met."

"Loose lips sink ships," Glass said, and it was borderline unkindly – but I deserved it. I really did.

"Who sold me out?" I asked a little put out.

"You sold your fuckin' self out!" Glass barked. "Ain't no one dipped in shit but you, right now."

I winced at the sharpness on my ears and how his voice thundered through my skull, but he was right. As much as my fuckin' mind was lookin' for someone else to blame for my stupidity, the buck stopped with me.

Mav was a little gentler when he said, "I need the full picture, bro. What did this asshole do to your woman that retribution so brutal and so swift without informing the rest of your club was required?"

I shook my head, grimacing, and said, "I already violated her trust once – maybe lost her forever for it. I don't want to fuck up like that again."

"We're your brothers, yo, not some rando motherfuckers off the street. Like it or not, as a part of this club, you made it our business last night lamenting how you fuckin' killed for her and shit. We need to know the fuckin' 'why' of it."

"Nothing you say goes past us, bro," Maverick declared.

I looked up at him and the sincerity in his dark eyes won me over. He was right. This wasn't the state pen, these guys were family beyond blood, thicker than the water of the womb.

I sniffed.

I told them everything. How he'd raped her, brutally. How she'd been so fuckin' brave, had gone to the cops, done everything a citizen was taught to do and how she'd tried to work within their fucked-up pretend system of justice. How they'd dragged her off in cuffs and beat her fucking ass half to death in some parking garage for it.

Glass's face held rage; Mav's was carefully neutral.

"With that kind of reasoning, I can't say either one of us blames you the slightest bit for going off the rails on this," Maverick declared.

"Still, there has to be some kind of consequence," Glass said.

"I'm getting my ass beat, aren't I?" I asked, wincing.

Both of them grunted and nodded. I winced.

Glass' fist came out of nowhere and crashed into the side of my face. It was fucking lights out all over again from that one punch.

I fucking deserved this.

aven...

"Hi."

"Be right with you, honey," I said without turning around right away as I slid the bottle of top shelf locally distilled stuff back on one of the higher shelves of the bar. This particular bourbon was from out in Auburn. One of the local native tribes had started distilling and aging and it was one of the best bourbon's the state had on offer. No one else could touch the simple fat round bottle with the orca whale on the label.

I turned around and stilled. One of the SHMC was sitting at my bar. One I vaguely recognized from the party the other night. The deeply dark black guy with the dreads… what was his name?

"Major, right?" I asked.

"Yes, ma'am." He grinned like he was pleased I'd remembered.

"What can I get you?" I asked.

"Uhhh, how 'bout an IPA – dankest you got."

"One dank IPA coming right up," I said and went to the tap to pull one for him. He slid onto a nearby barstool, looking around Shoreman's and giving some of the regulars up the bar some side-eye. I turned back to the line of taps and smirked. I guess Mace getting his ass beat here had given the bar itself a sort of reputation.

I went over, laid down a cardboard coaster, and set down his beer.

"You want to open a tab?" I asked, and he shook his head and slid a ten across the bar.

"Keep the change," he said, and I shook my head.

"I don't need any charity. What'd Mace send you here for?" I asked and scraped my bottom lip between my teeth. "To see if I'm big mad still?"

"Mace didn't send me," he said. "Don't get me wrong, I like Mace well enough, but I ain't Cupid or his fuckin' errand boy."

"So why are you here?" I asked.

"For a dank IPA," he said, grinning and taking another sip.

I rolled my eyes and moved up the bar, calling back over my shoulder, "Wave me down if you want another one."

"For sure, for sure," he called, and I got the distinct impression he was checking out my ass. I glanced back, frowning, and he gave me a shit-eating grin.

Yep. He had definitely been checking me out. Was that why he was here? Chum in the waters? Was Mace taking our break hard, and this guy thought he could sidle in?

*Gross... so much for bros before hoes or whatever,* I thought to myself as I went about my job, getting glasses to washing and working on other miscellaneous bar prep and cleanup. It was a busy night. The long-shoremen had work again down at Terminal 5, the biggest terminal in the city – even if it was in service to an oil rig about to deploy up north into the waters around Alaska.

It had all sorts of Green Peace eco-warrior types up in arms and there were some uncomfortable times knowing what some of my Burner friends would think about me serving up drinks to what they would consider the enemy.

I wasn't so hardcore. I realized that most of these men were caught up in the capitalism machine just trying to survive like I was, put food on the table for their families. It made me tired, but there were some things that, well, resistance was futile.

Like loving Mace… as hurt and as angry as I was, as upset as he made me… I loved him. Deeply. And I didn't know how long I would be able to stay away or stand on principle. Still, what he'd done couldn't stand without some kind of answer or consequence.

I was staying away from Angelica and my old life for a reason. To keep them safe, and I *really* hoped for their sake that Mace hadn't somehow fucked that up.

*Damn it.*

"Yo, Raven!"

I looked down the bar and Major held up his empty glass scaled with the remnants of his beer foam.

Guess he did want another.

"Be right with you, honey!" I called and winced inwardly. I was in full bar-matron mode and hadn't meant for the endearment – it was just habit. If Major was coming around to see if I were a suddenly eligible bachelorette, I didn't want to give him any ideas. Not that he wasn't nice to look at – oh, he was – he just didn't strike me as my type. Wrong vibe, you know? Certain people you just vibed with and could tell, and I could tell we were on completely different wavelengths… plus, I had literally *just* broken up with Mace – hell, I hadn't even broken up with him! I'd just said I needed a break which was true. I did.

The club and his life were somewhat overwhelming. Absolutely sure to draw law enforcement's attention at points, and I wanted to stay as far off law enforcement's radar as possible.

I got Major another beer and set the fresh glass in front of him, putting the other in the waiting rack to go in the washer. He watched me move, his gaze discerning as I moved with practiced rhythm, letting muscle memory practically carry me through the steps.

"So, why are you really here?" I asked after a moment.

"Why you think I'm here?" he shot back.

"Well, I sure as hell hope it's not to hit on me," I answered, tossing one of my long dreads from my freshly mended wig over my shoulder.

He grinned and winked at me as he said, "I thought about it, but you're still Mace's girl."

I narrowed my eyes and asked, "What makes you say that?"

"Mace ain't declared it quits yet, and Mace is the one with the final say on that. At least where the rest of us are concerned," he said with a shrug.

I didn't know if I liked the sound of that.

"Awfully misogynistic of you to say that, isn't it?"

He gave an infuriating gallic shrug.

"Club life ain't for the women. It's for us," he said succinctly.

And there was some of the heart of it. Adopting club life meant setting some of my feminism aside... not something I wanted to be parted with. I glared at Major, and he laughed.

"Don't shoot the messenger on that one, beautiful," he said, raising his long-fingered hands in surrender. I shook my head and went down the bar to refill the bourbon for a longshoreman they called Sharkey.

Major slowed way down after the first two beers, preferring to nurse the next couple over the remaining hours of my shift. I thought he planned on staying until I was off but about ten minutes before I started chasing the stragglers out of my bar after last call so I could lock the doors, he had disappeared.

I leaned heavily against the door once the last two patrons were out and threw the lock.

"Boy, I'll be glad to be outta here!" Manuk called from the kitchen.

"You and me both!" I called back before I shoved off the bar across the glass and with a heavy sigh, half-assed my way through final closing and cleanup. There wasn't much to do, and damn it, I was *tired*. Physically as well as mentally and emotionally. It'd been a damned long few days.

After finishing up my work and making the drop to the safe, I donned my light jacket and called out my goodbye to Manuk.

"You want I should walk you, sistah?" he called, and I shook my head.

"No, I'm good!" I called back.

He waved from the kitchen and I pushed back through the door into a cloud of fragrant green smoke. I looked over as I keyed the lock so Manuk wouldn't have to leave the kitchen.

"I thought you fucked off back to the club, or home or something," I said casually to Major who stood by with a spliff in his hand.

"Naw, figured I'd walk you home."

"Mace ask you?" I asked, curiously.

"Nope, Mav," he declared, falling into step beside me.

"Mav?" I asked. "Why would he care?"

"Like it or not, girly, you're still a friend of the club for what you did for Mace. Mace may have fucked up, but he still loves you. Mav asked that we all keep a lookout for you, make sure you were good. A brother asks for help, you help him. The president asks you to do somethin', well... that goes without sayin'."

"So, all that talk back there about whether I was available?" I asked.

He gave me that shit-eating grin again, his teeth very white in the dark, the shadows of the alley behind him engulfing him so his smile hung like a Cheshire cat. The visual made me smile in return, how could you help it?

"You know how I got the name Major?" he asked.

I shook my head. "I thought you weren't supposed to ask," I said.

He gave another one of his gallic shrugs.

"Some dudes care, some, like me, don't give a fuck."

"Okay, so how did you get the name Major?" I asked.

He stopped and put a hand on the door leading to my stairwell as I unlocked it. He dragged it open and said, "'Cause I'm a major pain in the ass."

I laughed, and he swept open the door for me. I stepped through, expecting him to follow, but he just let the door swing shut trapping us on either side of the glass, shot me a weird little salute, and jogged a little sideways out of view, in the direction of the club.

I shook my head, locked the stairwell door behind me, and went up to my door.

∼

"HEY, YOU!" I called the next night when Sauley slid onto the barstool across from me.

"Hey, Raven," he said, tossing his too-long brown hair out of his eyes. I sighed.

"Any word when they're going to let you cut it?" I asked, pouring him his usual beer.

"Probably when I start to look like a girl," he said laughing.

I shook my head. "I can't say I will ever fully understand it all." He shrugged, and I smiled and asked, "What brings you in?"

"Mace asked me to walk you home, then Mav ordered it," he said.

"H—" I hesitated on the question then decided I really wanted to know. "How's he doing?" I asked carefully, not looking at Sauley.

"Got his ass beat," Sauley said. I looked up sharply.

"What?"

Sauley swallowed his mouthful of beer. "Don't let *anyone* know I told you," he said. "It's technically club business, so that's all I can say. Don't pry for more – *please.*"

I nodded, unsettled and unhappy and asked, "Is he alright?"

Sauley nodded. "He's good. Sore for a while, but that's so the lesson sticks if you know what I mean."

I shook my head and leaned onto the bar and said, "I'm afraid I don't."

"Club's different, Raven. You fuck up, they let you know about it. The system of club justice is swift – you take your whoopin' and that's it. No dragging shit out through the courts or whatever. You pay your price and it's done. Mace fucked up, he got his ass kicked, and he won't fuck up again. That's how it works."

"It sounds brutal," I said sadly and Sauley nodded.

"Brutal, but efficient. No waiting or wondering if it's really over. Once it's quashed, it's quashed. It's *easier* than how citizens operate by far. Simpler. In the end? In a lot of ways, kinder."

I listened to him, absorbing his words, and finally nodded slowly.

"It makes sense," I murmured. "Even if I don't always agree with it."

He smiled. "You're more one of us than you are one of them," he said, jerking his head in the direction of the bar and the rest of the people in it.

I shook my head and sighed. "I honestly don't know *where* I belong," I said.

He searched my face, a strange set to his expression that I had no name or words for, and he said, "Honestly? I know he fucked up, but you know the answer to that just as much as I do, and I wish it wasn't so..."

His expression shut down then, sulking, sullen, as he took his beer back up and drank nearly half of it down in just a few pulls.

I straightened and blinked, a little shocked, as the implication of what he was saying sank home.

"I didn't know you felt that way," I said and felt the shock wash over and through me.

"I didn't either, but then there it was. Can you really blame me?" he asked.

"Uh... *yes?*" I asked. "I don't have any control over your feelings and I..." I squeezed my eyes shut and shook my head back and forth. "I'm no prized pig, Sauley."

He smiled at that and laughed a little. Nodding, he said, "You are too. Don't talk about yourself like that – and I'll get over it. I promise. It's just a little crush and I wouldn't dream of getting in Mace's way. Plus,

I see the way you look at him. I just hope someday a woman looks at me like that."

I blinked once, long, slow, and stupid. I literally had *no* idea.

"Why are you telling me this?" I asked.

Sauley shrugged.

"Don't make it weird," he said. "Just… if shit does fall through with Mace, I guess I just wanted to be on your radar."

Again, with that long stare in his direction with an equally long, slow, stupid blink.

"I'm not sure what to say…"

"Don't say anything," he said with a shrug. "You got a customer."

I shuddered as if coming awake and looked up the bar where one of the patron's had his hand raised, beckoning to me before lifting his empty glass.

I uncrossed and put my arms flat to the bar, gave Sauley one last wide-eyed and mystified look and pushed myself up to standing to stride down to refill the longshoreman's glass. He wanted to get salty with me about the wait and I just raised an eyebrow at him. His buddies shut him up. They knew the look, the one that said I was about to declare salty boy had enough to drink and it was time for him to move on.

Longshoremen were assholes, and I'd learned pretty quick, they wouldn't respect you unless you had no fucks to give about it and threw their shit right back at 'em. Plus, with the recent revelation from the biker prospect down the bar, I really wasn't in the mood. I was still honestly reeling a bit.

True to his word, Sauley hung around until after closing to walk me home. He even pitched in a bit and helped me close up. Once outside, I took a deep, refreshing breath of clean air.

"So, about Mace..." he said and that deep pang of resentment mixed with anger hit me dead center of the chest again, like a physical blow.

I shrugged one shoulder and wouldn't look at Sauley as I asked, "What about him?"

"He have any way to redeem himself?" he asked.

I looked up the street, away from the prospect, and sighed out, saying honestly, "I don't know. He violated my trust in a *huge* way. Went behind my back..." I turned back to Sauley and told the truth. "I just don't know."

He searched my face and nodded slowly and asked, turning to set the pace back to my place at a sedate and leisurely walk, "Even though he did it to protect you?"

"I don't know if that holds water, to be honest," I said.

"How's that?"

I buried my hands into the pockets of my felt asymmetrical and fairy-like hoodie and shrugged.

"He violates my trust and I'm supposed to trust that his intentions were pure simply because he says so?" I asked.

Sauley nodded and said, "Yeah, I can see how that cyclical thinking would be enough to drive you nuts... but you know Mace. You think he's honestly lying about something like that?"

"I don't know," I murmured. "That's what kills me. How am I supposed to believe?"

"And around and around she goes," he muttered under his breath. I smiled and laughed a little at that, knocking my shoulder into his.

"Yeah, well, I'm not sure what other direction to go in." I looked over at him and cocked my head slightly. "You confuse me," I confessed. "Not just you, but all of you."

"How's that?" he asked.

"Just an hour or so ago, you tell me you're crushing on me, and here you are now, and it sounds like you're actually rooting for me and Mace to get back together."

He smiled, bowed his head and nodded, letting it bounce on his neck a little before saying, "It's funny, sometimes, how loyalty works."

"To Mace or to the club?" I asked quietly.

"To both in this case, I guess."

I stopped and looked at him and he stopped too.

"You said he got his ass kicked because of me," I said and shifted on my feet uncomfortably.

Sauley shook his head.

"No, Mace got his ass kicked because of *Mace* and his own decisions and as far as ass kicking goes? It wasn't much of one. Not like the one that brought you two together." I felt the tension leave my shoulders as relief flooded my veins.

"He fucked up, he owned it, he took his licks – end of story on that."

"What did he do?" I asked.

Sauley shook his head. "That's club business, and the less you know the better." He raised his hand to stop me as I drew a breath to protest.

"It's not that we don't trust our women – far from it. It's that we love you, and part of loving you means keeping you in the dark about certain things to *protect you*. At least that's the way I've always understood it."

"A bunch of white knights falling on your swords?" I asked.

He shrugged, and it wasn't quite as gallic as Major's had been the night before, but it was equally as infuriating.

"Hey," he called as I went to spin on my heel and make my way up the sidewalk without him. I paused and looked back over my shoulder.

"Believe me, I get it," he said. "The need to have or be in some kind of control of your own destiny. How everything feels like it's spinning out of control around you and how you wish you could grab onto just anything to make the world fall back into place."

I startled slightly because he was right, I mean, it was like he *knew*… I *didn't* like things going on behind my back. I wanted to know everything and, I mean, could you *blame me*? Lack of control meant that I couldn't and wouldn't feel *safe*. I had for a time when I was with Mace and then he had to go and pull the rug out from underneath me – had to go behind my back.

I swallowed hard and *stared* at Sauley.

"We're on your side, Raven. You helped one of us and we're here and want to help *you*. You just have to trust us on certain things and one of those things is that we're moving the same direction as you. Toward freedom and our own type of security and safety for those we love."

"By doing dangerous and unsafe things?" I asked. "Isn't that, like, an oxymoron or something?"

He shrugged again and said, "I think it's more like a paradox, but it's no less true. We do things our way. Yes, sometimes our way isn't perfect or legal by citizen standards but by the same token, you think anyone is going to fuck with us or you? By default, you *know* how much of a fucking bad idea that would be. With us, you couldn't be safer and thus you can't know all the things, or you would be unsafe. Irritating, I'm sure, but no less true."

"You're making me tired and you're making my head hurt," I complained finally, and he chuckled.

He came over to me and touched my face. I froze like a deer in the headlights.

"Mace is lucky," he said. "I'm glad you two found each other."

"That's... charitable of you," I concluded after a long pause to find the words. I spoke carefully and Sauley grinned, looking so much younger, a man in his twenties with still so much ahead of him. It made my heart hurt for a moment for the girl I was. Before Max. Before all the pain and the heartache. For the girl who thought she'd been miserable and alone who didn't know what true misery was... not yet.

I looked up at Sauley in that moment, holding my breath, terrified he was going to do something stupid like kiss me, and half self-destructively wanting him to because the truth was, I was scared. I didn't think I deserved Mace, or this unexpected tribe of men and women that he was surrounded with who were willing to accept me warts and all. The truth was, for as much as society looked down on them, I still felt they were too good for the likes of me.

There was a certain amount of comfort in the sadness and melancholy of my aloneness.

"You deserve good things, Raven. You and Mace both, and I see what kind of peace you two bring to each other. Sure, he pulled a dumbass move, and if I were any less devoted to the club, I would probably blow my shot all to hell and gone and kissed you right now because I wish so hard to find someone like you."

"Like me?" I echoed, confused.

"Yeah," he said breaking into a grin and dropping his hand. "You're wonderful."

I shook my head, speechless, and he put an arm around me, almost brotherly, and walked me the rest of the way home.

"Do me a favor," he called as I unlatched the stairwell door. I looked back over my shoulder and a flash of guilt crossed his face.

"Keep this conversation between you and me?" I asked softly, and he cracked a smile.

"Yeah, if you would, please."

I nodded.

"I don't know if I can ever trust Mace again," I said and swallowed hard. Sauley nodded.

"I get it. Trust is in short supply, but Raven?" I looked up. "He would never do anything to hurt you. Me either. Not on purpose... and truthfully? We wish a motherfucker would try."

He looked scary then, so why did it warm me to my toes?

"Goodnight, Sauley. Thanks for walking me home."

"Anytime, gorgeous. Anytime."

I shut the door behind me and ascended the stairs, my mind reeling. I had a lot to think about.

$\mathcal{M}$ace...

"She good?" I asked, straightening up at the bar. Sauley opened his mouth and looking behind me, closed it.

"Off you fuck, Prospect," Maverick declared, and I turned to our president a little irritated.

"She's good." Sauley stood up a little straighter and put me out of my misery, stepping back out the front door of the club. Mav took a stool next to mine and raised eyebrows at Ms. Momma Kat. She rolled her eyes, put a beer in front of him and fucked off, too.

Mav turned to me and my cheekbone gave a throbbing ache from the punch Glass had laid my hungover ass out with a few nights before.

"We ain't really talked about it yet. You paid your price and all, and this conversation ain't about that... at least not really, so put your hackles down, bro."

I eased myself out of my unintentionally ready stance, perched on my own barstool and asked Mav, "What the fuck you talkin' about?"

"What you did for your woman, not a one of us who has one blames you for going there. Still, going there leaves a stain on the soul. How you doing with that?"

"Fine," I answered, clipped.

"You keep anything of this fool's?" he asked.

I pursed my lips and got into the small pocket in the front of my jacket meant for a lighter or pocket change or whatever. I slid the gaudy gold cross on its chain down the bar a few inches and Mav looked at it. He swore in what I think was Russian and shook his head.

"A real Chad motherfucker, huh?" he asked.

I nodded.

"Yeah."

"Ask you why you kept it?"

"To give to Raven at some point… when the time was right. So she could know she didn't have to be afraid anymore."

Mav nodded.

"You trust this woman enough to hand her the keys to the kingdom like that? To put your fate in her hands?" he asked, turning the cross in the light.

I raised an eyebrow.

"Already trusted her with my life once," I reminded him.

He grinned, shook his head, and said, "This is a mite different, bro." I felt my expression darken with the seriousness of it and nodded.

"Yeah, I know."

"There a reason you didn't hand it to her right after the deed was done?" he asked.

"We all got our trust issues, I guess," I said coolly.

He nodded slowly, absorbing what I said.

"Now's not exactly the right time," I said, turning to face the wall of liquor bottles behind the bar and taking a pull off my beer. "She's pissed at me, I fucked up… and I don't know that there's any fixing it."

Maverick sighed and pocketed the cross. I didn't say anything. I trusted Mav with my life. He was a crafty bastard, sure, but we weren't in any way crossways with each other. I had no plans or designs to cross him, either. If he felt better hanging onto it, then let him.

Besides, I felt my shit was precarious enough with the club. I'd made a bad decision keeping Mav out of the loop, but I didn't regret it – plausible deniability and all of that. I think he knew it, too. Otherwise, the beatdown would have been Fen or Dump Truck and I'd be doing a hell of a lot worse than a sucker punch when I was hungover.

"You're a good man," Mav declared.

"Thanks for saying so," I said, and he looked over at me sharply. I looked back, and he raised an eyebrow like he took offense at my disagreeing with his notion.

"Fine, then I take it back motherfucker."

I laughed, and the mood lightened, the heaviness dissipating.

"Prospect!" Maverick bellowed, and we laughed as something banged outside and Sauley cursed. He came in the door coughing, half a second later the smell of some of Major's dank ass weed wafting in behind him.

"Yes, sir," he spat out between coughs and Mav raised an eyebrow.

"Put Mace out of his misery," Maverick said. "Tell him how things went with his girl."

Sauley slid up onto the stool on the other side of me, and I turned my head raising my eyebrows. The kid blushed faintly, and I wasn't surprised he harbored a crush. It was hard not to. Raven was beautiful, smart, funny, kind, all the things you could want in a woman, her only flaw, her deeply held insecurities, which I found beautiful too. She was this wounded bird and it was hard to fucking resist, the combination intoxicating.

She looked at you and you felt every inch the man you were supposed to be. Her veneration a palpable thing, those stars in her eyes as I moved inside her. I felt every inch a god amongst men when she looked at me like that, and I knew it was just a part of her. That while I was special, she looked at anybody and they felt *seen*, you know?

She was oblivious to it, and it lent to her charm.

"All's not lost, bro. She's still just as nuts for you as she's ever been. She's just hurt. Her trust has been broken, but I don't really think it's as bad as all of that, you know?"

"No, he don't know, which is why he sent you to make sure she was good," Mav said and he made the remark slightly cutting. I knew he was just razzing the prospect, but the look on Sauley's face said he wasn't so sure. Good. He needed to keep on his toes if he was going to hack it in this life.

"She still pissed?" I asked.

"Oh, yeah." He nodded. "She's got a lot on her mind. She's a smart cookie, and I think part of her deal is she's worried this life ain't for her."

Mav laughed at that. "The fuck it isn't. She handled the situation with Mace like a fuckin' pro. Like she was *born* to this life."

"She doubts herself too much," I agreed.

"I'm right there with you on that one," Sauley said, and I cocked an eyebrow.

He ducked his head. "Sorry. Just my observation. I know you didn't ask for it and it doesn't count for shit."

"No, it does," I said. "Just wondering, did I make a mistake sending you over there so much?"

He shook his head and looked dead-ass serious when he said, "No way, bro. I like Raven but consider her the little sister that I never had."

"She's older than you, dipshit," Maverick said, and I laughed a little.

"It's cool, I get your drift, Sauley."

He nodded and a silent understanding passed between us. He loved her. Maybe like I did, maybe not, but he knew to stay in his lane.

I nodded back once and took another drink of my beer.

"I told her you got your ass kicked," Sauley said, and I frowned.

"Too bad Major's already got the name," Maverick muttered. "If he didn't, you'd be the club's major pain in the ass for that alone."

"Major sure lives up to that road name," I agreed. "But Sauley here?" I shook my head. "I ain't mad, bro, just tell me, what'd she do?" I focused my attention full on Sauley.

"Asked if you were alright," Sauley answered. Maverick clapped me on the back.

"You two lovebirds are gonna be fine," he declared, and I felt a knot in the middle of my chest loosen up some.

"Yeah," I agreed, relieved. "You're probably right."

"Just give it some time," Mav said, and I nodded.

"Yeah," I agreed, and we switched topics to bike mods and the next big ride. I knew Mav, though… the wheels in his head were turning. I just didn't know what road they were on, if they were chewing up asphalt or dirt, or where he was headed. Still, Mav was always the man with a plan, and he hadn't let any of us down yet.

# 24

*R*aven...

True to his word, Mace left me be. He never showed up himself, and he didn't push, but he still didn't let me walk home alone at night from Shoreman's. Someone was always there at the end of my shift and it wasn't always Sauley. Sometimes it was Major. Sometimes it was Nine or Squatch. Once it was Tic-Tac who bitched the entire time about having to do a prospect's job and fuck all to hurry my ass up so he could get back to his life. Tic, as they called him, was a real asshole. I was glad when he only showed up the once.

Tonight, it was the giant of a man leaning heavily on his cane. The one they called Dump Truck. He was ruggedly handsome, though his dark eyes tended to bore through yours uncomfortably, as though he was reading your soul like a book and he didn't always find what he'd read pleasing. I felt two inches tall under his gaze and wondered how his little bird managed to do it. Be with him, I mean. They couldn't have seemed more opposite but at the same time, they were thick as thieves. Anytime they were near each other it was like they inhabited their own parallel universe – one adjacent to ours where we could see in, but they couldn't see anything but the other.

It was sweet watching them together at the party two weeks ago, and I wondered if Mace and I could have been like that given enough time.

"What'll you have?" I asked as he settled his considerable bulk onto the barstool across from me, holding the thigh on his bad leg as he sighed out in almost relief. Now when I say *bulk* I didn't mean fat. Dump Truck was certainly not fat, not in the slightest. He was all muscle, with fists like cinder blocks. I would hate to be on the receiving end of one.

His smile, hidden in his dark beard, transformed his face, everything settling into gentle smile lines as he said, "Just a Coke if you got it."

"You got it," I said. "On the house."

"Thank you kindly," he said with a wink and my apprehension at his domineering presence receded.

I got him his soda and moved on to do some general bar chores before I started to close up. No one was in here tonight. It was the middle of the week and quiet for a change.

"Mace ask you to come?" I called down the bar after a moment of quiet. The last song had played on the jukebox and the next hadn't started yet. He nodded and his dark eyes roved over me.

"He misses you, you know," he said.

I couldn't look at him when I said, "I miss him, too."

"Yeah?" he asked. After the next song started, I picked up the remote to the system and turned it down so we could carry on a conversation.

"Yeah," I said.

"Then why haven't you reached out?" he asked, and it was a good question.

"I don't know," I answered, honestly. I didn't elaborate. I didn't want to go too deep with anyone. I was scared, maybe, that if I let this thing slide that I would let other things go and before I knew it, I would be in over my head. I was afraid that maybe Mace *was* the right man for me, and that would get him hurt or killed.

I felt like a walking poison with Max still out there, felt like the entirety of Seattle PD was on his side. I didn't know what the right thing to do was anymore. Should I run further? Harder? Was I just being stubborn staying here? I didn't know. I didn't have the answers.

All I knew is that I felt incredibly alone now more than ever. That I didn't feel like I could even talk to Mace about it after he had gone behind my back like he had and everything *hurt*.

An emotional raw and grinding ache, like my soul was broken and every time I moved, those broken pieces ground and grated together in the most unnerving way. I honestly didn't know what or how to sooth that hurt in any way.

"Want some unsolicited advice?" Dump Truck asked from down the bar, holding up his glass and looking at it, rattling the ice a bit and watching it swirl in the dark, syrupy liquid.

"Didn't you just solicit said advice?" I asked with a smile. He glanced at me sideways and grinned.

"I do believe I just did. Want it anyway?"

I nodded. "Shoot."

"Communication is key to any good relationship. You two aren't doing yourselves any favors sitting and stewing in your feelings not talking to each other."

I exhaled the breath I hadn't realized I'd been holding and nodded.

"You're right," I declared. "And I think I know that—"

"So, what are you scared of?" he asked.

I nodded slowly. "That's the million-dollar question, isn't it?" I asked.

"Isn't it just?" he asked then left me to my own thoughts on the subject.

Rather than face them, like the coward I was, I threw myself into closing in record time.

Dump Truck, to his credit, didn't push or pry. I think he'd achieved whatever goal he'd had just getting me to think things through on my own. He struck me as the wise beyond his years, Zen type. Patient, endlessly so... and I wish I was that way too, but alas I was me – a chaotic, anxiety riddled mess on the inside, and that was on a good day.

The walk home was slow, and we talked. I could tell he was asking questions without really asking; that he was prying apart the gordian knot of my feelings one strand at a time, trying to get to the heart of my problem. The thing I appreciated about Dump Truck's way was that he was patient about it, and was doing it in such a way that I could see and follow his reasoning.

He should have been a therapist, not a mechanic.

"I thought this was supposed to be my side gig," I joked as we rounded the corner to my building.

"What?" he asked with a chuckle.

"Listening to people's problems, throwing out a suggestion or two, and letting them sort themselves out."

He laughed. "It is sort of the bartender's way, isn't it?"

"Cheaper than therapy." I sighed miserably. Had I the access to mental health services, I would undoubtedly take advantage of them but alas, such was the way of American healthcare. The much-needed services were typically overloaded and out of reach unless you made a hundred thousand dollars a year or more.

We stopped in front of my door and I looked up at DT. He looked down at me and I felt incredibly small. Tiny. He was *massive*.

"Thanks for listening and for not judging," I said.

"No problem," he said back and cleared his throat. "It's how family is supposed to do. That's the thing about us. In a lot of ways, we work how society is supposed to but doesn't. At the same time, we don't always work how we're supposed to. It's a mess, but down at the bottom of it all, you won't find any other group of people half as loyal or dedicated to each other. We don't quit on one another when the shit gets real – remember that, Raven. I think you're the same kind of people and I would hate to see you quit while you're ahead. You and Mace both."

I nodded slowly and considered his words.

"I miss him," I said. "I just don't know how to get around this immovable object that is this break in trust."

"You hear him out, I mean really sit and listen. I think he might surprise you," he offered.

I nodded slowly, and we both looked up the street at the chug of an approaching Harley. Fenris swept up to the curb, and he looked at us both. He settled on me and a weird look flickered across his face.

"Mace," he said, and I felt myself blanch. I didn't even think about it. I just got on his bike.

## 25

*M*ace...

"Shit, man. I knew this was bottom of the barrel shit, but I didn't know it was this bad."

I looked up and over from the sheaf of letters in my hands to Mav picking his way through the shelves of pottery and shit up here to where my corner of the barn loft was at.

"It's not so bad," I declared. "What brings you up here?"

"Figured I'd come check things out for myself." He pulled over a milk crate and waved me down when I went to sit up off the mattress on the floor that I called my bed.

I kind of froze in a half sit-up crunch thing and finally eased back down.

"And?" I asked.

"And ask you some questions about your parole and shit, get caught up on what's going on with you other than Raven."

"Need me back on runs?" I asked.

He nodded. "Yes, but no at the same time."

I raised an eyebrow.

"We protect our own, you know that. I'm not going to ask you to do any shit that's going to get you locked back up and put another strike on you. That would be fucked up, and it's not how this club operates. Our members ain't disposable."

"We all take risks, Mav. We know that shit when we sign up. Nothing's changed about that."

"Calculated risks, bro… *calculated* risks. We live our own lives by our own creed, sure, but we don't go buck wild like the rules don't exist. We know they exist."

"We just don't care," I said grinning, and he grinned back and nodded.

I filled him in about how much time I had left with Kim and how that shit was going. He raised an eyebrow when I came clean and told him she's where I got the tea on Max and his whereabouts.

"For real?" he asked.

I nodded slowly.

"For real, and I didn't exactly ask," I told him. "She volunteered."

Mav gave a low whistle.

"Best keep Ms. Kim in your hip pocket," he said.

I nodded. You never knew when someone like Kim would come in handy.

"You playing model prisoner?" he asked.

I nodded again. "System had one thing right, Mav. I was and can be one angry S.O.B. It was a painful lesson to learn to chill the fuck out."

"Pick your battles," Mav agreed, and I nodded.

"I don't regret taking out that pig," I said. "I didn't do it from a place of anger or passion. The rage was there and real, but it was cold as ice. I was careful. I wanted you and the club to have plausible deniability."

"I know what you were doin' just like you know the rules and why Glass and I did what we had to do."

I nodded. I knew. They couldn't look weak. There had to be consequences for something like that. Doing something so large and that could impact the club as a whole without the club's knowing or a vote wasn't something you did. It just wasn't. It could give other brothers the wrong idea and as much as the citizenry wanted to look at us like we were a bunch of fuckin' animals – we weren't that. The rules we had were a lot fewer, and looser than society's, but they had to be ironclad. It was the only thing keeping us from going full *Lord of the Flies* or some shit which would just have all our asses up on charges and leave what families we had to struggle. We weren't about to fuckin' go there. Especially Mav who had Marisol and her kid brother relying on him.

We talked about a lot of things, basically catching up. Before I'd been locked up, Mav and I had been thick as thieves and right after? Well, his duty as pres kept him from visiting as often as he liked. We traded letters but most of them didn't get to me, intercepted by cops and the fuckin' COs looking for shit on the club. I don't know how much of my shit got to him, either but I was guessing not a lot. We talked about that some, and he pretty much confirmed my suspicions.

I'd sat up on the edge of the mattress, forearms propped up on my knees and he looked me over.

"You look exhausted, bro."

I nodded. "I am. Too many early ass mornings and even later nights."

"She worth it?" he asked me, searching my face, and I nodded.

"Can't explain it, but she's worth every waking moment and every breath I take. I don't regret a fucking thing, man... except maybe my order of operations. You know?"

He nodded and heaved a deep breath, letting it out slow.

"You put any thoughts toward the future?" he asked.

"With her?"

"Either way," he said with a shrug.

"I sure as hell don't see myself still living up here in five years, bro."

He laughed at that and nodded.

"Her place ain't much better," he said.

"At least it has a bathroom," I said, and he nodded.

"You coming to the club tonight?" he asked.

"You know I'll be there," I said.

"Ride with me. I'm headed back that way. Maybe we can come up with something to get you outta here and into something better. Something suitable to both of you?"

I looked off into the gloom of the loft and sighed. "The longer this goes without her contacting me, the more I'm starting to feel like it's going to be a future on my own. You know?"

"I wouldn't give up just yet. It's only been a couple of weeks and Raven strikes me as a complicated lady." I heaved myself to my feet and sighed.

"She's only complicated in her simplicity," I said. "She loves simple things, lives simply, and doesn't ask or require much, but she gets so inside her own head, lets herself overthink and over feel and things get complicated quick. I love her for it. Live for every minute of it. You know? She's a challenge but she challenges me to be better... *do* better."

He nodded and smiled. "I like you two together."

"Yeah, I like us together, too," I said quietly.

"C'mon, I'll buy you a drink back at the club."

"Ha ha," I muttered and heaved myself to my feet.

The ride to the club was cold and damp but not a soaker. One of those pervasive clammy chills that crept in under your riding leathers and made it hard to get warm without a hot shower or a shot of whiskey on the other side.

Unfortunately, the hot shower was out of the question. The showers at the club were still out of commission and needed to be properly plumbed. The whiskey, though? We had a damn decent supply of that on hand and coffee a plenty. I was in need of both.

"You boys look chilly!" Ms. Momma Kat declared.

"That we are, Momma, that we are."

"Get 'cha some Irish coffees?" she asked.

"You read my mind," I said to her and shot her a dazzlingly flirtatious grin. She blushed, waved me off and went to make up some coffee with some strong whiskey in it. I grinned at Mav and winked, and he chuckled.

Momma Kat was a treasure to the club and should always be treated as such.

Mav and I were bullshitting about this, that, and the other when we heard it – shouting, an altercation, whatever – and the back door of the club flew open hard enough to hit the wall.

"Help!" Tic yipped, and Mav and I hauled ass as one. Tic was lying on the floor, hands clamped over near his crotch, blood seeping out from between his fingers as a vehicle peeled out outside on fifteenth, Fenris bellowing rage.

"Fuck! Fen! Get in here!" Mav yelled.

"No! Go grab Raven!" I yelled over him, then looked at Mav. "This is bad. Help me get him in the chapel."

We hauled Tic up between us in the narrow hallway and Fen disappeared out the portal of the back door.

I had every faith my woman would know what to do.

## 26

*R*aven...

The cold and damp were biting for such a short ride, but I didn't care. All I could think about was Mace, and what could have happened. I tried to pretend the tears gathering at the corners of my eyes were from the wind, but the tightness in my throat wouldn't let me sell the lie to myself. Fenris pulled up to the front of the club, off sixteenth street, and I jumped off, tackling the front door and barreling through. I stopped short at the sight of Mace, hands slicked and smeared with blood, in the hall toward the back door.

He froze when he saw me and Maverick came out of his office with a super large, soft-sided, med kit. The kind that paramedics carried.

"Raven," Mace called. "Help me!"

My medic's training kicked in and with a slight shake of my head, I strode forward and took the kit from Mav and asked, "What's happened, who's hurt?"

"It's Tic, in here." I followed Mace as he pushed through the door across the hall to the chapel. A room he had shown me, and that was tight, but impressive. Tic was lying on the table, bar towels soaking crimson as he shook and shuddered, trying to apply pressure down low to one side near his right hip.

"Getting a little lightheaded here, bro!" he rushed out, voice shaky. I set down the kit and ripped open the top.

"What happened?" I demanded.

"Fucker stabbed me," Tic uttered.

"Shit," I muttered and pulled on a pair of gloves. "How bad, do you know?"

"Not bad but fuck, it won't stop bleeding!" Mace declared.

I handed him some compresses and ordered him, "Use these."

I snatched the trauma sheers from their place in the top of the kit and started low on Tic's pant leg cuff, heading up his leg.

"Hey, hey, hey, hey, hey!" he cried and writhed to get away from me.

"Stop it!" I snarled. "I'm trying to save you!"

"Fuck!" He was sweating and panting. When I got through his waistband and peeled the blood-soaked denim back, I almost froze at the gleaming silver cage around his cock and balls.

"Who has the key?" I demanded.

"Dahlia," he said, and his pallor was going a whiter shade of pale, whether from blood loss or for having been exposed, I didn't know.

I looked up at Mace, put my gloved hands over his and applied pressure like a motherfucker on Tic's wound.

"Find Dahlia, get the key," I demanded.

"Got it."

"Oh, man, don't let anyone know!" Tic begged.

"Secret is safe with me, bro. Just don't fuckin' die!"

Tic made a frightened noise, tears slicking down his sweat-soaked temples as he stared at the ceiling and I promised him, "You're not going to fucking die. Not if I have anything to say about it."

He nodded but wouldn't look at me. He was scared, bottom lip trembling, and he needed to be. He was losing *a lot* of blood. I took Mace's place and glimpsed Maverick on his phone in the hallway. He looked in and he looked afraid for his man on the table. I made sure to block all view of Tic's manhood with my body, preserving his modesty until the door swung shut.

I assessed quickly how bad it was and where the blood was coming from.

What a fucking mess, and definitely high and almost outside my skill set. I had stitched wounds before, but nothing this bad. However, I *had* assisted on an emergency one at Burning Man where a nicked vein was concerned. I think this was what I was looking at. I just needed to get in there, get it clamped, and figure out what to do from there.

"I'm sorry, Tic, hang in there for me. This is going to hurt," I warned him, and he nodded without looking at me, staring hard at the light fixture over the table.

I gritted my teeth and dove right into what needed to be done.

Mace ducked his head into the room and said, "Just stabilize him. Eulogy is on his way, so is Dahlia."

"How long?" I demanded.

"Dahlia, in a few minutes. Eulogy, we got lucky – he was in Centralia which is an hour and a half. Sooner if he rides like a bat out of hell."

"Shit," I muttered. "Don't let Dahlia in here, just get the key and get him unlocked," I said.

I applied more pressure and swallowed hard. I didn't know how long an artery or vein could stay clamped without permanent damage. That was beyond my knowledge. I was hoping the Oregon doctor guy for the club could get his ass up here sooner rather than later and I could hand this off.

*Shit. Fuck. Goddamn. Motherfucker,* I thought savagely and took a deep breath. This was *not* a time for me to panic. This was a time for me to get my fucking shit together, do what needed to be done, and get the job handled. I could fall the fuck apart later.

"Who stabbed you, Tic?" I asked. I needed to keep him focused on something. I needed to keep him talking, from slipping completely into shock.

"Some fuckin' meth head, man! I don't know!"

"Okay, why?"

"I don't really know that either! Something about turf and us not being so bad!" I barked a laugh.

"Boy, did that dude fuck that one up!" I said.

Tic laughed slightly, an edge of hysteria to it and nodded a little too fast. "Yeah! Yeah, he did!"

"Okay, I'm going to take this compress off and I'm going to go digging. I know it's gonna hurt and I'm sorry!" I said, and I pulled the packing away.

Tic bit down on a yelp.

The wound wasn't too deep, he was right. Clean, about two inches, maybe three inches long; the meth head must have twisted or something at the last second. Still, it was deep enough, past the fat layer. I had stitched worse; the problem was finding where all the fucking bleeding was coming from!

I probed the wound with a fingertip and Tic screamed and hollered. I reassured him the best I could.

"Okay, okay! It's okay, you scream, you curse, you cry and call me all sorts of names. I know it hurts and I won't take it personal. You're doing good! Ah! Don't *move!*" I shouted when he moved his legs, his heels skidding along the tabletop. He gripped the edge of the table in a white-knuckled grip and blood spurted. I saw it. I spotted it, but I didn't have anyone in here to hand me the fucking clamp out of the kit.

"Mace!" I bellowed, and he appeared in the doorway. "Clamp!" I cried, and he handed me a pair of locking forceps. "Yes!" I took them but there was too much blood again. I shoved the packing back against the wound.

"Damnit!" I muttered fiercely and shook my head. "Okay, take the packing, that's it, keep the pressure on, okay?"

I stilled and made eye contact with Mace. His darker gaze met my lighter one and something passed between us, as though we borrowed strength and a calmness from one another.

"When I say, move the packing so I can get in there and try and find this thing and clamp it."

"I got you," he said with a nod.

I turned my attention back to Tic's hip and said, "Okay."

He moved the packing. I probed and there was a spurt. The offending vein didn't want to hold still but after a moment, some grunting out of Tic, and listening to his white-knuckled grip squeak against the edge of the sealed wood of the blood-smeared table, the forceps clicked in my hand and I let out the breath I had been holding.

"I got it!"

Mace's breath left him in a whoosh and I stepped between Tic and the door, making sure to shield the mess of his hip and the cage around his cock with my body as someone, maybe Fen, said behind me, "Dahlia's here."

"Go," I told Mace, and he left my side. I made eye contact with Tic who panted and nodded, gratitude flashing across his face.

"You're going to be alright," I said. "Just a little while longer."

"Thank you," he said, and I could tell it was for a lot more than just stopping his bleeding.

I got him unlocked and out of his cage with the key Mace provided after speaking with Dahlia and secreted it away.

"Thanks for that, too," Tic said without making eye contact.

"It's no problem," I said. "Any of it." The first fine trembling started in my hands. *I wouldn't crash.* This wasn't over yet.

"You did good," Eulogy praised as he put the final stitch into Tic's hip. He'd shot him up with something for the pain and it was a heavy enough dose, Tic was out. I was grateful for that. Tic had been a trouper and through enough pain.

"Thanks," I muttered softly.

"No, I mean it. You did real good, Raven."

I handed him some triple anti-biotic ointment to smear along the fresh line of stitches and he set the needle and pair of forceps he was using aside in the metal tray that'd appeared, and sighed.

"You doing alright?" he asked, eying me.

I nodded. "I'm fine."

"You don't look fine."

I shook my head. "I'll crash later, but right now, I'm fine."

He nodded and something like pride crossed his face, or like he was impressed. I bowed my head and started cleaning up.

"Leave it," he said. "You've done way more than enough. I can get it." He sounded genuinely grateful, and I was honestly exhausted and on the ragged edge of my adrenaline petering out, so I graciously stripped my gloves and bowed out.

"Thanks," I said and discarded the gloves in the black garbage bag that'd somehow appeared in the midst of all of this.

His breath hitched on a scoffing laugh. "Heh! Thank *you*, darlin'. You definitely kept him from bleeding out."

I nodded.

"Let me know if there's anything else I need to do."

He looked back at Tic and shook his head. "Nothing left now but to get him full of fluids and let him recover naturally. I got all that, though."

I'd started an IV after I'd gotten him stabilized but he would be in need of a new bag in a few. I let Eulogy handle it.

Out in the hall, I took a deep, cleansing breath that didn't hold the sour note of fear and the copper tang of blood.

"Hey." I looked across the hall in the direction of Mav's office where he leaned in the doorway. "Before you go down that way," he said, nodding in the direction of the barroom, "come talk to me in here a minute if you don't mind."

I slipped into the office behind him, and he went around the desk, dropping into the seat behind it and gesturing. I took the seat across from the cluttered desktop and felt like I'd gone from the conquering hero to being called into the principal's office in the blink of an eye.

"You look like you could use a drink," he said as the sweat still cooled on my clammy hands from being trapped in the latex gloves for as long as they were.

"I could," I agreed. He reached into the file cabinet drawer, the loud clang of the old, metal, 70s desk making me jump.

"Whoa there, relax. You're cool," he said, and I nodded. I was back to being jumpy. I think it was part of the impending crash and burn.

He poured a measure of vodka into two glasses and nudged one in my direction. I leaned forward and took it, downed the contents, and held out the glass for a little more. He raised an eyebrow and obliged me, his smile slow and easy.

"Can I get personal?" he asked.

I nodded slowly, not sure what he was going to ask but guessing it had a lot to do with Mace.

"This thing between you and Mace, this blowup or whatever—"

"It's not a blowup," I said defensively.

His smile grew. "Apologies," he said and cocked his head. "I'm gonna be straight with you. The way you came through that door and the look on your face when you saw him, you thought it was him didn't you?"

I stared at him impassively, not really wanting to give anything up, but yeah, I had and Fenris – he was so on my shitlist for it, too.

"Might I suggest," Mav said carefully, "that you aren't as mad as you think you are, and that maybe you're only as mad about whatever it is as you want to be?"

I thought about what he was saying for a second and chewed my bottom lip and finally nodded. He was right. I knew that. Loving Mace was easy. *Being loved by Mace,* that was scary. I had a lot of trust issues, not just from the whole thing with Max, but from before that.

The only thing I feared more than death was being some sort of a failure, or disappointment to the ones who loved me. It made for some interesting struggles sometimes. It was something I was thinking about – especially the last few days.

"I think you might be on to something there," I said softly, and Mav nodded slowly, his deep blue gaze level with mine and unwavering.

"You want I should bring Mace in here so you two can talk?" he asked gently, and I nodded carefully. I did want that. I wanted that very much. What I didn't want was to fall apart in front of Maverick, who I didn't know.

It struck me then, that despite how Mace went behind my back, contacted Angelica, went to my old house, I still managed to trust him, and deeply at that. With the important things, at least. With my heart, and my emotions.

Mav heaved himself to his feet and stopped next to me. I looked up at him and he put his hand on my shoulder and said, "That man loves you more than life itself. More than freedom, and, I reckon, in some ways as much if not more than this club." He reached into his pocket and held something in his hand. He rubbed his lips together and searched my face. Making some sort of decision, he took my hand from the arm of the chair and upended it, spilling something on a length of chain into it.

He curled my fingers around it, my gaze never leaving his and said to me, "Trust us and we trust you. Cross us, and... well... I think it goes without saying. Twice now, you've proven to be one of us and if you're amenable to it, it's no greater sense of family, safety, or purpose you could hope to find."

He bent at the waist and kissed the top of my head. He said, "Thank you, Raven, for saving and patching up my boys. We'll never be even, but maybe this gesture, this token of appreciation can give you some kind of idea how grateful we really are."

I looked at his retreating back as he went for the door. He stopped with his hand on the handle and turned to look back at me.

"You have Mace to thank for what you've got in your hand there, and the keys to the proverbial kingdom. I hope you realize that."

And with that, he went out, closing the door behind him.

I dropped my eyes to my hand and uncurled my fingers. It took no time at all to recognize the cross in my hand. I had stared at it long enough while Max had been raping me. Had had the dangling, crucified figure and its gold filigree haunt my dreams for countless nights.

I looked up sharply, just as Mace's familiar and comforting figure filled the door. His expression at once wounded and guarded.

"Close the door," I said a bit sharply, and he stepped in and did.

I stood as he turned back around to me and I held out the crucifix as though a venomous spider were perched in my palm.

"Did you really?" I asked. "Did you kill him… for me?" I asked.

He searched my face and nodded once, carefully. I dropped the metal as though it burned me and flew into Mace's arms.

He didn't hesitate, his arms going around me tight as he held me close, and I crashed. I crashed into him and from the adrenaline and under the sheer, monumental weight of the absolute crushing relief that fell from the sky as quickly and as hard as that foul gold necklace had fallen to the floor.

## 27

*M*ace...

"Shhh, I've got you," I soothed as she trembled, clinging to me tightly. She didn't cry loudly, instead, her body shook with silent sobs that I couldn't see. Not with her face buried in my shoulder like it was. I put my lips to the curve where her long, slender, beautiful neck sloped in that perfect sweep to the rounded cap of her shoulder, and I breathed her in deep – that rich, organic, herbal scent – green, alive, and underneath just purely *her*. *God,* did I miss the silk of her skin, her smell, just everything about having her in my arms.

"I'm so sorry," she sniffled, and I shook my head.

"No, you were right. I'm the one that should be sorry," I told her, and it was true.

I shouldn't have gone behind her back and ham-handed the situation. Even if my heart was in the right place where she was concerned, I'd violated her right to privacy and it'd been stupid. It'd almost cost me everything.

"No, about being a stupid hot mess," she said, and I chuckled and held her a little tighter.

"I love you," I murmured and marveled at her ridiculousness. She was anything but. She was more human than any other human I'd encountered, and it was one more of the things I loved about her.

"Let me take you home," I whispered into her hair and she nodded against my shoulder. We stood there for I don't know how long, and I just simply held her. No rush, she needed it and I needed her. It was such a perfect moment, a sweet reunion, I didn't want it to end right away either.

Eventually, she reluctantly pulled away, sweeping her middle fingers under her eyes to wipe away the last vestiges of her tears.

"You good?" I asked gently, and she nodded.

"Better," she said with a weak smile. "Thank you."

I nodded and reached out. She put her hand in mine and I gave it a gentle squeeze.

"I need to take a quick leak," I told her, and she nodded. I opened the door to Mav's office, and we stepped out into the hall, both of us pausing outside the chapel door. The door was opened narrowly, and we glanced in.

Dahlia was sitting at the head of the table, Tic's curly blond head of hair beneath her palm which was gently stroking his forehead and smoothing over his hair as she murmured low to him. Her voice was too low for us to hear but clearly soothing, her touch loving and light; and Tic? Tic looked up at her with this level of adoration I didn't think he was capable of.

I looked at Raven and was surprised to find a raw, naked *want* in her expression as she looked at them. I looked back, my mind working to decipher the meaning of that look on my girl's face, saddened to realize what it could mean… that Raven didn't feel that bond from me. That she didn't feel that she was loved like that, and I wondered how much of that was what'd I'd done, going behind her back the way I did.

If only I could make her realize that I loved her *more* than what she was looking at. I put an arm around her waist, a hand on her hip, and drew myself closer to her, leaning over slightly and pressing a kiss to her temple. She startled and looked to me, and I slipped off to deal with the urgent need from my bladder.

When I stepped out, she was right where I left her, staring at the floor with a light blush on her cheeks. I looked back to Dahlia and Tic and the door was firmly shut.

*Ah...*

"C'mon, I'll take you home," I murmured, and she slid her hand in mine and nodded. We went out through the front, past the rest of the guys so I could tell Mav what was up. He nodded, told me to ride, and made sure we'd lock up like a worried dad or some shit. I nodded. There would be church over this, but it wouldn't be until the rest of the boys could get in here, so I had some hours yet.

I would take Raven home, love her, and we would sleep for a time. I think she needed it. She still trembled finely under my hands as I led her out the door in front of me, my hands on her hips.

She went out ahead of me into a blast of frigid air and I wanted to pull her back against me, wrap her in my jacket and cut against my chest and warm her with my body heat. As impractical as it was, it was my first inclination, but I resisted the urge in favor of just getting her home to show her just how much I loved and adored her.

The trip back to her apartment was blessedly short on the bike, but definitely enough to chill my woman behind me. Her teeth chattering, her slim body shuddering as she unlocked the door at the street level for us. I trailed her up the steps after making sure that the street-level door was secure behind us before we went.

She opened her apartment door with an audible sigh of relief. I shut it and locked the line of bolts behind us with an equal sense of decompression.

Raven turned to me and I felt my shoulders drop at the exhaustion on her face.

"Come here," I murmured, and she did, stepping over to me and burying herself against my chest. I held her tight for several long moments again, waiting for her to soak in her fill and when she had, she sighed out and relaxed beneath my touch. It was as though we both let go of our last vestiges of apprehension with each other, with the situation, with everything. It was nice. It was really nice.

"My turn for the bathroom," she murmured, and I chuckled as she pushed back from me and I let her go.

"You go on," I nodded, and I trailed her into her bedroom. She gave me a backward glance as she shut the door to her tiny bathroom, as though she didn't quite expect me to be there when she got out.

Like I would go anywhere else.

I slipped out of my jacket and cut and set it aside, then pulled my layered tee and thermal off in one piece over my head.

By the time she was washing her hands, I was toeing off my boots. By the time the bathroom door opened, I was working my belt and the front of my jeans open. She paused and looked me over and I stripped for her hungry yet reserved gaze. She was tired, maybe even exhausted. The sun would be up in a few more hours, and she needed rest. To rest, she needed to relax.

"Come here," I said and crooked a finger, my cock twitching, starting to rise as she drifted over her bedroom floor like some sort of ethereal sprite or Fae-like being.

I kissed her, settling my hands on her hips, and smoothing my hands over the natural fibers of her clothing.

I broke the kiss to whisper against her lips, "I'm going to take all of this off of you a piece at a time, lay you down, and treat you," I promised, and she made a small noise of want in her throat.

Good, that was good, she had no idea what she was in store for.

I kissed her, gently divesting her of her clothing a piece at a time, letting it fall to her floor. When she was nude, I laid her down on her bed, on her stomach and carefully straddled the backs of her thighs. She was a sight, her back strong and the lines of her lean muscles and dancer's body so very pleasing to the eye.

I could weep at the sight of her, trailing fingertips lightly over her back in sweeping patterns, deepening the touch into a massage that made her groan in pleasure, teasing the knots from around her spine and out from beneath her shoulder blades firmly but gently, wishing I had some lotion or oil to make my hands glide better.

I asked her, "Got any lotion or…?"

"Lotions in the basket on the milk crate over there," she said, voice heavy and hazy with the effects of my love and attention.

I went and got the bottle and returned, liberally applying some to my hands, sweeping them over her upper back and shoulders, working my way through muscling the tension out of her, feeling her turn liquid with relief beneath me.

I worked her quietly, listening to her soft little moans of pleasure and sweet surrender under my attentions and it was a hell of an aphrodisiac, let me tell you.

I was as hard as iron when I replaced my hands with my lips at the back of her neck, draping myself over the back of her, caressing her down her sides as I kissed my way down her back. She rose to meet my lips, writhing unconsciously beneath me, and that was so incredibly hot, fucking sexy, she had no idea the things she did to me, but I damn sure knew what I was about to do to her.

I had intended to cut her some slack when I'd started. That I would just give her a little massage and back off, lying beside her, gather her into my arms, but with the way her breath fell from her lips in these soft little gasps of wonder, the way she whimpered and moaned in pleasure, I just couldn't keep my hands off of her. She was so sweet, so perfect, so supple and soft beneath my hands and the way she became yielding under my touch?

Goddamn, she made me feel like some sort of virile sex god and I couldn't keep my hands off of her, my lips off of her, and God willing, my cock out of her if she'd let me go there tonight.

I helped myself to a handful of each globe of her ass and prized her cheeks apart, thrusting my tongue into her wet and waiting cunt, teasing her opening, and reveling in her scent and her taste.

She cried out, deep and throaty, clutching at the sheets beneath her as I lapped at her slit from behind and tease her forbidden, more sensitive areas with the tip of my tongue.

She panted, and the noises she made just encouraged me.

"Mm, I need to be inside of you, is that alright?" I asked, and she nodded.

"Yes!" she cried in desperation.

I climbed her prone body the same way I'd made my way down, pressing lips against her skin, pressing kiss after kiss, trailing kisses and light nips along her skin and taking pride in the goose flesh that rose in the wake of my attentions.

I kneeled, my knees to either side of her thighs, fisting my cock, stroking myself lazily as she rose her hips off the bed in supplication, in offering. I eyed her glistening opening and lost myself in the vision of her in front of me, the feel of my cock, running myself through my hand for just a moment as I imagined how fucking wet, how tight, and how silky she would feel wrapped around me.

"Mace, *please*," she begged, and I smiled.

"I've got you, baby. I've got you," I murmured and dropped to one hand that I planted over her shoulder. The other, I used to guide myself to her entrance.

Sliding into her was pure heaven. I mean, there wasn't anything or anyone like it. I could feel my eyes roll back in my head at the pure nirvana she inspired as I took my hand from between us and palmed her hip, sliding in all the way home.

This position was *nice*, intense; with her prone and her legs together like she was, she felt tighter somehow, snug around my invading cock as I lay over the top of her.

I had to be careful in this position. Without a pillow under her hips to hold her up for me, it could be all too easy to slip out, and I tell you what... she felt so fucking good, I never wanted to be parted from her again.

"Raven," I breathed. "God, I've missed you."

She arched beneath me just a little and wiggled her hips just enough that it was everything in me not to explode like some inexperienced teenager.

I choked off a cry and thrust deeper. She made this wonderful, deep, throated gasp that ended on a strangled cry of her own.

I wasn't about to rush this. Oh, no. This time was meant to go slow; this woman was meant to be savored, and that was what I was going to do.

# 28

*R*aven...

God, I *loved* him like this. He pressed me into the bed beneath us and at this angle, he felt like he went impossibly deep. I pressed back onto him and it was everything I could do to keep my hips raised to continue to give him access but this felt *so good*.

He stroked slow, long, hard, and sure but at this incredibly controlled pace that left me quivering and on the ragged edge. The marvel of it was that he kept me in the pleasure, in the moment, on that precipice. I panted and gasped and just let him ride me because it felt so fucking incredible. So incredible, I didn't care if I even came as long as he just kept doing this forever.

I gripped the sheets beneath us and eventually, my hips failed me and collapsed to the bed. He slipped out of me and I swore. He chuckled darkly and grabbed a pillow from beside us.

"Hips back up, baby," he urged and stuffed the pillow beneath my hips, then took another and doubled them up before saying, "Back down, that's it."

"Oh, that's perfect," I told him as he slid back inside me. God it was, too. The wadded-up pillows giving me just enough support, raising me up at not quite the same angle, but a good angle that felt just a little less good but still phenomenal. I bit my lips together and hummed in appreciation as he slowly took me back up among the stars.

I panted and whined, and he kept his pace steady and moaned his appreciation, the vibration of it through my back making my nipples tighten against the sheets, his thrusting doing magical things not just to my chest, but to my clit which bounced and ground against the pillows, touching off sparks of diamond pointed light, lighting the sparks that would eventually be fanned into roaring flames.

I went up like flash paper, burning into smoldering ash beneath my lover's touch, shuddering uncontrollably beneath him, listening to him laugh and delight in blasting me apart. He continued to ride me through the tremors, my pussy impossibly slick around him, coating the insides of my thighs, as I whimpered, a spent mess.

"Shhh, that's it," he praised and drove deep, a little harder, a little faster, the possessiveness of it a total turn-on as I lay almost limp from my life-shattering orgasm just the moment before.

My breath quickened almost before it even had the chance to recover, and I tightened up around him.

"Oh, God, yeah! That's it!" His voice was strained, he was close, and God, I wanted him to come inside me. I wanted it so fucking bad.

He tried, he kept at me, fucking me so good, but finally with a frustrated grunt, he pulled out of me and said, "I need you on your back."

I rolled, and he pulled the pillows out from beneath me and made sure they were behind my head, taking the moment away from his own climb toward release to care for me. God, his dark eyes boring into mine was so hot. He got between my thighs and reintroduced his body into mine and drove into me, hard, but not fast. His movements were deliberate, hands going to my hips where he kneeled up above me and watched me. I put on a bit of a show, caressing down my body, pinching my nipples as much for his gaze as for my own pleasure as he struck a steady rhythm.

"I want to watch you come for me," he growled, and the pad of his thumb went to my clit, slicking through my wetness where his body met mine as he rode me.

I closed my eyes and gave myself over wholly to the sensations he wrought. Writhing for him like a candle flame on a lit wick, and I felt just as hot. His phoenix, rising from the ashes of my past. I burned for him, and I loved it.

"That's it, baby," he ground out from between gritted teeth. "That's it, come for me."

I bit my bottom lip and watched him, my pussy tightening up around him as he moved inside of me, stroking over that *spot*, right there, stoking the flames of my desire for him with every thrust, his thumb skimming over that sensitive bundle of nerves, adding fuel to the rising pyre inside me. I moaned on every breath I let out, the peel of them high and feral, something wild.

"Mace!" I cried and my body jerked, spasming, legs locking around his hips, as he collapsed over me, catching himself with his one arm as he tortured me so sweetly, a beautiful agony rippling through me from my oversensitive clit as my pussy convulsed around his cock, milking his own orgasm from him as he cried out, grunting, his thrusts losing their controlled rhythm as he bucked into me wildly.

I screamed a little as his touch against my clit became molten and he recognized the sound as less pleasure and more distress. My nervous system on complete overload as I shuddered and shook uncontrollably beneath him. He braced himself on his arms and lowered himself over me, resting his ear between my breasts, against my chest, listening to my thunderous heartbeat as the organ battered against my ribs, feeling like it was trying to batter its way out from the cage of my ribs.

"Oh, God," he groaned, spent, shuddering himself as he pulled himself from me. I cried out and gasped at the joyous but unexpected sensation and basked in the glow of his love, melting into the bed beneath us as he settled carefully against me, holding me tight, and I believe, basked right back in the glow that emanated from me.

"I missed you," I confessed, and he turned his head to press his lips over my fluttering heartbeat.

"I was always right here, baby. Always," he said.

"I know, and I'm sorry," I murmured.

"Don't be," he said. "I fucked up, I get it, believe me."

I didn't know what to say to that... like, you're never really prepared for someone to own their mistakes. I mean, it so very rarely ever happened.

"Thank you," I said finally.

"For what?" he asked, raising his ear from my chest, and propping his chin there, holding his weight off of me, careful not to make me uncomfortable with the point of his chin, or to crush me.

"For apologizing, for giving me the time and the space to sort myself out..." I trailed off. God, for *everything*. I mean, this man whose dark brown eyes I gazed into from mere inches away, who touched me so gently, so sweetly... he'd *killed* for me. Quite literally had ended my worst nightmare. Had become the thing my fears feared and my shield.

I caressed his short hair lightly and watched as he closed his eyes in pleasure when I lightly scratched my nails through it and over his scalp. He sighed in sheer, unadulterated, contentment and I felt my own heart give an echoing happy sigh. I smiled, I couldn't help it, and he just laid there, eyes closed, face schooled into a mask of contented bliss. He was *painfully* handsome – so beautiful to me, so gorgeous in a rugged way.

That sleek alley cat with the notched ear and missing patches of fur, used to scrapping and claws sharp, but so sweet and practically purring in my lap.

"God, I love you," I said and let my head fall back and my eyes close.

"I love you so much it hurts," he responded, laying lips against my skin in a gentle kiss; right between my tits, over the plate that protected my cracked heart that I swore was mending right before my eyes thanks to his love.

We closed our eyes and drifted then. Sleep claiming us both, even though we were wrapped up in each other in a less than ideal sleeping position.

I don't think either of us cared. We were happy to be whole again.

I WOKE, who knows how long later, sticky between my thighs, covered to my chest as I slept soundly but seriously lacking in Mace's warmth.

I turned onto my side from my back to see him mere inches away, head propped on his hand as he watched me. I blinked, slightly dazed, and settled facing him, tucking my hands beneath the pillow, under my cheek.

"What are you doing?" I asked with a slight smile and laugh.

"Watching you," he answered.

"Why?" I asked laughing. "That's so weird!"

"It's not weird," he countered and reached out a hand, smoothing it in a caress just above my hip and down over its curve.

"It's a little weird," I said, biting my bottom lip to keep from smiling. He grinned slowly and shook his head, his expression clearly enamored as he looked at me.

All I had ever wanted was for someone to look at me like Mace was looking at me right now, and my heart, I couldn't tell if my heart were tying itself in a knot in the center of my chest or if it were melting away completely.

Maybe it was both at once.

"What?" he asked, concern sliding over his expression.

I shook my head slightly, a confession of that magnitude a scary one to make. I didn't want to admit how much my emotional well-being was tied to him. I mean, how co-dependent was that? Totally unhealthy... and yet...

"Raven what is it?" he asked, his concern only growing. He touched the side of my face, sliding some of my hair in a light caress to trap it behind my ear. God, I must have looked dreadful first thing in the morning like this, but here he was all concerned because around him, I couldn't seem to keep any one of my thoughts or emotions off of my face and despite it all – he loved me. I could see how much in his dark eyes as they roved my face. I knew now, just how much in that gold necklace Maverick had put into my hand mere hours ago.

"I've never loved someone like I love you," I rushed out. "It's terrifying. I'm scared—"

He touched a fingertip to my lips to hush me and cocked his head slightly.

"I'm sorry I let you down," he said finally, and my heart broke just a little at that.

"It's not that," I whispered. "I just... I'm bad at saying how I really feel. I've been hurt so much and I'm trying not to be that way with you."

He looked thoughtful for a time and finally nodded. "You don't ever have to be that way with me," he said. "I want to know it all. The good, the bad, and the downright ugly. If I *ever* do something to fuck you up, you *have* to tell me, and I will do *anything* and *everything* to fix it. You're the best thing that's ever happened to me, Raven, and I hope you know just how much and how far I'd go for you."

I thought about that damn gold necklace and nodded. "I do know, and—"

"And that scares you too." He smiled faintly and sighed. "I get it. If I could do whatever I did to ol' Max, what would I do to you?" He gave a sad and broken little half-smile and I felt so shitty saying it but...

"Yeah."

"I would never hurt you," he said, and I sniffed. He kissed my forehead. "But you've heard that before, huh?" he asked and gathered me close against his chest.

"Yeah."

"Then I'll spend the rest of our lives proving it every damn day if I have to," he said fervently and the vehemence he said it with made me jerk my head up to look at him. He was serious. Dead serious.

"You don't have to," I said automatically, and he chuckled and held me a little tighter.

"Too late," he murmured. "I've already committed."

I laughed slightly and said, "That's ridiculous."

He smirked and kissed the top of my head and in a funny voice said, "You're ridiculous." Which struck my funny bone and made me laugh more. Then the tickling started, then before I knew it and before the laughter died, he was sliding back inside me and the giggles turned to moans, and the moans to gasps and the gasping into cries of sheer ecstasy.

God, I loved this man and what he did to me so much.

## 29

*M*ace...

I left Raven to sleep after our second round of love-making that morning and took my ass to the farm to work. I met up with Fen as I pulled up.

"How're things, brother?" he asked as I shut off the bike.

"Good," I told him. "Okay for now."

He nodded and sighed, saying, "You know, shit may have gone easier for you if you'd given me up to Mav when it came to that fuckin' pig."

I shook my head and said, "Wasn't gonna happen."

He nodded and reached out and clasped hands with me. We pulled each other into a hug and let go.

"Any word on what's up with Tic getting stabbed?" I asked.

"Word is a gang of tweakers wants to move into Rat City with the meth trade." He shook his head.

"Yeah, that ain't gonna happen. You have to be a tweaker to think that this shit was a good idea."

"Word."

"When's that meeting supposed to go down?" I asked.

"Church tonight at eight," he said, sucking his teeth.

"Plenty of time to get through the chorin'," I said, looking out over the goat pens.

"Yup, so let's get to it, princess."

I rolled my eyes and forged out toward the barn. It was mucking out stalls today.

"What exactly did you say to Raven last night that had her so freaked out coming through the door?" I asked midway through the first stall.

"Ahhh, yeah... that may have been a manipulative little dick move on my part," he confessed. I leaned on the shovel and cocked my head, slightly hostile in his direction suddenly.

"Fen, what did you do?" I demanded.

"Ehhh, what I was *going* to say was 'Mace needs your help,'" he said. "What maybe came out was just 'Mace.'"

"Goddammit, man! That *was* a dick move!" I cried, throwing down the shovel.

"I know! I know but look at me. Both of y'all were fuckin' miserable for no damn reason other than generating your own angst and drama. Hate me if you want, but you guys are good now, right?" he asked.

I scowled and retrieved my shovel out of the muck and said, "We're going to be alright. Fixing things is gonna take time, but I ain't afraid to put in the work," I said.

Fen nodded. "Good! Good... see, it all worked out then."

"Fuck you," I said. "It was a dick move."

"Yeah, well, I'm a dick and I'm alright with that," he said with a casual shrug. I rolled my eyes and dug in, shoveling the muck into the waiting wheelbarrow.

"So, what's your next big move?" he asked.

I shook my head. "Keep looking for work in the field with which I'm actually fuckin' good at and find a place."

"You know," he said casually. "Raven's place isn't a *bad* place, it just needs fixing up. It'd actually be hella convenient for you – being close to the club and all."

"You been thinking about this," I said, leaning on the shovel and looking him up and down.

"No offense, brother, but you deserve a hell of a lot better than my fuckin' barn loft, and my couch when it's too cold for that. As much as I appreciate the help around the farm, I can't pay you for shit and this is a teenager's work. Prospect's work. You're skilled labor and this ain't skilled."

I nodded. "As much as I love you, I do not enjoy shoveling goat shit," I agreed. "But you gotta do what you gotta do and you're keeping me in good with the parole board."

"I honestly don't think it would take much on that score after what your P.O. did," he said. "I think you might be her class favorite."

I chuckled and nodded. "I do what I'm supposed to when I'm supposed to do it. You'd be surprised at how many of these guys can't seem to do even the bare minimum."

"No, no I would not," Fen said, shaking his head.

We both had a laugh at that.

"You really think it'd be worth fixing up Raven's place?" I asked.

"Okay, you really think this was my idea?" Fen asked, giving me a look like "bitch, please" and I smiled wryly.

"Mav?" I asked.

"Yup. He just asked if I'd bring it up."

"What's he thinkin'?" I asked dryly.

"Cut a deal with the landlord, fix up Raven's place for you and her, bring that shit up to code, fix up the other three units up there, pay the dude to keep his fuckin' mouth shut and have a place for brothers to crash that's not at the fuckin' club. Off the radar of LEOs."

"Not bad, not bad." I nodded along, picturing things.

"Could definitely be some help if we're going to start a war," he said, and I raised an eyebrow.

"You really think this is going to be some kind of war?" I asked.

"A bunch of tweaker freaks?" Fen asked. "Shit no, it's going to be a slaughter, but no telling how ugly it's going to get. You know what I mean?"

I nodded. "That I do, bro. That I do."

We liked to do things quiet like, as much as possible. Mass murder in one fell swoop wasn't something you could pull off easily, but by the same token, doing shit quietly and in such a way that you kept your ass from getting caught? That left room for retaliatory maneuvers on their part. If they could fuckin' even get it together to pull that shit off.

Dealing with a bunch of fuckin' tweakers could make that complicated.

"Think while you shovel, dude. We got other shit to do."

"Right, sorry." I went through the rest of the day of chorin' doing a whole lot of thinking.

"Hey!" Raven greeted me like she was startled to see me in her bar. I smiled and slipped up onto the same barstool, at least I think it was the same one, as the night we'd met. There was a whole lot about that night that was hazy, and a whole lot more that I wished I could forget, but watching her perfectly toned ass as she walked the length of her bar to serve other customers? Nope, I wanted that memory burned into my brain for-fucking-ever.

"Hey, baby," I greeted her. "Gimme whatever's on tap that's good."

She smiled and bit her bottom lip and pulled me a beer from the multitude of taps, bringing it over.

I slid a twenty at her and winked. She frowned and pushed it back and said, "Fuck that, no! On the house." She leaned way over the bar, holding herself up on her arms and leaning forward to present her lips for a kiss. I kissed my girl to a rowdy compliment of cheers from a bunch of the asshole grizzled fuckin' longshoremen littering up the joint.

A few shouted lewd suggestions later, but they settled down and smiling happily after rolling her eyes, Raven lowered herself back to the floor on the other side of the bar from me.

"What brings you in and so early at that?" she asked.

"Oh, just thought I'd swing by before church," I declared, and she nodded.

"Meeting up about that thing with Tic?" she asked, and I didn't say anything, I wasn't supposed to, but she was turning into a keen ol' lady and she knew how the street worked, so I just nodded.

"Be careful," she cautioned and gave me a raised eyebrow in warning that I'd better watch my ass. I smiled and sipped my beer.

"As a virgin on her wedding night," I declared, and she laughed

"Be right back." She wandered up the bar to a beckoning customer.

I loved it when she was "on" and her insecurities weren't raging. It was like she stepped into this role, and it was hot. Likewise, though, I loved it when she was vulnerable with me. I may not always know what to do in the face of her vulnerability or insecurities, but goddamn did it make me feel like a man, like the only man for her, when I got it right.

She came back this way and wiping down the bar asked me, "To what do I owe this unexpected pleasure?"

"Oh, now see, that just tells me that I don't come and see my lady where she works nearly enough."

"You've had some good reasons," she said, letting me off easy.

"Not anymore I don't," I told her. "So, how's about I walk you home tonight?" I asked.

"Staying over?" she asked, and her expression was hopeful.

"I'd stay with you forever if I could," I said. "How would you feel about me maybe making that happen?"

She cocked her head curiously and said, "I'm intrigued."

"Talk about it more tonight?" I asked.

"Absolutely," she said.

I watched her work for a while before I had to git to make it to church on time. As I sat there, I realized, I couldn't wait to take her on some adventures on the bike. Just her and me... and I wasn't talking to Black Diamond Bakery or anything as pedestrian as that. I wanted to take my earthy fire maiden witch girl places like the lavender fields in the summertime, and out to the beaches on the coast. I wanted to get her out of the city and make love to her under the stars high in the mountains.

I wanted to go places with her, show her things that she'd probably only dreamed of. Introduce her to things and places, *people* like us – free spirited and the like.

I wanted to grow old with her, watch her hair turn white, give her a house with a garden for her to tend like she'd told me she wanted in her twilight years, where she could make things and sell things at a little roadside stand.

I got up, left the twenty pinned under my empty glass on her bar, and she waved at me from where she was taking a food order and blew me a kiss. I caught it with a wink and tucked it inside my jacket and cut near my heart and left.

The ride to the club was short, but with sufficient enough wind to carry most of my troubled emotions away. The little anxieties of just how I was going to manage to pull a bunch of shit off. I felt like I had a weight on my shoulders balancing more than a few things like a house of cards, but then Mav met my gaze off the back porch and gave a nod and the rest of those little worries and penny ante shit just fell away.

I didn't have to do shit on my own. I wasn't locked up anymore. I was free, and I had the love of a good woman and my club to help me. I needed to remember that. I needed to let some of that shit *go*.

I went up the back step and Mav blew out a fragrant cloud of green smoke and held out the spliff to me. I took it and filled my lungs, holding it and nodded, handing it back.

"You good?" he asked, and I nodded, holding it some more. Finally, I blew it out in an explosive exhale, my tight shoulders starting to relax some.

"I'm good, man."

"How's Raven?" he asked, and I nodded.

"She's good, too."

"Fen talk to you?" he asked,

"He did."

"Thoughts?"

"I'm on board, just tell me what you need."

"Landlord's name and number to start with," he said.

I nodded. "I got you," I declared.

"Good deal."

I went in the back door and into the chapel which smelled strongly of disinfecting cleaners and under that, still the coppery tang of Tic's blood. At least to me. Maybe it was my imagination, but there was really no telling.

I went around the table and took my place.

"Dude, Mace, you give up your phone?" Sauley asked from the doorway.

"Oh, shit. I'm losing my mind," I declared and pulled it from my pocket and tossed it across the table to him. He caught it one-handed.

"No big deal this time," Mav said, edging in around Sauley and going to the head of the table. "Nothing's started, yet."

"Thanks, man. Good looking out," I called to Sauley, and he nodded and went around collecting the other brother's phones.

When everyone had arrived, Mav shut the door to the chapel, and called shit to order.

"So, this is what happened…" Glassjaw filled us all in.

Seems that a local gang of white supremacist tweaker fucks were getting some big ideas about moving out of Des Moines and into Rat City just sort of skipping Normandy Park all together in their march north. Tic was out back when a few of them slow rolled it on by, talking shit and one of them jumped out the back of their fuckin' pickup, opened up a knife, and went to gut our boy, stabbing low and going for his junk. Tic's version of events was he twisted and raised a leg and the dude got him in the hip. I think that metal cage he wore to get off or whatever the hell it did for him might have had something to do with deflecting the blow, but fuck if I was going to say any of that shit out loud.

Tic-Tac's extra circulars were Tic-Tac's business and nobody else's.

At any rate, these fuckin' tweakers had done fucked up by pulling such a ballsy move. It wasn't going to end pretty for them, but we had to play our cards right. Doing something big and flamboyant wasn't our way. That's how the cops got involved and not to put too fine a point on it – fuck the police.

"I know we want some heads on some fuckin' pikes, gentlemen," Maverick said. "Nobody wants that shit more than me, but like I always keep telling you – order of operations, boys. Order of operations."

"How we playing this, then?" Dump Truck asked. "Gonna let 'em think they scored a blow? Let 'em think we're scared?" He grinned, and it was fairly savage, but it didn't have shit on the smile plastered on Fenris' face. Fen looked like he was a kid in a fuckin' candy store.

"You've got the right of it," Maverick declared. "And don't you worry, Fen. I'll be letting you off your leash, eventually."

"Reconnaissance then?" Cipher asked.

"You got a toe in that world based on how you came up," Maverick said and there wasn't any reproach to his tone, just a matter of fact.

"Unfortunately," Cipher said nodding, and he sucked his teeth distastefully. "I'll put out some feelers."

"I know you and your bro ain't close and I hate for you to put yourself out," Maverick said, and he sounded sincere, but Cipher stopped him with a raised hand.

"I appreciate it, Mav, but if ever there was a time to put myself out, this would be it. I mean, *fuck...*"

Mav nodded.

"Glad we're on the same page, brother," Glassjaw murmured. Cipher nodded.

"Opportunistic scraps?" Squatch asked.

"Have at," Mav said. "We don't have any control over that shit but if it comes up, you fuckers better make it fucking count."

There was a ring of chuckles sweeping around the table.

"So, holding pattern," Nine said and didn't sound one hundred percent happy. That made all of us, but it was what it was.

"Order of operations," Mav declared.

"Don't you worry," Glassjaw said. "There's enough of these fuckwits to go around. Everybody's going to get a piece."

Nine nodded, and I smiled. I wanted my pound of flesh and pint of blood just as much as anyone else around this table.

"What other business have we got?" Major asked.

"Why, you got someplace else to be?" Glass asked with raised eyebrows.

"I ain't saying that," Major said. "I just want to know what's up – damn."

"No, you're right, there's other shit in the works. An opportunity's come up, but it might stretch some of our resources," Mav declared.

"Oh, yeah? What you got?" Derry asked, curious.

"We've had two major medical emergencies inside the last quarter or so," Maverick said. "Lucky for us, both times, Raven – Mace's new woman – was there."

"What you thinking?" Cipher asked, brow crushing down.

"He's thinking she's taken care of us in our time of need, maybe it's time we take care of her back a little," Glass said.

"What'd you have in mind?" Dump Truck asked, leaning back in his seat.

"Most of you have seen her place," Mav said.

"Fuckin' shithole," Fenris declared.

I nodded. "It is that," I agreed.

"Now, we still have to get in contact with her landlord or whatever," Maverick started, and Fen snorted.

"Slumlord is more like it."

"All that aside," Glass said firmly and shot the big man a look. Fen grinned a twinkle of mischief in his bright blue eyes. I grinned and hung my head to hide it some.

"I'm thinkin' we fix up her place for her and Mace – it's nice and close to the club, and then we fix up the other three units up there to rent out as a crash pad. It's within walking distance of the club and they're not bad little units all things considered."

"Use a shell corp to rent 'em out, make everything on the up and up." Cipher nodded, and I could tell he was a million miles away running the numbers through his brain like grains of sand through a normal guy's fingers.

"Not bad, not bad." Dump Truck nodded. "All but invisible from law enforcement, those other three units. Like hiding in plain sight."

"My thoughts exactly," Mav said, leaning back in his chair.

We sat in silence for a while letting the idea soak in for all the other brothers. Nods started appearing and Mav asked, "Shall we put it to a vote then?"

"I second," I declared.

It was unanimous. Dudes were willing to put in the time and effort, might even get some skilled labor in from some of the surrounding chapters. I mean, it would benefit them too.

There was some other random loose shit to cover, but that was essentially the bulk of the fucking meeting.

By the time we were out, it was still some hours yet before Raven would be free, but I bounced anyway, preferring to spend my time at the end of her bar than with the rest of the boys hashing over the same ol' shit. Raven was much more interesting than bitching about a bunch of tweakers.

About the only thing I gave a fuck about right now was how Tic was doing and the answer to that was resting comfortably at Dahlia's in a drugged-out stupor for his pain, healing up as fast as his body could repair itself.

When I swept back into the bar, Raven's smile said it all. I couldn't wait to talk to her about what the club wanted to do. No more secrets, nothing behind her back. I wanted to do this one right.

"Welcome back, lover," she said with a kiss and a wink before she went to pull me a beer.

"It's good to be back, baby. You have no idea."

"I have a few hours yet, you good to wait?" she asked.

"Sure am, you think you got a minute for me?" I asked.

She looked around.

"It's pretty dead, now. Everyone's got work tomorrow. Let me come around."

She came around the bar and hopped up on the stool next to mine.

"Everything okay? How's Tic?" she asked. I absently put my hand on her knee and massaged up and down her thigh.

"Tic's good. I wanted to talk about you and me," I said.

"Oh? What's up." She leaned back subconsciously, and I grinned.

"The club wants to say thank you, for everything you've done," I said carefully. "We'd like your landlord's name and number to see if he would be amenable to us fixing up your place. Professionally. Not any half-assed janked repairs, or anything. A bunch of us know what we're doing. We want to see if he'd let us fix up your place and the other three apartments and let us rent 'em out from him. Raise his property value a bunch, give him a fair rate, all of that."

"Really?" she asked, bewildered.

"Only catch is, he doesn't raise your rent any. You get a lifetime lease if you want it."

She looked thoughtful and shrugged. "What's the worse he can do? Say no?" she asked.

"That's what I was thinking," I agreed.

"Well, I guess he *could* kick my ass out," she said and smiled.

"If he did, I would have us in a better place in nothing flat," I vowed.

"Can I think about it?" she asked.

"Sure can." I nodded.

She smiled then and said, "Thank you."

"For?" I asked.

"Telling me. Talking to me and not trying to go behind my back."

"I learn from my mistakes, baby," I said and leaned forward, kissing her cheek.

She blushed prettily and smiled at me.

"I love you," she said, and I grinned.

"I love you too."

"What about that other thing?" she asked, her stormy steely blue eyes clouding over with worry.

"That I can't talk about, just know that it's being handled."

She nodded carefully. "You'll be careful?" she asked.

"With my current status as a watched man, I'll more than likely be out of it for this round until the heat is off of me." I scowled.

Her expression softened. "I can't say that's too upsetting for me," she said honestly, and I nodded.

"I figured you wouldn't have much to complain about there," I said wryly.

"Can we go somewhere?" she asked me suddenly after a silence.

"Just the two of us, for a day or two? No club, no bar, just you and me?" I asked.

"Yeah," she said.

I grinned.

"I thought you'd never ask."

## 30

*R*aven...

"Now please, don't anyone get stabbed, or shot, or beat up, or otherwise need any medical attention for like the next three days!" I called to the track of masculine laughter around my apartment.

My apartment was emptied of all my belongings which were being stored upstairs in the clubhouse's second floor. They'd put the brakes on finishing the club's upstairs, yet again, to do this renno on my apartment first, then the rest of the units surrounding mine. I don't know what they'd said or done to convince my landlord, and personally, I'd been surprised he'd gone for it, but here they were, working away; everything covered in plastic and a layer of plaster dust and God knows what else. I wouldn't be surprised if there were things like asbestos and shit in these walls... which is why we were all wearing respirators and other protective gear. It was a last look at the place, a final "before" before we left on our long weekend away – just me and just Mace.

The weather was warmer, spring had sprung, and we were going for a long ride that I knew involved at least one ferry ride. I still had no idea where we were going, though. Mace was being close-lipped. It was an adventure in the making and I, for one, was excited.

I needed the vacation, as small as it might be.

"This place will be mostly done by the time you get back," Glass Jaw vowed.

I shook my head in wonder. "I seriously just don't see how," I said. I mean, there was *so much* to do.

"Leave it to the professionals, sweetheart," he said with a wink through his goggles. He moved around some of the other men in their Tyvek moon suits and I shook my head and smiled, though you probably couldn't tell through the bulky respirator unit on my face.

"Go on, get out of here!" Glass shouted, his voice muffled, and I did, stepping out into the hallway and going down the stairs, waiting until I got outside like I was instructed to get everything off.

"So, was it as cool as you thought it was gonna be?" Mace asked casually from the back of his bike. I rolled my eyes as one of Glass Jaw's guys from his regular day job as a contractor of some sorts took my protective gear from me.

"Sort of, I mean, they're taking sledgehammers to the walls! There're all kinds of weird stuff in them, too. Like old newspapers from the forties."

"Yeah, they used to use that shit as cheap insulation back when," Mace said nodding. I handed over my oversized moon suit thing to the guy who nodded and stepped into it.

"Thanks again," I said, and he grinned.

"Boss says jump, we jump and ask if it was high enough," he replied back. I laughed. That sounded like Glass. He was a hard-ass and somewhat of a perfectionist but his finished product really spoke for itself. He'd fired two guys about a month ago and had hired Mace to replace one and found he didn't need to replace the other. Mace knew what he was doing and was damn good at it. Of course, I knew that already.

"You ready?" Mace asked me as I settled onto the bike behind him.

"I am more than ready!" I declared. "Take us out of here!" He handed me back my helmet, and I put it on my head as he started up the bike.

I grinned in excitement and had to laugh a little at myself. To think, only a few months ago, I had been *scared* of the idea of getting on his bike, but by now I was thoroughly addicted to the ride and letting the wind sweep my cares away with every single mile that passed beneath its tires.

We rode down to the Seattle waterfront where we boarded the Bainbridge Island ferry for the half-an-hour ride across the sound. We stood on one of the top decks breathing in the fresh and salty air and indulging in the wind off the water, taking selfies with the Olympic mountain range far in the background against the backdrop of a blazingly brilliant blue sky.

The ride on the other side took me through places I'd never heard of or known until we ended up in a little slice of heaven known as downtown Poulsbo which is where we stopped for lunch and to explore a bit.

"How did I not know about this place?" I asked as we waited on our food at this little Italian place that Mace swore was the absolute best.

"I'd like to know that too, 'Ms. Been to the Nevada desert for Burning Man.'" He wrinkled his nose at me, and I stuck out my tongue.

"While I've *been* places," I said. "I guess I haven't gotten out to explore locally, much. Like, I bet I could show you places in Ballard and Fremont that you didn't even know were there."

He conceded that point. "Haven't spent much time in either neighborhood, so I bet you could."

I held up my wine glass, and he held up his beer. "To weekend adventures until we die," I declared, and his eyes sparkled.

"That's a lot of weekend adventures with me," he said. "You sure you're down for the whole 'until we die' part?"

"Mr. Anderson!" I cried, and he laughed at me. "What is the point in being your ride or die if I'm not in it until we die?" I asked.

He grinned and said, "Fair point, well made, my lady. Fair point, well made."

We clicked glasses and drank our silly little toast just in time for my linguine with fresh clam sauce to be set in front of me, and Mace's lasagna with meat sauce to be set in front of him. I smiled, and we both ate until we were stuffed.

After, we decided to ride right away would be foolish – especially with such a lovely and wonderful slice of downtown to explore. A lot of the shops and things were, granted, touristy, but several were super cool. There was a little grocer that had hundreds of varieties of black licorice, just everything you could want from Australian, to Swedish, to Finnish, to German varieties, from salted to soft eating licorice, to hard pastilles, I was in love!

Mace, on the other hand, thought my fascination with the stuff was gross but that was the nature of black licorice – either you loved it, or you hated it. I don't think I had ever met someone that was just kind of meh about it.

Still, despite his strong feelings about the stuff, Mace bought me some, and with the plain little white grocery sack looped around my wrist, we continued on, hand in hand to the bakery down the way.

This place was totally Mace's jam and smelled absolutely divine.

"What should we get?" I asked as he eyed a pull apart bread, sticky with cinnamon and melted sugar, lousy with raisins that was in the window.

"Breakfast?" he asked, nudging his chin toward the confection.

"That sounds good," I declared. "Do we have room on the bike?"

He grinned.

"Where there's a will there's a way," he said, and I laughed.

"Oh, lord of light and lady of night!" I knew what that meant. The pink box in its plastic bag would be riding around my wrist to wherever it was we were going for a final destination.

The last stop we made along the little historic main drag was a bookstore and bath supply place. It was a unique but perfectly suited combination, let me just say that. While I was engrossed in perusing the books they had on offer, Mace snuck up to the register with some bath treats. By the time I had caught him, they were already wrapped and bagged, and he wouldn't tell me what he'd bought.

"You'll find out later," he said, kissing me soundly, and I knew when to quit while I was ahead.

The ride from Poulsbo was beautiful, with towering trees high to either side of the highway, and points where we dipped out onto a wide, flat floating bridge across the Hood Canal. We even saw porpoises on crossing that bridge which was just phenomenal to me!

We turned through a small town called Chimacum, where he pointed off to one side at the only little four-way stop and a fancy in its rusticness.

"Yeah!" I called out, letting him know that I was seeing what he was pointing at, and he turned left down the way and up into the lot.

"Oh! I didn't know you meant to stop – but hell yeah, I'm in," I declared.

"Good deal, they have really damn good cider here."

"You know, you're absolutely spoiling me," I said, getting off the bike so he could back it into a space etched out in the gravel.

"Ah ha, good to know I'm succeeding at my goal here."

I grinned stupidly, he had that effect on me, as I took off my helmet. We went up to the hostess hand in hand and she asked us if we wanted to be seated at the bar or out in the orchard. We opted for the orchard, seeing as how beautiful it was today.

We were seated at a glossy, live edge picnic table among the trees which were budding green, their petals all fallen to the grass like snow.

"You hungry?" Mace asked, as we perused the menu on his phone, a little card in the center of the table with one of those QR codes printed on it, an effort to be earth friendly and green, to reduce waste.

Lunch had been only a few hours ago, and I was thirsty more than anything, but I looked at the snacks on offer on the menu and said, "I could go for one of their pretzels."

"Sounds good."

We each ordered a pretzel and a flight of their ciders they had on offer. He ordered one set, and I ordered another, so that we could try them all.

"Good day so far?" he asked, as I watched birds dart through the tall grass and wildflowers beyond the orchard where we sat.

"The best day," I told him with a smile. "Feels good to be out here."

He smiled back and nodded. "That it does, but only because I'm out here with you."

I blushed, he always seemed to have that effect on me. He showered me with compliments near constantly and they just never got old.

"So, am I allowed to know where we're going yet?" I asked.

"We're almost there," he said. "Another twenty minutes, maybe."

"Yeah?" I asked, shading my eyes from the sun to look at him.

"Yup."

"You're a little infuriating, you know that?" I asked, and he laughed.

"You really don't like surprises, do you?" he asked, and I thought about it for a second.

"No, I do," I said slowly.

"But?"

"No but," I said. "I mean, I used to love surprises, but I think now maybe I just have a few too many trust issues."

"You don't trust me," he gently teased, and I shook my head.

"No, no, no! Don't you even suggest that! I do. I just think this might be a new 'me' problem that I need to work on."

"Babe, tastes change over time for a variety of reasons. It's okay if you don't like something you once did anymore. It's really no big deal. You have plenty of reason to feel the way you do. Your feelings are valid," he said.

I smiled gently and reached a hand across the table. He put his in mine and I gave it a squeeze.

"You always know just what to say to make me feel better," I said, and he smiled.

"Good," he said. "That ever changes, you need to let me know right away, okay?" he asked, giving my hand a little shake.

I smiled and nodded, the waitress returning with our cider flights.

"Those pretzels are coming right out," she said. "In the meantime, can I get you anything else?"

"A couple of those glasses with your logo on 'em, please?" Mace said.

I cocked my head as the waitress nodded and wiping her hands on her apron turned to walk back across the expanse of grass toward the building and shelter that housed the bar.

"What's with the glasses?" I asked.

"So that we can remember the day," he answered. "I'd kind of like to get a pair every place we go."

I raised an eyebrow and smiled. "So there are more places like this one in our future out here?" I asked.

He laughed and nodded. "Yeah. A few more."

I looked out over the rolling green around us and smiled.

"I am getting thoroughly spoiled this weekend, aren't I?" I asked.

"If I have anything to say about it, yeah."

He sipped the first cider and said, "Ooo, that's a good one. Here try this."

He passed me the glass, and I sipped. It was dry, my mouth puckering slightly, but held notes of bright apple and hints of fresh vanilla and something slightly spicy, but not cinnamon. Something almost peppery. You wouldn't think it would go together, but the flavors complimented one another nicely.

"That *is* nice," I agreed, handing it back. "I prefer sweeter myself, though."

"They get sweeter as they go," he replied and added, "Try your first one."

"This is the blackberry," I said and sipped, nodding. I handed it to him with a bit of a face on me. "Too bitter for me."

We tried them all, loved a few, only one of them mutually, and he placed an order for some bottles. We would have to jockey a few things around in the saddle bags to accommodate things, and I would indeed end up with the baked goods in my lap the rest of the way to where we were going, but that was alright. Totally worth it.

# 31

*M*ace...

I'd rented a cabin, sort of isolated, with a view of the Strait of Juan de Fuca. It was one of those glam type places, all-natural glowing wood and warmly gleaming copper fixtures. One big room, the kitchen area, bed, and bath all sharing one open concept space and it was something I knew would be right up Raven's alley.

It had a big deck overlooking the water, and a stone fire pit out on that deck to sit under the stars and have a nightcap. I was looking forward to the peace, the quiet and solitude, just me and my girl.

We had to drive through Port Townsend to get to it, and I took the long way through so we could go down the main drag of the Victorian port town. It was artsy and held a bunch of Bohemian charm and again, I knew it was right up Raven's alley.

She put her hands on my shoulders and levered herself up for a better view as we rolled through and I thought to myself, *jackpot*.

It was a bit treacherous getting down the dirt track driveway to our cabin, the pine needles shifting under the bike's tires making for some majorly slow going, but eventually, I was able to cut the engine on the cement pad near the building just as the light began to fail around us, the sun beginning to dip over the horizon.

"Holy shit, Mace. This is *wow*," she said getting off as I heeled down the kickstand on the cement pad that served for parking.

"You like?" I asked.

"It's beautiful out here," she said, looking up into the trees. "Do you think there are owls?"

"I bet there are," I said, really having no idea, but this was the Pacific Northwest at its best and when it was at its best there were all sorts of critters.

"Someday, I want to go to Vancouver Island," she said wistfully, looking out through the trees and down over the glimmer of the setting sun rippling over the surface of the straight.

"Oh yeah?" I asked, lifting things from the saddle bags to bring in. "What's there?"

"There are white ravens on Vancouver Island," she said coming over to take things off of me. One of the many things I loved about her. She wasn't afraid to pull her weight no matter if things were big or small.

"White ravens? What, like albino or something?" I asked, curious.

She shook her head and shouldered her pack.

"Not albino," she said. "They're white because of a genetic defect, but it's not albinism. Their eyes are blue, not red."

"No shit?" I asked, leading the way down the steps and around the back side of the cabin that faced the water.

"I've been fascinated with them for a while, was thinking about doing the other arm with one if I could ever get the money together."

I glanced back at her and she stopped looking at the floor-to-ceiling windows, the entire back half of the cabin nothing but large panes of glass.

"Whoa," she murmured.

I went to the French doors leading inside and keyed the code I'd been given into the lock box hanging off the handle. It opened right up, and I took out the keys.

"Welcome to our home away from home for the weekend," I said, pleased at her expression.

I let her go in ahead of me and watched her mouth drop open in surprise.

"Holy *shit*, Mace!"

It had vaulted ceilings, all-natural glowing wood, and a king-sized bed against the back wall facing the windows. There was a small kitchenette just inside the door and she absently slid the bag of her gross candy and the box of pull apart bread onto the little kitchen counter by the farmhouse sink basin.

I'd been through listing after listing online looking for the perfect place for us, and this one had been booked fucking solid for months. I'd put myself on the waiting list in case of cancelation and it must have been meant to be or something, because at the eleventh hour, it'd opened up and I can't tell you how fast I smashed the booking link in that email with my finger.

By the look on my girl's face, it was totally worth it.

She drifted through the place, past the low dividing half wall hiding the toilet from view of the rest of the cabin to go over to the copper tub. She put a hand on the rim and turned back to me, blinking like an owl she seemed to so badly wanted to see.

"This is… this is *stunning*," she said.

I smiled and cocked my head and told her, "Only the best for you, babe."

She dropped her shapely narrow butt to the edge of the tub, completely knocked off her feet while I put the cider in the mini fridge to chill.

"You good?" I asked.

"I'm more than good!" she cried, stunned.

"I'm going to get a fire going out back," I said. "Why don't you settle in?"

I left her sitting on the edge of the copper tub, which I was pleased to see was big enough for the both of us, and went outside. Availing myself of the woodpile just off the deck to get a fire going in the pit the deck was built around.

There were a couple of Adirondack lounge chairs out here that we could make use of. A couple of blankets to drape over our laps inside. All in all, it was about to be a cozy evening out here.

I looked up and caught Raven through the glass, making up some of her tea that she'd brought at the little kitchenette. It made me smile. By the time the fire was going, she was slipping out the back door with a couple of steaming mugs.

"Oh, hey, thanks," I said, taking the one she offered me.

We settled into the couple of chairs and basked in the fire's glow as the sun finished setting somewhere off to our left behind the trees.

Raven sighed in contentment.

"It's so quiet," she said, and I smiled.

"Whole point was to relax and unwind, right?" I asked.

"Absolutely," she answered and leaned way over the arm of her chair with her lips puckered invitingly. I met her halfway and kissed her softly, and *damn*. It didn't matter, the first time, this last time, every time she kissed me, I got hard.

We sipped hot tea in the cooling evening temperatures by the fire and laughed and talked. It had been a long day on the road, even with all the stops, and we were tired. After about her third yawn, I had to smile and say, "Alright, sleepy girl. I think it's time for bed."

"Mm, I can't argue with you there," she said.

It was then an owl called somewhere out in the night and the look on Raven's face, her eyes lit up, her excited grin was everything, and damn if I wasn't hopelessly in love with her.

THE NEXT MORNING, I woke my sleeping beauty with a kiss on every rose of her darkly colorful tattoo. She smiled, and breathed in deep, stretching luxuriously like a cat, reaching back to cradle the back of my head and draw me closer.

"Good morning," I murmured against her skin.

"Good morning," she greeted me back and tipped her face back to kiss me.

She hummed in pleasure, and I trailed a hand down her body, caressing her silky soft skin with my rough palm.

"How'd you sleep?" I asked, wanting nothing more than to make love to her right here and right now, but exercising restraint. If I started now; we would spend all damn day in bed. I wouldn't let her out, and there was far too much I wanted to show her out here.

"Mm, good." She bit her bottom lip, her smile escaping the hold of her teeth, her eyes alight with joy and I caressed her cheek, committing her face, this moment, to memory.

"Hungry?" I asked.

"Starving, actually."

"Let's have some breakfast." I pecked the tip of her nose and she crossed her eyes and laughed.

We got up, and each used the restroom and got dressed. She made some hot tea while I heated up the pull apart and we breakfasted out on the deck listening to the morning birdsong and watching the morning light filter through the mist and trees.

"What are we doing today?" she asked.

"I thought we'd poke around Port Townsend and check out some of the shops. Maybe have some lunch and take a hike out to the sea glass beach."

She perked up.

"Sea glass beach?" she asked.

"Ahhh, I thought you might like that," I said.

"Absolutely! Sounds wonderful."

That's what we did. We took a ride into Port Townsend, stopped for some coffee in this quirky little strip mall since the tea didn't really do much for me by way of caffeination, and leaving the bike parked with three others, struck out on a walk down Water Street and the main drag through town.

A lot of things weren't quite open yet, so we just meandered along picking out the places we wanted to go when they finally were open. There was a steampunk shop that had some clothing pieces in Raven's aesthetic, and a metaphysical shop she got excited over. There were bookstores and antique stores that I admittedly got a little excited to check out, and a rock and gem shop that looked promising.

We held hands and walked along at a sedate pace and looked at just about everything there was to see before going in anyplace.

One of our first stops was the metaphysical shop and I swear Raven could have gotten lost in there for *hours*.

It was a bit of a crash course in her Pagan faith which she shyly and patiently told me about, and I had to say, a lot of what she talked about made sense to me. I didn't know if I would be converting, or signing up or whatever, but it made a hell of a lot more sense than anything else I'd encountered so far.

From the metaphysical shop we ended up in an antique shop where she perused stacks of old artwork and books. I was passing by the jewelry counter, eyeing an old lighter in the case when the ring caught my eye.

Gold with white gold accents, a square-cut diamond at its center. The thing had to be from the 1930s. Art deco period, there were a bunch of buildings in downtown Seattle with the same kind of facing and that's what they called them. Art Deco.

"Excuse me, how much for that ring?" I asked the lady behind the counter.

"Oh, good choice!" she declared. "It's nine-hundred-and-eighty-nine dollars," she said pulling it from its felt and reading the tag.

"I can give you seven-fifty cash for it right now," I said.

She blinked at me and said, "You know, it's been here for years and I think I know who it's for... sold."

I grinned and handed her my reserve wad of cash out of the top of my boot, glancing around to make sure Raven was otherwise engaged, hoping that if all went well, we would be by the end of this trip.

"I hope it fits," she murmured, handing the ring over.

"You know what, me too," I said and handed her the cash.

"Mace?" Raven called, and I stuffed the ring in my pocket, deep.

"Yeah, I'm over here!" I called back and the woman behind the counter winked at me and drifted away to count her money and put it away.

"There you are." Raven beamed at me.

"You find anything?" I asked her.

"Oh, lots of neat stuff, but nothing I want to try and carry back with us." She laughed.

I hooked an arm around her shoulders and pressed a kiss to her temple.

"What about you?" she asked as we wandered out the front door and back into the sun.

"Oh, I saw a thing or two. There was a really cool lighter back in that case."

"Oh yeah?" she asked. "Why didn't you get it?"

"I mean," I shrugged, "how many lighters do I really need?"

## 32

*R*aven...

     We walked all over Port Townsend and ended up having lunch on the breezy back deck of a pub with a mermaid for the sign. The food was fantastic, a shrimp pizza with a white garlic sauce, artichoke hearts, spinach, mushrooms, and fresh tomatoes. All the vegetables locally sourced, real farm to table fare. The cider and beers were local and craft, too, real artisan stuff. I loved it.

Afterward, we needed to walk off such a carb heavy lunch, and so we started our trek to the sea glass beach, an easy hike but one that required low tide to get around to where we were supposed to be at.

We double-checked the tide tables, figured it out, and set off down easy walking trails and eventually, over rocks crusted with barnacles and around some shallow tide pools that were teeming with life.

"Oh, would you look at that!" I covered my mouth with my hands after my excited utterance, the sea glass beach was beautiful. All white, brown, and green glass worn smooth by the sand and churning sea. Here and there it was dotted with blue glass pieces that were just brilliant.

"I wish I'd brought something to collect some," I pouted.

"Psht! I got you," Mace said and produced a tan Crown Royal bag out of his jacket pocket.

"Oh, my God, you're the absolute best, you know that?"

"I try, but only for you," he said with a grin, handing the bag over.

We chatted, and I picked glass from the shore.

"You know what you're even going to do with this?" he asked me at one point, laughing.

"Not a clue, but I bet you I'll find something to do with it. Something good."

He laughed and said, "God, I love you!"

"I love you too," I said smiling and bent to pick up a sizeable piece of blue glass worn smooth by years of turbulent ocean, polished to a silky matte finish by the sand.

"You ever think about the future?" he asked quietly, stooping to pick up a bit of green and holding it out to me. I smiled and held out the bag for him to slip it inside.

"Sometimes," I answered. "I don't like to too much," I confessed.

"Why not?" he asked, picking up an opaque white stone and casting it aside when he realized it wasn't glass.

"Because I'm afraid sometimes," I said.

"Afraid of what?" he asked frowning.

"Afraid that this is all some beautiful waking dream and that any moment, I'm going to wake up to the nightmare," I said quietly.

"Oh, baby," he murmured and reached out, capturing my hand and towing me in against him. He wrapped his arms around me and kissed me soundly.

"It's not a dream," he said, looking me in the eye. "This is real. As real as it gets," he looked me over and let me go.

The vibe suddenly shifted, and I frowned slightly.

"Mace?" I asked.

He dropped to one knee in front of me.

"I want forever with you," he said and held up a gold ring. "I want to make you my wife and ol' lady if you'll let me. I want to hold you every night and wake up to you every morning. I want to make love to you as often as possible and I want to grow old with you and pinch your ass from my fuckin' wheelchair."

Strong emotion, the strongest I'd ever felt, seized me. I sniffed and swallowed hard as happy tears stained my lower lashes and made the beautiful ring pinched between his forefinger and thumb blur.

"Just say yes, that's all you have to do."

I felt my mouth work, open and closed as I tried to force the word past the knot in my throat.

"Yes!" I finally cried and he let out an explosive breath, surging to his feet.

He practically tackled me in a hug, holding me tight, kissing me fiercely with the fire of a thousand suns.

I looked down as he slid the beautiful ring onto my finger and marveled that it was a perfect fit.

"Meant to fuckin' be," he whispered and after staring at it for several heartbeats longer, I looked up and he claimed my mouth in a kiss all over again.

It was surreal, being and feeling so incredibly loved by a man such as Mace, and it was a sensation that I would *never* get tired of.

"I can't wait to make you Mrs. Mace," he said with a grin and I grinned too.

"I can't wait to get you back to the cabin," I murmured and plucked at his vest.

"No time like the present," he said. "You ready to head back?"

"Absolutely."

We picked our way back across the beach slowly, choosing the best pieces of worn glass along the way.

Back at the cabin, Mace went to the tub and started it, drawing a bath.

"Come here, you," he said crooking a finger at me, and I wandered over. He lifted a paper bag from the bath and book shop in Poulsbo and said, "Choose your poison."

I picked through the bag and several bath bombs and handmade soaps and chose one of each that complimented each other.

"K, get naked and in the tub," he said, and I grinned.

"You joining me?" I asked.

"Maybe later, I want to spoil you tonight – so let me."

"Ooo la la, who am I to argue that?" I asked, and he grinned.

I stripped slowly, making a bit of a show of it and he held out a hand to help me over the high lip of the tub. I settled into the water with a contented sigh, and he dropped the bomb in. I was suddenly surrounded by fragrant foam as it whirled and twirled in the water, fizzing and bubbling away.

I sank into the soft, fragrant heat, my hair already twisted up and secured by a pair of hair sticks. Mace took off his shirt and watching him do it was a treat. It always was. I hummed in appreciation of the view and he gave me a lascivious smile.

He kneeled by the tub and dipped a hand in, trailing fingertips up my leg from the top of my foot, skimming along my shin and over my knee, stopping there. The way he looked at me, God and Goddess, I felt like the sexiest woman alive.

"You really want to marry me?" I asked softly, and the smile that touched his lips – so patient and so kind.

"All I want to do is marry you," he murmured.

I had always dreamed of a love like this. That I could love and be so loved, and it really did feel as if it were a dream. A beautiful waking dream that I never wanted to end.

We kissed, and his hand crept up my leg further beneath the water.

"Mm," I moaned into his mouth and he took it for the plea that it was, his fingers rubbing at the top of my sex, fingers delving between the folds, seeking out that knot of pleasure. He pressed firmly but gently and made a slow, lazy circle.

My hips rose unbidden from the bottom of the copper tub to press myself more firmly against his fingertips as his tongue delved between my lips, past my teeth, to stroke provocatively against my own.

I groaned into his mouth, my hands coming out of the water to clasp his face between them gently, holding his mouth to mine as we kissed passionately, and he worked me into a slow burn.

God, I wanted a deeper touch from him. He was working my clit so sweetly, and I was rising to a low simmer, but *fuck* I needed a deeper touch. I ached for it, and as though he read my mind, he gave it to me, sliding his fingers down between my thighs and his middle one up inside me, the pad of his thumb replacing his fingertips against my clit.

I sucked in a breath around our kiss, my hips jerking unbidden, and I ground my pelvis down on his hand. He chuckled darkly against my mouth and pressed his finger in deeper, moving it slightly against my walls to drive me fucking *wild*.

I moaned into his mouth, whimpering, begging my body as much as Mace to push me just that last little bit to the precipice. He worked me sweetly, roughly, expertly into a near frenzy and when I came, it was in an explosion of light behind my eyelids.

I came down slowly, panting, languid in the tub, muscles loose as he stroked my pussy lightly, eventually removing his hand from it when the tremors sliding through me lessened.

"You are the hottest little thing when you come for me like that," he said, his voice pitched low and sexy, caressing my sense of hearing like sable soft fur.

"Kiss me again," I murmured, and he bent low, over the edge of the tub, to press his lips to mine.

With love and laughter, and more than a bit of mischief, I pulled his ass in with me – jeans and all.

He collapsed half over me laughing and tore his mouth from mine, crying out, "Okay, okay! I'll join you!"

I giggled lightly and let him get undressed and into the bath with me proper. It felt so fucking good lounging in the hot fragrant water wrapped in his arms.

He massaged my shoulders, he washed me from head to toe, and I swear it was like the stains of my past came clean out of my soul under his touch and I felt like a new woman – because I was. *His* woman.

"You think about seeing your friends when we get back home?" he asked a time later as we cuddled in the cooling bath. Neither one of us quite ready to get out.

"I'm not sure they would want to see me," I said a bit of sadness creeping in.

"Oh, baby, I don't think that's true," he said.

"Maybe," I hedged. "Would you go with me?"

"Absolutely, if you want me to."

I nodded against his chest and he tightened his arms around me, I squeezed his fingers, interlaced with mine, the palms of his hands resting along the backs of mine.

*He felt so good.* I would never get tired of this.

"I don't know how to do it," I said.

"Do what?" he asked.

"Merge my old life with my new one. It seems like an almost impossible task."

"I don't want to take you away from anything, babe. That's not me, that's not healthy," he said.

"No, I know... I don't know, I guess I just feel like I've grown, I've changed, and that life it just doesn't suit me anymore, but that doesn't have to do anything with *you*, or the club." Which was true, it didn't.

It had everything to do with things being post Max... it wasn't that I *couldn't* go back, I just... I didn't feel like I needed to. I didn't know if I wanted to.

"Nothing has to be decided right now, baby. Give it as long as you like. I'll be there for you, whatever you decide."

I smiled at that and pushed back slightly, so happy it was crazy. I believed him. I believed wholeheartedly everything that he said.

I tipped my head up and back and he smiled before claiming my lips with his once again.

# 33

*M*ace...

Once out of the bath, her nude form was like a siren's call I couldn't resist. I gathered her up, laughing, shrieking in joy, and carried her to the bed and threw her on it. I followed her onto the sheets, and wedged my hips between her thighs, spreading her legs, my cock sliding up and down her slick, wet, pussy lips.

"Fuck I want to be inside of you," I growled, and she gasped as I put my lips against the sweet spot on the side of her neck and both breathed her in and tasted her, teasing the erogenous zone with my lips and tongue, nipping at her shoulder lightly to give it a slight rest before attacking it all over again.

She twined her arms around me, her body rising and falling as she writhed beneath me – like she couldn't get enough skin-on-skin contact and I knew the feeling. It was never enough. Sometimes, even being balls deep inside her didn't feel like quite enough.

She was so fucking beautiful laid out beneath me. I smoothed my hands over her stomach, up her body, over her beautiful tits, sweeping my fingertips out along her collar bones and over her shoulders, over the colorful ink under her skin and down to her hands where I locked my fingers with hers. I rode her, worshiped at the altar that was my beautiful girl on my knees, sliding my cock's shaft up and down her velvet pussy lips, edging myself, edging her.

I would say we were dry humping like teenagers, but fuck – there wasn't anything dry about her hungry little pussy. It was getting harder and harder not to slip inside her by accident. When I finally penetrated her, I wanted it to be intentional. I wanted to drown in the storm-swept sea of her eyes as I sank into her slowly, inch by fucking inch until there wasn't any going further. Until we were one fucking person, and I touched my lady soul fucking deep.

"Mace, *please...*" she begged, voice high and breathy with need and desire and who was I to deny her anything?

I stopped fucking around and drew my hips just a little further back, the head of my dick finding purchase and parting the entrance to her sweet pussy. I held back, sinking in slowly, relishing the red rush to her chest, watching that blush climb into her cheeks as her eyes slipped shut and she relished in the feeling of my body in hers.

I couldn't close my eyes if I wanted to, the sight of her spread beneath me, arching for me, her lean body rising up in offering to me – there wasn't another sight like it that could stir me as deeply.

"Fuck, baby, *yes*," I praised. "So fucking beautiful, so fucking hot."

She bit her bottom lip and looked at me, eyes heavy lidded with desire and it was everything in me not to explode inside her right then and there.

I rolled my hips, and she cried out, head falling back as she surrendered to my ministrations so sweetly.

I would die for her, I had killed for her, and I would do it again in a heartbeat. I would love her, knight for her, be a monster for her, *anything* for her. Whatever she needed, because damn if she wasn't *everything* I needed.

A princess, a saint, an angel, a goddess, just everything one woman could be and more… she healed parts of me that I didn't even fucking know were broken. She accepted all of me, forgave me, and I would do whatever it took from here until the day I died.

I picked up my pace, giving her the short little thrusts that I knew drove her right up to the edge of that silver abyss. I kept her there too, for as long as possible, gritting my teeth as it took me right up to that razor's edge. So hot, so wet, her pussy velvet where it gripped me tight and tighter still.

"Oh, God, *Mace…*"

"That's it, baby. That's it," I praised.

She threw her head back and arched, crying out, her body drawing taut like a bowstring and I waited, she was close, she was so close, her pussy gripping so tight it became hard to thrust. I kept pace, moving for her, everything for her, anything for her.

When her pussy rippled around me and she lost it, I lost it with her. I came so hard it was like an out-of-body experience. *Goddamn*, it felt so good it hurt, my cock jettisoning over, and over, and over. Thick, hot, white streamers of cum decorating her stomach, all the way to her tits as flashbulbs went off behind my eyes calming to the occasional silver tracer or spark at the edge of my vision.

I collapsed over her, her fingers twining in the back of my hair as I rested, panting, my cheek against her shoulder, sweat dewing our skins, cooling in the ambient air of the room that was deeply perfumed with our sex.

"That was…" she gasped, gulping in air, "amazing."

"You're amazing," I returned when I could breathe again.

She laughed, her legs quivering around me.

"I think we need another bath," she murmured.

"Just let me get my legs back," I said, and she laughed again, the sweetest sound at once rich and soothing to my soul.

~

"You maybe wanna tell us something?" Dump Truck asked, eyebrow raised upon mine and Raven's return.

I put my arm around her shoulders and drew her into my side where she put her hand on my chest.

"What's he gotta tell us?" Nine asked, confused.

"Keep lookin' you'll figure it out or you won't," Glass Jaw said, grinning.

"Oh, shit! Is that what I think it is?" Cipher crowed.

"Boys, I asked my woman here if she would do me the honor of being my ol' lady and my wife, and she did, in no uncertain terms, agree," I said.

"Yeah!" A loud whoop went out and the barroom of the club burst into cheers and applause.

"Well, that's a fuckin' world class party," Maverick declared, holding Marisol on his lap. "Boys, let's light it up!" he shouted.

The jukebox was put on blast, the liquor flowed, and it was a big damn party after that with the finest green and the top shelf shit making an appearance.

Through it all, Raven stayed close as club members and their women came up to congratulate us one by one and two by two.

We were asked all sorts of questions; did we have plans? Did we want help with the planning? Where were we getting married? Who was doing the honors of marrying us? Did we want Deacon or Mav for such an auspicious event?

Food, music, liquor, weed, and finally to cap off the night, sex. I couldn't stand it anymore. I needed a break from everybody but my woman, who I took upstairs amidst the drop cloth draped pile of our shit, backed her into a private corner against a wall, and went to my knees to pull down her leggings and to bury my mouth against her sweet cunt.

"Oh, God, Mace," she moaned and tangled her fingers in my hair, pulling my mouth tighter against her.

I lived for it, for this, giving her pleasure while the party raged downstairs. I jabbed my tongue at her clit and she writhed, fucking my face with her wet pussy. The alcohol and weed lowering her inhibitions and turning her loose and wild in my arms.

"Fuck yes! Fuck yes! Fuck yes!" she cried, and it was the sweetest sound.

She shuddered in my arms, her back thumping against the wall as she came for the first time. I held her tight and looked up that wonderful lean body of hers and into those heavy-lidded, storm-swept eyes of hers.

Fuck, I loved the way she looked at me. Like I was the only fucking man on earth for her.

"I need you inside me," she murmured, and I got to my feet. She watched me undo my pants hungrily, the way she looked at me making me believe that I was the sexiest fucking man alive, and I lived for that expression on her face.

"Turn around," I ordered, and she did, putting her hands against the wall and pushing her bottom out, arching her back provocatively, putting her pussy on offer for me. I throbbed in my hand, eyeing her glistening slit and put a hand to her hip, massaging through the tail of her asymmetrical shirt.

"Mm, baby you have no idea how good you look right now." I sucked in a breath between my teeth and let it out in a rush. "Fuck yes."

"Mace..." her voice held a note of warning, like if she didn't get me inside of her *right now*, she was gonna be mad about it.

I chuckled and pulled back on her hip slightly, she bent forward just a little bit more, and I slid right in to her waiting wet heat.

"Oh, God..." she choked on her words slightly and it was the hottest thing. I took my hand from between us where I'd guided my cock inside her and put it to the back of her shoulder, pulling her back and down onto me.

I was in the mood for a rough and dirty fuck up here, the place and setting perfect, the heat between us scorching, and yet I would be lying if I said I wasn't low key worried about her and how she would take it.

She told me to stop, I would stop, but I really hoped she would trust me to take her on this wild ride like she had for me to take her on all the others.

I plunged into her balls deep and squeezed my eyes shut. She felt so fucking good, and I wasn't ready. Not yet. I wanted to last for her. I wanted this to last as long as I could make it.

She whimpered and pushed back to meet me and I made a strangled noise, barely hanging on from going *off*.

She made the sweetest sounds, her voice light and lilting, emanating from her without words yet full of purest emotion and it was those sounds, in combination with the feel of her body wrapped around mine that did me in. I fucked her up against that wall in the corner and I wasn't good for more than a dozen strokes, burying myself deep and deeper still as I lost all semblance of control and came deep inside her; glad she'd gone down to the free clinic and had gotten herself on some hearty birth control so I could do this with her, because there wasn't anything better than emptying my balls deep in that hungry little pussy.

"Oh God!" she gasped as I withdrew from her, damn near losing my shit at how oversensitive my dick was after such a mind-blowing orgasm.

"You good?" I asked, breathless.

"More than, lord and lady you feel so fucking good." She turned around and put her arms around me and kissed me deeply. I stood, caressing her body through her tunic or whatever, and smiled against her mouth.

"Let me see if I can't find our mattress under all this," I murmured.

"I'll go clean up," she whispered.

"Sounds good."

She pulled up her leggings and looked back over her shoulder, sultry and cool all at once as I tucked myself back into my pants. That last lingering look she gave me over her shoulder before stepping into one of the bathrooms up here had my cock rallying already.

There would never be getting enough of her. Never ever...

# 34

*R*aven...

It was just us upstairs, listening to the bass thump through the floor beneath our mattress. We were both curled up together in our clothes on the bare mattress on the floor as we were unable to locate any sheets or even pillows, Mace's head propped on his rolled-up jacket, the leather of his cut slick beneath my fingertips as I rested my head on his shoulder, snug against his side.

"I can't wait until the day we aren't sleeping on the fucking floor anymore," he confessed, and I laughed.

"Right? I think this weekend sleeping in a real bed spoiled me, too."

He laughed and held me a little tighter.

"I can't wait to see what you do with the apartment."

I tilted my head up to look at him and he looked down at me.

"What?" he asked.

"It's your apartment, too…" I murmured, and he smiled.

"Yeah, but I'm not really good at that girly decorating shit. I figured I would leave that up to you," he said and I smiled and sighed.

"You get a say, too."

"I'll totally give my opinion if you ask it," he said, and I could hear the smile in his voice. I laughed at that.

"I'll just bet you will," I said, and he chuckled, squeezing me tight and kissing the top of my head.

"Get some rest, baby."

"It's hard to," I confessed. "I'm excited."

"Not sure how much there's going to be to look at," he cautioned.

"Three days isn't a lot of time, I know," I agreed.

"Enough time to get the drywall up in most of the place," he said.

"Paint?" she asked.

"Maybe, maybe not."

"In any case, it will be nice to have walls without any cracks or boards showing through," I said.

"True that," he agreed, and we settled in.

I must have been more tired than I thought because I was asleep before I knew it.

"Is that where you two got off to," Maverick said the next morning as we came down the stairs. His voice held a note of disapproval. He wasn't any worse for wear from the night before, in fact it looked like he and Marisol had gone home, slept well, had showered and returned.

"Yeah, sorry about that – sort of didn't have any place else to go," Mace said chagrinned.

"Just don't be making a habit of it, k?"

"No sir," Mace said, and cast a wink at me – it was quickly becoming the universal sign of 'tell you later' between us.

I know he was telling me things that he shouldn't, but he had been absolutely serious when he'd said no more secrets, nothing behind my back, and his secrets and by default, the club's secrets were absolutely safe with me because I'd absolutely learned… fuck the police.

When we stepped outside with our coffee and he was sure we were away from any ears that could overhear he murmured, "Staying the night at the club is forbidden, you sleep here it gives any enterprising cops the creative leeway to get a warrant for the place based on it being a residence."

"Ah," I murmured and nodded.

"Hence the apartments," he said.

"Gotcha." I smiled at him. "Speaking of which…"

"You ready to go look?" he asked grinning.

"Maybe after you take me to breakfast," I shot back. "I'm starving."

He laughed and nodded. "Huckleberry Finn's?" he asked.

"Absolutely," I agreed.

"Let's round up who's here and find out who's down."

"Sounds good."

We had a decent sized pack of us that ended up going up Ambaum Boulevard to Huck's, it was a fantastic breakfast joint that mostly catered to families and the older crowd. We were a rag tag crew and completely out of place, but Huck's was sort of a neutral place, the

Switzerland of the area if you will, and thus we were welcomed as any other guest and seated as soon as a table large enough opened up.

Their food was both cheap, and good, and they served breakfast all day. I loved their spinach, chicken, and mushroom omelet.

I was talking and laughing with Little Bird, Mace at the other end of the table heads together with Glass Jaw over the apartment more than likely and I was struck by how much and how quickly this felt like *home* and *family* even more than living among the burners.

Mace caught my eye from the end of the long table comprising of several tables moved and pushed together and his smile in my direction was everything.

I smiled back and Little Bird sighed happily, "Feels good, doesn't it?" she asked as Dump Truck squeezed the top of her thigh beneath the table.

"Yeah, it does," I agreed.

After breakfast, we went back to the apartments and I let out a shuddering breath outside the ground floor stairwell door.

"Nervous?" Dump Truck asked from nearby, leaning heavily on his cane.

I nodded, and frowned slightly, "Yeah, it's weird," I said.

He shook his head, "Naw, your world's changing. For the better, but it's still change. It's only natural."

I thought about that for a minute and finally nodded.

"Yeah, you know, you're right. Thanks for that."

He smiled a small thing and tipped his head down in a slight nod.

"You ready?" Glass Jaw asked.

I nodded.

"Ready."

We went upstairs, and he unlocked my apartment door for me and *oh, my gods...*

I stepped into a living room with vanilla walls, light and airy, the smell of fresh paint assailing me. The floors had been stripped, sanded, and re-stained a deep golden oak, yet still retained enough scars and discoloration in places that it was honestly *perfect*. The character and the history etched in their surface.

I felt my hands over my mouth before I even knew they were there and edged further into the apartment. The kitchen was completely new, still lacking cabinets and countertops, but the backsplash was already so modern, glass thin strips of tile in grays, whites, and blacks. The floor set with black-and-white tile that was just exquisite.

The bedroom was done, the walls a light sage green, the bathroom so close just in need of faucets and fixtures.

"We'll get it done, just needs a day or two for the tile to cure," Glass Jaw declared and I rounded on him.

"Are you kidding me? It's beautiful!" I sniffed, teary-eyed and looked from him to Mace to a track of 'Awww's' from the doorway. Mace came to me and hugged me tight as I cried happy tears.

"Welcome home," Glass Jaw said.

"More importantly," Maverick interjected. "Welcome to the family."

Home. Family. Yes... wasn't it just?

# EPILOGUE

*Two years later*

*G*lass Jaw...

"Gah! Damnit!" Mace cried, and I frowned, looking up from my call with one of my suppliers.

"Alright now, thanks," I said and hung up the phone, calling from the kitchen down the basement stairs "What's the problem?"

Laughter filtered up, and I rolled my eyes.

"Quit fuckin' around down there and get it done!" I yelled. "The home buyer's coming today, and I don't need you all making us look like a bunch of fucking jackasses!"

We were working in the basement of a house built in the 1940s. It was a multi-tier repair, some foundational shit, new sump pump installation, mold removal; that sort of thing. The current homeowner? What a fucking bitch. I was hoping the buyer, who was coming in from across the country, would be easier to deal with since the repairs were going to overlap and go past closing which was supposed to be tomorrow.

I mean, honestly – who the fuck bought a house sight unseen from across the fuckin' country like that?

"Hey, boss!" Mace called. "Come and look at this and tell me what you want me to do."

"Fuck," I muttered and went down the stairs into the unfinished basement. That wasn't good, that was *never* good.

I went down to deal with whatever bullshit had come up and sighed.

"This cheap-ass white-trash fucking cunt ain't gonna pay for it," I said, looking up under the fireplace at the severely rotted wood. It wasn't too bad of a repair, not bad at all, but I wasn't about to do any more shit for this woman.

"What do you think?" Mace asked. "Point it out to the buyer after close and go from there?"

"Yeah, maybe." I rubbed my chin and closed one eye looking up at the flaking dry rot going on. The whole corner of the beam was starting to come apart.

"Man," Mace said shaking his head. "I don't know what show this bitch watched to make her think flipping houses was a good idea, but she watched the wrong fucking one."

I barked a laugh and said, "Who you telling?" Finally, I sighed and said, "Let me look at this inspection report again. The buyer's inspector was really fuckin' thorough – I don't see how he could have missed this."

"Yeah." Mace nodded.

It was a real odd situation, this whole job. The *buyer's* agent had reached out to me for one – which that almost never happened and after meeting the current homeowner, I understood why.

She wasn't interested in anything except getting her money, period. Gold digging hooker. She'd even had the nerve to get up in my face about shit and I was fuckin' trying to help her ass – giving her options. Not my fault she wanted top-tier everything at bargain basement prices. That wasn't how this fucking shit worked.

"Jared?" a female voice called from upstairs, and I frowned and looked at my watch.

"Yeah, just a sec!" I called back.

"Holly?" Mace asked.

"Sounds like it, also sounds like she's early."

"Fuckin' great."

I huffed a laugh and slapped him on the back.

"Time to be the bearer of bad news," I said and turned toward the stairs. Holly was the buyer's agent – and thus, she was on our side.

"Hey, Holly," I said as I came up the stairs.

Holly was the quintessential bubbly blonde, buxom, too – which I could appreciate both. She blinked wide blue eyes at me and said, "Uh oh, you don't look happy. Homeowner or…?"

That was the other thing I appreciated about Holly – she was sharp as a tack. Today, that worked against me, some.

"I don't know yet, give me half a second here," I said and went over to the kitchen counter. That was the one thing they'd done right in this place – or at least on the surface. Granite countertops, gleaming white cabinetry, and brick facing for the backsplash, the kitchen looked sharp all except for the shitty, half-assed paint job in the same unrelieved gray throughout the whole fucking house.

I swear to God, the woman selling this place was painfully fuckin' *cheap*. She probably had her fuckin' kids paint the place.

Holly waited while I flipped through like the fifty-four-page printout that the fuckin' inspector had handed her on the house. Yeah, it seemed like a lot, but a lot of it was penny ante shit. Nothing to write home about when just about every fuckin' house in the history of ever had the same shit going on.

I tapped the third page and said, "Gah..."

"What is it?" Holly asked, looking over my shoulder.

"Your guy was maybe a little too thorough. Yhis is a problem that really needs to be addressed but he's got so much penny ante shit packed into this report it got overlooked."

"Oh no," Holly said dismayed. "Show me."

I took her down into the basement and showed her she covered her mouth with her hand and shook her head.

"Jared this is really bad... the negotiations have been made, and the contract has been signed, how immediate of a repair is this?" she asked.

"It's bad," I agreed. "It really shouldn't wait."

"How much are we looking at, though?" she asked.

"There's the good news," I said with a sigh. "I mean, I could do it for..." I ran the calculations through my brain and shrugged. "Five-seventy-five, maybe."

Holly let out her breath in a woosh. "Okay, that's not completely awful, but Jared I don't know if my client can do it," she said. She looked worried, and that was weird. Like, who was this woman that was buying that Holly was *this* invested?

"What's going on, Hols?" I asked her.

"She's a really nice lady," Holly said with a sigh. "And she's really been through it. Single mom, husband left her and tried to leave her cold. It's just her and her son and she got a job out here, but they weren't going to pay for her relocation fees. She's spent just about everything she's had on securing this house and of course we get so far into the process and the woman that owns this place—" I raised my hand to stop her.

"Say no more on that last one," I said.

Holly looked at her watch and said, "She's supposed to be here any minute."

"The seller?" I asked. "Or the buyer?"

"Oh, God no! The buyer! The seller was warned away from the walk through. My client doesn't want to have anything to do with her, she's been jerked around so much. Between you and me," Holly made a cringy sort of face.

"Always, Hols. You know I take care of you," I said, and it was true; in a business sense, I did. Always had and always would. That was why she and her real estate group were one of my best repeat customers.

"Jared, she's really been through it and I don't know that she can take much more bad news," Holly said. She genuinely sounded like her heart went out to this lady.

"Got pretty close with her, huh?" I asked.

Holly nodded. "She's an amazing person." She sighed, chewed her bottom lip, and drew herself up to her full height which was only like five foot six which to my six one, looked adorable.

"I'll pay for it," she said. "Out of my finder's fee."

"Shit, you're fuckin' serious," I said wide-eyed and surprised as fuck. I'd never seen her do anything like it.

"As a heart attack," she said solemnly.

I sniffed. "You know, you've brought me a lot of business and shit over the years, I can't do it for *free*, but I'll go halves with you. Two-seventy-five." I stuck out my hand, and she smiled and shook it.

"Thank you, I'm glad you're here," she said and then her eyes went wide as her phone went off in her hand. "Oh!" She looked at the screen and smiled.

"She's here!"

"Well go on," I said. "I got some shit to handle down here. I'll be up in a bit."

"Okay."

She went up the stairs, and I put my hands on my hips and shook my head. Well, that was something.

"Hi!" I heard Holly's enthusiastic voice at the back door and a peal of feminine laughter.

"It's so good to finally meet you!" another woman's voice cried.

"Hi," a boy's voice said, cracking, so a teenager maybe.

Hm.

I went around looking at my crew's work nodding and finally took myself upstairs. I had no idea where the women had got to, but there was a teen in the kitchen. Skinny, tall, hadn't equaled out yet but maybe sixteen? Seventeen?

"Hi," he said and waved.

"Hey, how's it going?" I asked.

He tossed back brown hair that was getting too long in the front, bangs sweeping into his brown eyes.

"Good to be stopped," he said with a reckless grin.

"Aw, yeah? Where you come from?" I asked.

"East coast," he said.

"Shit, that *is* a long way away," I agreed.

"Marc, who are you talking to?" A woman's voice called from the stairwell up to the second floor. Her flats hit the hardwood floor, and she stepped around the corner into the dining room where I could see her and holy shit… she left me eating asphalt.

She was fucking gorgeous.

Long, sleek brown hair waved around her face which was angular and super model perfect. Wide brown eyes swept over me uncertainly and softened when Holly came around from behind her and introduced us.

"Oh, Cadence this is Jared; Jared, this is our buyer, Cadence."

"Hi." My brain finally caught up to what I was supposed to be doing versus what I *was* doing which was staring gobsmacked at the woman.

"Jared Ronald Allen Smith," I said. She hesitantly put her soft hand in mine and barely gripped it, shaking weakly.

"Oh, like the trucks outside," her boy said, and I startled slightly, forgetting he was even there.

"Yeah, I own the contracting company," I said.

"It's nice to meet you," Cadence murmured and without any more preamble, said, "How bad is my house?"

Direct. I liked that.

Shit, I was in trouble here…

# ALSO BY A.J. DOWNEY

### *The Sacred Hearts MC*

1. Shattered & Scarred

2. Broken & Burned

3. Cracked & Crushed

3.5 Masked & Miserable (a novella)

4. Tattered & Torn

5. Fractured & Formidable

6. Damaged & Dangerous

### *The Virtues*

1. Cutter's Hope

2. Marlin's Faith

3. Charity for Nothing

4. Stoker's Serenity

### *The Sacred Brotherhood*

1. Brother to Brother

2. Her Brother's Keeper

3. Brother In Arms

4. Between Brothers

5. A Brother's Secret

6. A Brother At My Back

7. A Brother's Salvation

Synchronicity

# ABOUT A.J. DOWNEY

A.J. Downey specializes in writing real and relatable contemporary romance stories. She's from Seattle, WA and loves the Pacific Northwest. She finds inspiration from her surroundings, through the people she meets, and likely as a byproduct of way too much caffeine. An avid reader all of her life, it's now her turn to try and give back a little, entertaining as she has been entertained.

Stalker Information:

Website
www.ajdowney.com

Sign up for her newsletter at
http://eepurl.com/dkQiIH

Facebook Group - AJ's Sacred Circle
https://www.facebook.com/groups/authorajdowney/

f facebook.com/authorajdowney
🐦 twitter.com/authorajdowney
📷 instagram.com/ajdowney
BB bookbub.com/authors/a-j-downey

www.ingramcontent.com/pod-product-compliance
Lightning Source LLC
Chambersburg PA
CBHW050739230626
47052CB00004BA/712